# A
# Sticky End

# A

# Sticky End

James Lear

CLEIS
PRESS

Published in the United States by Cleis Press Inc., 2246 Sixth St., Berkeley, California 94710.

Printed in the United States.
Cover design: Scott Idleman
Cover photograph: © David Vance.
Fine art prints available at: www.davidvance.com.
Text design: Frank Wiedemann
Cleis logo art: Juana Alicia
First Edition.
10 9 8 7 6 5 4 3 2 1

ISBN: 978-1-57344-395-1


Library of Congress Cataloging-in-Publication Data

Lear, James, 1960-
A sticky end / James Lear. -- 1st ed.
    p. cm.
ISBN 978-1-57344-395-1 (trade paper : alk. paper)
1. Gay men--Fiction. 2. London (England)--Fiction. I. Title.

PR6069.M543S75 2010
823'.914--dc22

                                    2010004487

# Chapter One

ONE LOOK WAS ALL IT TOOK TO KNOW THAT MORGAN was in serious trouble. He stood at the door of his family home in Wimbledon, his face haggard, his eyes bloodshot, his clothes, usually immaculate, crumpled. He'd sounded fine on the phone, a little hurried, perhaps—but I put that down to his eagerness to get me over to the house now that the coast was clear, so that I could fuck him.

He'd been keeping me at arm's length ever since I arrived in London, which I understood—he was a married man, a father of two small children, and it was not always conve- nient to entertain your old college pal, especially when the entertainment involved cock, rather than cocktails. Now, however, his wife had taken the children to stay with friends, he was a bachelor again—and he wanted good old Mitch to come around and give him what his wife never could. I was ready for him; it had been over a year since I last had my dick in Morgan's tight ass, and by the time the train had rattled its way from Waterloo down to Wimbledon, I had a healthy hard-on in my pants. I'd take him straight up to the bathroom, I thought, as I walked through the leafy sub-urban streets, bend him over the sink, grease him up with a blob of Brylcreem, and fuck him good and hard before we even said hello.

But the moment I saw Morgan, my dearest friend, standing distraught and disheveled on the doorstep, the blood rushed from my cock to my brain. Something was wrong—and I wanted to know what. I'm ashamed to say that I felt a shiver of excitement; here was some mystery I would get to the bottom of. Not the bottom I'd been hoping for, but not a bad alternative.

"Morgan! What is the matter? You look like death."

He drew breath to say something, but nothing came out. He turned the color of porridge and swayed a little, catching hold of the column that held up the porch to prevent himself from pitching headlong down the steps. I grabbed his arm and guided him indoors. He walked unsteadily, as if drunk. So much for chasing him up to the bathroom, ripping his pants down, and parting his cheeks; it was the most I could do to drop him on a chair in the dining room, where he sat gasping, staring into space. I poured him a brandy.

"Drink this, come on."

He looked at me, and looked at the brandy glass, as if he had never seen such things before. I took his hand—it was as cold as ice—and carefully put the glass between his fingers. Gradually, we got it to his lips, and tipped a little of the golden spirit between them. It seemed to break the spell; Morgan swallowed, gasped, and started to breathe again.

"My God, Mitch," he said, as if he had only just noticed I was there.

"What the hell is going on, Boy?" I've never been able to break the habit of using the nickname he earned at Cambridge for his fresh looks and high spirits—but at that moment he looked anything but boyish. Dorian Gray had changed places with his picture. His eyes were bloodshot, sunken in rings of shadow, his lips, usually so full and laughing, were thin and bloodless.

"Dead," he said. The word came out in a ghastly croak, and he started coughing. Now his face turned an awful, livid purple, as if he were being gassed. A thick vein stood out in his forehead, framed on either side by Morgan's dark hair, falling almost into his eyes. I held him until the fit had passed, and then pushed his hair back, an action I had performed so many times before in more pleasant circumstances. His forehead was burning hot.

So that was it—he was running a fever. That would explain the grim looks, the bloodshot eyes, the distracted manner. It was a relief—for a moment I thought something was badly wrong. Now I realized he was just ill. Perhaps he hadn't said "dead" but "bed"—which is exactly where he needed to be.

"You're sick, Morgan. Why on earth didn't you tell me?"

He was shivering now; yes, this was a real lulu of a fever, and he needed to be looked after. Lucky for him that his best friend, Edward Mitchell, was a doctor. I had planned to get him into bed for different reasons, but at least he was in good hands. I hoped it was not influenza; I had no desire to ruin my longed-for vacation by catching that. If I was going to be ill, I wanted to do it on company time. I spend all my working hours caring for the sick in the hospital in Edinburgh where I work; it seemed unfair that I should have to play nurse on my vacation.

"He's dead."

The voice was clearer now, the word unambiguous. I snapped out of my selfish reflections.

"Dead? Who's dead?"

He said nothing, just stared gloomily at the brandy glass on the table in front of him.

"Morgan, for God's sake! What are you saying? Who is dead?"

His eyes moved slowly, horribly slowly, to meet mine, and I saw in their depths a misery and desperation that I hoped never to see there.

"Who, Morgan?"

"Bartlett." His voice caught, and I thought he would start coughing again, but he swallowed and cleared his throat. "Frank Bartlett."

"Who is Frank Bartlett, Boy?" I realized I was speaking as I would to a child.

"My...my friend..." His eyes were darting from side to side now, unable to hold my gaze.

"You've had some bad news, Morgan. I'm so sorry. If it would help to tell me about it..."

He looked puzzled, as if I were speaking a foreign language.

"Did someone call you on the telephone? Did you have a telegram?" He shook his head, said nothing. "Was this after you spoke to me? Morgan? Come on, please, tell me what's going on!"

"I think I'm going to—" He leaned over the side of the chair and retched; nothing came up but gas. When he sat up again, I noticed that he was blue around the lips. I grabbed his wrist and felt for his pulse; it was fast and weak. He was exhibiting all the symptoms of shock.

The doctor in me sprang into action. I got him into the lounge, laid him down on the couch, and put two cushions under his feet; that would get the blood flowing back to his heart. There was a thick woolen blanket over the back of the couch, which I tucked around his body, and placed a rug on top of it. Morgan was shivering violently now, his teeth chattering so much that he could not speak. I took off my jacket, unbuttoned the front of my shirt, pulled back his covers, and lay down beside him, pressing my body against his, trying to warm him. We lay like that for ten, maybe 15 minutes until, gradually, the shivering subsided and he began to breathe more regularly. I took his pulse again; it was stronger and slower this time. The crisis was past. I stood up, buttoned my shirt, and tucked it back into my pants, taking the opportunity to rearrange the completely inappropriate erection that had been straining painfully down there ever since lying beside him. I'm not above taking advantage of a man when he's down, but there are some depths to which even I won't sink.

I sat on the edge of the couch, smoothing his hair, holding his hand. He kept his eyes tight shut, like a child pretending to sleep. Whatever had happened, he couldn't yet face it. I would have to wait.

I have lived in Britain for long enough to know that what was needed at this point was tea—hot, strong tea with plenty of sugar. I rang the bell for the maid.

There was no reply.

"There's no one here," said Morgan, in a weirdly normal, controlled voice. "I gave the servants the weekend off."

"I see." Was this part of his plan—to have the house to himself so that we could fuck uninterrupted? If so, why the hell hadn't he called me yesterday? We'd wasted a whole day and a night. As usual, I was letting my dick do the thinking. I found my way to the kitchen—this was my first visit to Morgan's new family home, but it was modeled on traditional lines—filled the kettle, and lit the gas. The kitchen was scrupulously clean, the floor scrubbed and shining, the grate clean, the pots and pans neatly ranged on shelves and hooks. There was a vase of lilacs on the windowsill, and the fresh, sweet perfume filled the room. Nothing here was out of place. It was exactly what I expected. Boy's wife, Belinda, would know just how to run an orderly, pleasant house. A cook and a maid were all she would need; she would take care of everything else, looking after her husband and two small children as if it were the easiest thing in the world. I admired Belinda tremendously, despite the fact that she was married to my dearest friend, the man who, of all the men in the world, I most enjoyed fucking. More than Vince—my own husband, or wife, or whatever the world would call him. My own beloved Vince, with whom I shared my life and my home. Who was now in Paris, on publishing business, negotiating British rights for American books, and wanted me to go with him, but I had invented some nonexistent medical conference as an excuse to get down to London and see Boy Morgan.

The kettle boiled, and I made the tea to the best of my ability; Vince said that no American would ever make a really good cup of tea, but grudgingly admitted I had just about risen above the dishwater level. Vince again. I hadn't done anything with Morgan, and already I was feeling guilty. I shouldn't have come. I should leave.

And perhaps I would have left—turned on my heel and left Wimbledon without a word to Morgan, taken the boat train over to Paris and surprised Vince...

But then I saw the blood in the hallway.

I hadn't noticed it before. How could I miss it? A dark red smear on the black-and-white tiles, about two feet from the door, drying now to brown but still unmistakably blood. I've seen enough of the stuff in operating theaters to know what it looks like.

There was a fair-sized patch of it, perhaps four inches long, roughly the shape of an elongated leaf, with a few sprayed droplets at the end. From this angle, it was as clear as day. I must have overlooked it before. Yes, from the other side the light from the fanlight above the door fell strangely, and it looked no more sinister than the scuff mark from a rubber-soled shoe.

I bent down for a closer look. It was still tacky. This blood had been spilled within the last few hours.

I set the tea tray down on the living room table. Morgan was sitting up a little, and the color had returned to his cheeks.

"Tea."

"Thanks, Mitch."

I poured, added milk and sugar, stirred, and handed him a cup.

"That's better." He sighed. "I'm sorry about that little performance. Don't know what came over me."

"Morgan," I said, "there's blood in the hall."

"Blood?"

"Blood. A great big puddle of the stuff." I needed to know what was going on, and saw no harm in exaggerating, if it would prevent Morgan's upper lip from restiffening.

"Ah."

"I think you'd better tell me what's going on."

He sat with the teacup poised between saucer and mouth. "Yes," he said at length, replacing it in the saucer with a dainty tinkle, "I suppose I'd better."

We sat in silence for a while, sipping our tea, for all the world like two old maids whiling away the hours before death. The clock ticked, somewhere a bird sang, and we listened to horses' hooves approaching and then departing along the street outside.

"Mitch?" He put his teacup down and stood up, brushing some creases from his trousers. I thought he was going to ask me to leave. "Would you mind awfully," he said, "if we went to bed? I think I might start crying, and I would feel a lot better if I was in your arms."

It wasn't long before we were lying in his bed—his and Belinda's bed, a large, comfortable piece of furniture with a handsome Turkish rug thrown over it. The curtains in the bedroom were closed, shutting out the light and sounds of the day. We had undressed to our shirts and underpants. Morgan lay on his side, and I lay behind him, holding him the way I'd held him so many times before under happier, hornier circumstances. Of course he felt my hard cock pressing against his ass, and he even backed up against it, wriggling those firm, rubber buttocks the way he always did—but we did these things without thinking. Perhaps, later, we would fuck. But right now, he had to talk, and I had to listen.

"I found him in the bathroom," he said, and let out a great sigh; I felt his rib cage rise and fall, and his heart pound. "He had cut his wrists. There was blood everywhere—all over the bath, the sink, up the walls. It must have taken him a long time to die." His voice broke again, and I held him tight, waiting for the crisis to subside, gently kissing his neck.

"Oh Mitch, I can't bear it. Everything is wrong. What am I going to tell…" He couldn't go on, but I knew what he was going to say.

What am I going to tell Belinda?

"It's okay, Morgan. There's nothing that we can't sort out together. You and me. The old team. Come on. Tell me everything."

"I suppose I must."

"I think you'd better."

He took a deep breath, and began.

"The door was locked. I'd gone to bed, oh, hours before. Bartlett was staying for the weekend—he's an important business associate, and he's become a good friend. Of both of us," he added, hurriedly. "Belinda's gone to stay with his wife, Vivie. They've been awfully good to us. They don't have children of their own, and I think they've rather taken a shine to Margaret and Teddy… Oh God…" He was weeping now, as silently as he could, ashamed of his tears, but I could feel the shaking of his body. I held on tight, soothing him, kissing him.

"I woke up at about three o'clock, and he… I realized something was wrong. I got up. The bathroom door was locked, and the light was on inside. I knocked, I called him, but there was no reply. I thought at first that he might have fallen asleep in there—like we used to do at Cambridge sometimes, remember? When we'd had too much to drink?"

"I remember."

"But I kept knocking and calling, then banging on the door, shouting out—and still there was nothing. And so I... I broke a pane of glass in the door and unlocked it and... Oh God, Mitch, it was horrible. He was lying on the floor, half propped up against the side of the bath. There was an open razor lying beside him. The blood... God, there was so much blood. And his eyes..."

"I know. I know. It's dreadful when you're not used to it." I've seen many dead people, but I will never really become accustomed to that eerie stare.

"I tried to do something—to save him. But there was nothing I could do. He was...gone."

"Did you touch the body?"

"What? Of course I touched the body. I thought I might be able to...to help him."

I wanted to say "You should have left him alone"—but I didn't think that was what Morgan needed to hear at that moment. "So what did you do?"

"I called the police. They were very good, I must say. They came round right away."

"And what did they say?"

"Well, it was pretty obvious, I suppose. Poor Frank had committed suicide. It's awful, Mitch. It's so awful. How am I going to tell his wife?"

I thought about the scene that presented itself to the police officers who arrived on the scene—a dead man in the bathroom, another man in his pajamas, presumably covered in the dead man's blood. They would not be quite as eager to write it off as suicide as Morgan might believe.

"Are they coming back?"

"Yes. They said that someone would be here later this morning to ask a few routine questions."

"And the bathroom?"

"They put a padlock on it."

"What about the body?"

"They took him away on a stretcher. He was still bleeding, Mitch. Oh God." That explained the stain in the hallway.

"What else did they take?"

"Stuff from the bathroom, from the guest room. Stuff he'd brought with him. I don't know. I wasn't really paying much attention. They were looking for a note, I suppose."

"Did they find one?"

"Not as far as I know."

"So—this Bartlett. What's the story? He turns up at your house to discuss business, locks himself in the bathroom, and slashes his wrists. Why?"

"I... I don't..."

"Who was he, Boy? What's this all about?"

His breathing became heavy again, and he whimpered. I felt powerless. I wanted to make things better for him, to make the pain go away, to break through to the real Boy Morgan. I wanted to kiss him on the mouth, to pull his shirt over his head and see his fine, pale, athletic torso, to run my hand over his muscular stomach and inside the waistband of his shorts. But I could not do that. I felt paralyzed.

"Frank Bartlett and I met about a year ago," he said, when he'd finally gained control of his voice. "He's a partner in a City law firm, Bartlett and Ross—he and Walter Ross built it up after the War, and they've been very successful. International shipping, mostly. Complicated stuff. Pots of money. Anyway, they brought their business to the bank, wanting help with investments, and so on—all the stuff that I do every day of the week, although not usually with quite so many noughts at the end. I was assigned to manage the Bartlett and Ross account, and over the course of a few meetings I got to know Frank Bartlett pretty well.

We hit it off. He's a nice chap. Was. Was a nice chap."

I didn't want him to start crying again, or the police would be here before I'd had a chance to get the full story. I felt sure that, if I were going to help Morgan out of this jam, I needed to know as much as possible—things, perhaps, that he would only tell me, from whom he had nothing to hide.

"What did he look like? I mean, what sort of age, build, coloring?"

"He was in his mid-forties. Average height, a bit shorter than me, but then I'm such a beanpole. Bit taller than you, shortarse." This was better; Morgan was more like his old, bantering self. "Dark hair, what was left of it; he told me he started losing his hair when he was an officer in France. He saw some terrible things over there, Mitch. He was a hero, you know. Distinguished war record. Decorated, and everything. He wasn't one of those awful old men who try to hide it by brushing their hair over the top; he wore it cut short on the back and sides, with a good pair of side-whiskers that he always kept very neatly trimmed. I remember thinking, when I first met him, what a neat, clean man he was. He always looked freshly barbered, freshly shaved…"

A shudder went through Morgan's body—and through mine. We were both thinking of the razor. I squeezed him tight, and he continued.

"Anyway…" He cleared his throat. "He was in very good shape for a man of his years. Most of the chaps in the City get very flabby once they're over thirty, but not Bartlett. He played a lot of sport, trained with weights at his club, had a lot of massages and steam, and so on. His gut was as hard as mine; harder, actually. He was strong and wiry, with a lot of dark hair on his chest and stomach and arms and legs. To look at him, you'd have taken him for ten years younger, at least."

"So you got to see quite a lot of him?" I couldn't keep a suggestive tone out of my voice.

"Yes, well... I mean, like I said, we got on terribly well. He invited me to his club. You know, the Parthenon, in Saint James's."

I whistled.

"Oh yes, he had everything of the best. Very nice, the Parthenon. Excellent food, and excellent facilities. They have a Turkish bath in the basement. You can exercise down there on all sorts of pulleys and contraptions, then you can get a jolly good rubdown and a steam bath."

"I see."

"And... Well, Mitch, you know what I'm like." He sounded ashamed, as if he'd been caught with his hand in the cookie jar.

"I do."

"We were there one evening after work. It had been a long day; Bartlett was preparing a report for his shareholders, and we'd spent hours going over and over a load of figures until my eyes were rolling around in my head. So he suggested we go for a massage and a spot of steam. And it jolly well did the trick. Those Turkish chaps, they can really work the knots out of you. Have you ever tried it?"

"No. Go on."

"Well, afterwards we were relaxing in the steamroom. It's marvelous, all done out in oriental tiles, and so on, with little cabins that you can rest in, get a bit of shut-eye."

"I see."

"And so we were lolling around in one of these, just with towels wrapped round our waists, and I got...you know. A stiffy."

"You would."

"I didn't really notice particularly, I just felt so relaxed and good after the massage, until I noticed that Bartlett was staring rather hard at the front of my towel. So I shifted my leg to try and, you know, hide it a bit, but that didn't work, because the towel started to come undone, and the old feller was about to pop out, so instead I rolled over on my front."

"And what did he do?"

"Blow me if he didn't start stroking my backside."

"Through the towel?"

"At first. Then his hand went up my leg. He had big, strong hands, and he was grabbing me—not roughly, but very firmly. Like he was playing with a football."

I knew exactly what he meant; I have done the same to Morgan's ass myself a hundred times. It's one of the most grabbable asses I have ever seen. I couldn't fault Bartlett's taste, even though I found myself hating him for touching something that, in some way, I thought of as "mine."

"So what did you do? Tell him to get off?"

"I suppose I should have done. Business and pleasure, and all that. But—well, it felt good, and you know what I'm like when things feel good, Mitch. I find it very hard to say no."

That's one of the reasons I love you, I wanted to say.

"Then he pulled the towel off me completely, and got both his hands on my bum, kneading it like dough. God, that made me so hard. It had been ages since anyone had touched me there. Not since you and I... When was that?"

"A while ago," I said, not wanting to remember the strained atmosphere at our last parting.

"And then I felt his face pressing between my buttocks, kissing, his tongue pushing between them. I said he was always clean shaven, but by now it was early evening, and there was a bit of stubble on his chin. It scratched and scraped; I love that feeling, and my legs just opened up. His tongue was straight in there, and it hit my you-know-what. It was incredible, Mitch. His tongue was so firm—it felt like... Like a cock."

I was hard myself, and pressed against him. He moaned softly, and wriggled back into me.

19

"I had my forehead resting on one forearm, but with the other hand I reached round and found his cock. It was like an iron bar, Mitch. It was so big and hard. When I grabbed it, he groaned like a soul in torment. I looked up, and there was the most extraordinary expression on his face—I couldn't decide if he was sad, or happy, or angry. We looked at each other for a while, and then... And then... He kissed me."

"I see."

"God, it was wonderful, Mitch. Not like you—with you I always feel good, and happy, and alive. But this was something different—something serious, and intense, and dangerous. He kissed me like it was the only thing that mattered in the world. It wasn't a bit of fun between two chaps who happen to like each other a lot—this was like...like it meant everything to him. Life and death."

I felt that stupid stab of jealousy—I, who was betraying Vince just by being here. "And then he fucked you, I suppose." I couldn't keep the bitterness out of my voice, but I don't think Morgan even heard me.

"There wasn't much we could do, right there and then; someone could have walked in. I suppose things go on in those steamrooms all the time, don't they? But it wouldn't do to be caught with one's legs in the air, not in the Parthenon Club, not with an important client like Frank Bartlett. But we carried on kissing as if we couldn't stop, my hand on his cock, his hand on mine, sitting side by side, kissing and wanking each other until suddenly we were both coming at the same time, breathing in each other's mouths, sharing the same feelings, as if we were one body. It took both of us a while to come round. Anyone could have stumbled in and found us; we were awfully lucky. Afterwards, we just got dressed. We had a quick drink at the bar, but we didn't have supper or anything. We both suddenly remembered that we had important reasons for getting home. It had taken us by surprise, rather."

"I imagine it had."

"But we both knew that we were going to do something again. There was no going back. I don't know how other chaps feel after things like that—I suppose for some people, that sort of business doesn't mean a lot, just a quick fiddle with another fellow and that's it, full stop. But it wasn't like that for me. I couldn't stop thinking about him. I was all keyed up for days. Even Belinda noticed. I didn't hear from Bartlett for a while, but there was no reason for him to speak to me. We'd done all we needed to do."

"And then?"

"He just turned up at the bank one afternoon. He told my boss that he needed to consult me urgently on a business matter. There was a taxi waiting outside, and we drove out to a hotel near Euston. We didn't say anything. We were both looking out the window, pretending that nothing was happening, but I was as stiff as a pole and I'm sure he was too. He had a copy of the *Times* with him, and he lay it on the seat between us, and took off his glove. Our hands met underneath the newspaper, and we held on tight to each other. The driver didn't suspect a thing."

"And what happened when you got to Euston?"

"I..." His voice was low and gravelly. "Mitch, will you do something for me?"

"Anything, Morgan. You know that."

"I know this sounds completely insane, under the circumstances, but will you..."

"Yes?"

"Will you fuck me?"

"Now?"

"Yes, please. Now. Fuck me. As hard as you can."

# Chapter Two

I GAVE HIM WHAT HE WANTED, AND THEN SOME. I KNOW Morgan well enough to anticipate his needs, to deliver a fuck that will satisfy him on all levels. I started with a finger, warming him up, and when his hole seemed to be sucking my finger in, I judged that the time was right for the main event. There was no time to run around the house looking for lubricants, and unlike my own bedroom, there was no handy little jar of Vaseline on the nightstand, so he would have to do with spit. I knew he could take it. We'd done it this way often enough before.

So I hawked into my hand and rubbed it all over my stiff dick; there was enough of my own slick precum there to make me nice and slippery. Still lying on my side, I pulled down Morgan's pants, lifted one of his legs, and positioned the head of my cock at the target. One firm push, and I was in. Morgan gasped, and I forged ahead, encountering very little resistance. Usually, when fucking Morgan, the first assault is a tactical matter of advance and retreat; now he yielded completely and immediately. Obviously the late Frank Bartlett had been giving him a lot more than furtive hand jobs in the Parthenon steamroom.

I started fucking him slowly, checking that he was enjoying himself by grabbing his cock and stroking it gently; he was fully hard, as I knew he would be. Morgan loved to be fucked—it was the one thing that prevented him from being the hundred-percent-hearty family man who, in every other respect, he was meant to be. Soon he was pushing back against me, hungry for more; the time was right to change position. I pulled out, grabbed his calves, and rolled him onto his back, pushing his thighs against his stomach. He reached down and pulled his ass open, impatient for me to get back inside. I didn't keep him waiting.

This way I could fuck him with all my body weight pressing into him, and I could watch his face for clues and cues as to where to go next. At first he kept his eyes shut tight, his mouth set in a grim line, as if this were a punishment that he had to endure, that he deserved. But then I kissed him, fucking his mouth with my tongue as I was fucking his ass with my cock, and he came back to me. His eyes opened and looked into mine, and we spent the next few minutes searching the depths of each other's soul. At least, that's how it felt at the time. These moments of profound communication sound ridiculous in the cold light of day. But as I fucked him, and looked into those big, dark, troubled, honest eyes, I felt that I would never know or love anyone as deeply as I knew and loved Boy Morgan.

It couldn't last for long; we both needed release. He bucked his hips, and I picked up the rate of my pounding, and soon I was burying my face in his neck and emptying my balls into his guts. He wrapped his legs around me, and with one fist on his cock he pumped himself to a climax just as I thrust the last, longest time into him. We lay like that for a while, my cock buried deep in him, our stomachs glued together with spunk, until finally I withdrew with a plop and a squelch, rolled off him, and held him in my arms.

We must have slept for an hour.

I woke with a start. What were we doing? The police would be back any moment, and I still didn't have a clue what had happened. Morgan was still lying beside me, but he wasn't sleeping. His eyes were open, staring up at the ceiling.

"Christ, Boy, we need to get up! Come on!"

"No… I want to stay here."

I pulled the covers off him; his naked body was beautiful, the hair on his stomach and chest still matted with cum.

"You're in a big heap of trouble, Boy. You can't just stay in bed and pretend you're not."

"I can."

He sounded pathetic and petulant, and I told him so. He scowled at me, and very grudgingly got out of bed. The bathroom was out of bounds, but there was a jug of water and a basin in the bedroom; we freshened up as best we could with that, and got dressed. We must have stunk of sex; anyone with a nose for these things would know exactly what we had been doing.

"When are the cops coming?" I asked.

"I don't know. They don't give exact appointments."

It was well after ten o'clock. "They could be here any minute. What are you going to tell them?"

"The truth."

"The whole truth?"

"Well…"

That, of course, he could not do. To admit to any kind of improper relationship with Frank Bartlett would have landed Morgan himself in the dock, possibly in prison, certainly out of a job and out of a marriage. I hoped to God that there was a damn good solid reason for Bartlett's suicide—something that didn't suggest to the police that there were other, unmentionable motives at play.

"So why'd he do it?"

That took him by surprise. "What?"

"Your pal Bartlett. Why did a successful lawyer come around to your house for the weekend and cut his wrists in your bathroom?"

"I... I don't know..."

"You better have some idea, Morgan, when the police arrive."

"Oh God."

"Because if they think for one moment that there was some kind of lovers' tiff—"

"Don't be disgusting."

"You were lovers, weren't you? You and Bartlett."

"I didn't mean to—"

"Weren't you?" It was obvious from the deep blush on Morgan's face, and from the ease with which I had penetrated him, that I was right. This had gone a lot further than a bit of slap and tickle between two married men, the sort of thing that happens every day in every town. Morgan was keeping something from me.

"Yes."

"Tell me why he did it, Morgan. Please tell me that he was in trouble at work—that he'd been caught with his hand in the till, that he'd forged a document or given false evidence. Tell me that this was a decent, honorable suicide."

"I don't know."

"You must."

And to underline my words, the doorbell rang. Morgan jumped, then froze.

"Answer it," he said.

"That's going to look suspicious. You answer it." Already, I realized, I was acting as if something had to be covered up. Could it possibly be that Morgan was—what? Guilty? In the wrong? Hiding something? There was no time to think. The bell rang again, and Morgan marched out, looking every inch the successful young City banker enjoying a bachelor weekend in his comfortable suburban family home.

"Ah, hello again, sergeant," I heard him say from the hall.

"This is Constable Knight," said a stern, deep voice.

"Constable. Come in, both of you. My friend Edward Mitchell is here."

Morgan showed the two cops in, and for a crazy moment I hoped that I might be in for a repeat of some of my earlier, friendlier relations with the British police force. These two certainly looked appetizing enough in their uniforms. The sergeant was tall, with dark-brown hair and a strong jaw and chin; his constable was somewhat shorter, fairer, and younger. They both carried their helmets under their arms.

"Mr. Mitchell," said the sergeant. He did not offer to shake my hand. I nodded coolly.

"Mitch, this is Sergeant Godley. And Constable... Sorry, I've forgotten already."

"Knight," said the younger man, who stood at the door—as if to prevent any escape bids.

"Please, sit down," said Morgan. Godley obliged, his constable did not. "What can I do for you, sergeant?"

"Just a few routine questions, sir." He took out a note-book. Morgan sat, his hands pressed between his knees; he looked anxious.

"You don't mind if Mitch sits in, do you? I'm afraid I'm in a bit of a state. Mitch is a doctor, he's good in a crisis."

"That's quite all right, sir," said Godley, eyeing me coolly. Did he guess, or suspect, the nature of our friendship? If he had seen what we'd been doing just a couple of hours ago, would he have busted us? Or would he have laid his helmet to one side and joined in? And what about the little blond? Would he—

"How did you know Mr. Bartlett, sir?" asked Godley.

"He is a client. I work at the London Imperial Bank. I manage Mr. Bartlett's business affairs."

"And how long have you known him?"

"Let me see… A year? No, it was before Teddy was born, before we moved here. Eighteen months, I suppose. Yes, that sounds about right. It was autumn, I think, when he first came in. I seem to remember the conkers were on the trees."

He was babbling. Godley watched him, and waited for him to stop.

"And why was Mr. Bartlett staying here?"

"What, Frank?" Morgan's mouth hung open, as if he could not think of an answer. "Well, he was… I mean…"

"He was here to discuss business," I said. Godley scowled; obviously I was not expected to speak.

"That's it," said Morgan. "His firm was about to acquire a new building in Chancery Lane, huge great place, brand-new. Costs a fortune. I advised against it on the ground that it would overextend their credit. Not what the bank ought to tell a customer, that, eh? But he wanted to go over all the pros and cons because I think he'd rather set his heart on it. So we packed the ladies off to his place in Teddington and we were planning to spend the weekend plowing through the figures."

"Do you have the paperwork to hand, sir?"

"What?"

"The figures that you and Mr. Bartlett were going to, er…" Godley referred to his notebook. "Plow through."

"No. He brought it with him, I suppose, in his briefcase. We were meant to be starting this morning. Oh God…" Morgan went very pale, and put a hand to his brow. I suppose anyone would do the same under the circumstances, but my heart pounded; I wanted him above all to remain calm and businesslike.

"Was there anything else that you and Mr. Bartlett had planned for the weekend?"

"No... I mean, we had a walk on the Common to clear our heads, but there was a lot of work to..."

"Plow through," supplied Sergeant Godley. I was starting to hate Sergeant Godley. I wanted to interrupt, ask him what the hell he was driving at when he could see my friend was distressed, but I didn't think that would help.

"Were you aware of any irregularities in Mr. Bartlett's financial affairs?"

"Good Lord, no. Bartlett and Ross is one of the most highly respected law firms in the City."

"I didn't quite mean that, sir. I was thinking more of his personal financial affairs."

Morgan caught the meaning, and responded perfectly. "Oh, no, sergeant, you've misunderstood. I was not Frank Bartlett's personal bank manager. I handled business matters for him, that's all. I believe his personal account was with Lloyds. Yes, I'm fairly certain. Couldn't tell you the exact branch. Obviously I'll have a record of that somewhere."

"So your dealings with Mr. Bartlett were strictly professional?"

"No."

"Ah?"

"We became jolly good friends. It was through the girls, really—I mean my wife, Belinda, and his wife, Vivien. They hit it off from the start. Vivie rather took Billie under her wing, helping out with the children, and so on. They don't have any of their own, you see—not quite sure why, that's just the way it goes sometimes."

"How many children do you have, Mr. Morgan?"

"Two, sergeant. My daughter, Margaret, is nearly two and a half now. The boy, Edward, is coming up to one."

"They must be a handful."

"They are," said Morgan, beaming—it was like someone

had turned on a light—"but I wouldn't have it any other way."

"Thank you, sir. That's all for now." Godley got up, and Knight opened the door. "Will we be able to find you here for the rest of the day, sir?"

"Yes, if you want me. I'm not going anywhere."

"Is Mr. Mitchell staying with you?"

That's none of your damn business, you arrogant prick, I wanted to say.

"Yes, I hope so. Don't much like the idea of being alone."

"Has anyone told Mrs. Bartlett?" I asked.

"Oh God, Vivie! I hadn't even thought... How awful. She must be in bits."

"Yes, she has been informed. I believe your wife is staying with her for the time being. Perhaps," said Godley, "you should telephone her."

He raised an eyebrow, maybe surprised that Morgan hadn't thought of doing it already. I was surprised too. Morgan had been so determined to get fucked, he'd forgotten to call his wife.

"I'm all at sixes and sevens," said Morgan. "It's the shock of all that...blood. I'm sorry." He coughed, pulled himself together. "I'll get on the blower right away. Good morning, gentlemen."

"Oh, just one more thing," said Godley. "Don't go into the bathroom under any circumstances. It's a crime scene now. Good morning."

We listened to the heavy tread of their feet until they disappeared. Morgan put his head in his hands.

"Oh God, Mitch, this is a ghastly business."

"It would help if you told me all about it."

He looked up with hope in his eyes. "Really? You won't be...angry?"

"Morgan, the only thing that is making me angry is the

29

horrible feeling that you're holding out on me."

"Then I suppose I have to tell you everything, don't I?"

"You sure do," I said, putting a hand on his shoulder and squeezing. "But first of all…" I picked up the telephone and handed him the receiver. "Your wife."

I left him to it. Apart from not wishing to eavesdrop on what was bound to be a painful conversation, I had some thinking to do.

Morgan was in trouble, that much was clear. But how much trouble? What did he know of the reasons for Bartlett's suicide? Was he himself one of the reasons? How could he explain that to the police? And if, as I guessed from Sergeant Godley's questions, there was some suggestion of financial wrongdoing, was Morgan implicated in that as well? I did not for one moment entertain the idea that Morgan had deliberately, knowingly involved himself in any shady business—but I could not rid myself of the suspicion that, somehow, he had got himself tangled up in another man's crime, and now he had blood on his hands. Or at least on his pajamas.

He came out of the drawing room, pale but calm.

"She's staying with Vivie for a while," he said. "Jolly good of her. Poor thing is in a terrible state, apparently."

"She's just lost her husband."

"Quite so, quite so…" He seemed distracted, unable to grasp the reality of Vivie Bartlett's bereavement.

"Morgan…"

"Hmmm?"

"Penny for your thoughts."

He'd started to put on his coat and was stepping into his outdoor shoes. "I thought we might get some fresh air."

"The police told you to stay put."

"I don't think they meant that I couldn't take a walk on the Common, old chap. Come on. I've got to get out of here. You'll make sure I don't do anything silly, I'm sure."

"Like what? Run away? Is that what you were thinking of doing?"

"Don't be daft," said Morgan, and knelt down to tie his laces.

Wimbledon Common started just two streets away; the solid suburban houses stopped suddenly, and nature, or some well-managed version thereof, took over. It was a pleasant enough day, and it felt good to be out of a house where death had come so recently, so violently. Away from that locked bathroom, and the horrible imagining of red blood on white tiles. Morgan took huge strides with his great long rower's legs; I almost had to trot to keep up with him.

"There's a pleasant spot just up here," he said, after we'd walked for ten minutes in silence. "Nice view, and a bench to admire it from. Come on."

The bench was on top of a little hill, well away from paths. We could see anyone approaching from some distance. I assumed this was not accidental. I lit cigarettes for both of us, and we looked out over the golf course and the horse rides. I could see from the expression on Morgan's face that he was working up to a confession.

"That first night in the hotel," he said at last, "I knew that this was going to be a serious business. You know me, Mitch. I take life pretty much as it comes. I'm not a deep thinker. Things usually work out for me—I mean, look at you, and Belinda, and the little ones. My job, my new house—it's all fallen into place, hasn't it? You and I have been in some funny old scrapes"—I thought that was a strange way to refer to two murder investigations in which we'd nearly lost our lives—"but things have always turned up trumps. You and I have a bit of fun, and that's nobody else's business but ours. It's not as if it matters to anyone."

Keep saying that, I thought, and maybe one day you'll convince yourself.

"But this was different. There was something about

31

Frank Bartlett—I knew it from the very first moment that I met him, to tell you the truth—something deep and...well, serious."

"I see."

"I don't mean that we were ever real friends, not in the way that you and I are, Mitch. You're like a brother to me."

A brother who fucks you.

"But he was something else. At first he was a sort of father figure, I suppose. He was so much older and wiser and more successful than me, but he took an interest in me and seemed to want to help me."

He wanted to get into your pants.

"But after that first night..."

"Wow," I said, trying to keep the tone light, "he must have been one hell of a fuck."

"Yes," said Morgan, "he was."

That took the wind out of my sails; I was hoping to hear that Bartlett couldn't hold a candle to me. Then I realized that I was feeling jealous of a man who was lying in the morgue, minus several pints of blood.

"That hotel that he took me to wasn't the nicest of settings, to be honest—but I didn't notice. It could have been the Taj Mahal or a Whitechapel slum as far as I was concerned. Mitch—I've never felt such power coming from another man. It was as if he'd hypnotized me. He just drew me in, and when he shut the bedroom door, we were in another world. He took my clothes off—I stood there like a stuffed dummy—and when I was completely naked, he kissed me all over. I was trembling, and he took me to bed, stripped, and—"

"Pounced?"

"I suppose so. But it didn't feel like that. I knew what to expect, of course—I mean, we've done it often enough, and I've always had a jolly good time—but he took me by storm.

It was as if I was drunk, or flying, or falling, or something. I've never experienced anything like it."

"What, then," I said, sounding like a bitter old maid. "He fucked you, did he?"

"Yes. And then I fucked him. And then he fucked me again. And then, afterwards, we took a bath. It was a dreadful old rustbucket of a bath, all the enamel chipped off, great brown water stains under the taps, and to be honest the water was none too hot when it came, but it didn't matter. We could have been floating in the Pacific Ocean. He washed me, so gently and tenderly, like you'd wash a child. And then, when it was really too cold, he dried me. And then—"

He stopped, swallowed hard, and stared out over the Common.

"What, Morgan?"

"He shaved me."

"He shaved you?"

"Yes. He stood behind me at the sink, his cock was hard again, pressing into my arse, mine was hard, resting on the edge of the sink. He ran a little more hot water, he lathered up my face, and he shaved me. It was the best, closest shave I've ever had. Better than you get at the barber. Much better than I can do myself. He took his time, stroking the blade over every part of my face, so softly, like I was being tickled by a feather. Afterwards, my skin felt like silk. I don't think I've ever done anything so exciting."

"Wow." I was hard again too; why hadn't I thought of shaving Morgan, damn it?

"Afterwards, he rinsed off the razor and put it very carefully back in its case." Morgan shuddered, thinking, I suppose, about the razor's ultimate use. "And then, with what was left of the lather, he soaped me up and fucked me again.

"My God. The man was an animal."

"It was like he was making up for lost time, Mitch. He told me afterwards that he and Vivie no longer had relations. I'm not sure if they ever really had. I think it had been a long time since he'd been really satisfied. I had trouble keeping up with him."

"What was he like when you finally finished?"

"I don't know. Quiet, I suppose. I tidied myself up and got dressed in the bedroom. He stayed in the bathroom for a while, cleaning his teeth, gargling with mouthwash. He was always very particular like that, especially after...you know. He spent ages brushing and slooshing and spitting. I suppose it made him feel clean again. That's why last night, when he didn't come to bed..."

"So it wasn't just a business visit."

"Of course not." Morgan sounded angry, impatient. "That's what I'm trying to tell you. After that first time, we were together as often as we could be. Sometimes we went to that same hotel, sometimes we stayed at his club, but we had to be so dreadfully careful there. Sometimes I had to accompany him out of town on a business trip—you'd be surprised how many business trips he arranged."

"Didn't Belinda suspect anything?"

"Good Lord, no."

"But weren't your tanks rather low?"

"She was expecting Teddy by this time. I think she was rather glad that I wasn't pestering her in that department. I kept up a decent show of willingness... God, what a cad I am. How could I do this to her?"

"You didn't mean to, Morgan." Like hell—he'd cheated on Belinda since before they were even married, with me. And with who knows who else? I felt a wave of indignation, until I realized that I, too, had been consistently unfaithful to Vince. But it was different for me, wasn't it?

Of course it wasn't. I was just pissed because I thought Morgan was mine—at least, that part of him. Now I knew what it was like to be deceived. It hurt, just as it would hurt Vince and Belinda.

"No, I didn't mean to. I was carried along. And then the girls got to know each other, and it became even more complicated."

"How on earth did you let that happen?"

"I couldn't very well avoid it. I mean, we were spending so much time together, it would have looked very odd if we hadn't met socially. Bartlett was a great one for appearances. And so he invited Billie and me over for dinner at their house in Teddington. Lovely place. Huge great villa near the river. Billie was right at home, but, of course, she comes from that kind of background. I was a bit overawed, kept tripping over things, didn't know which spoon to use and all that. But Vivie is a lovely woman, and she put me at my ease, and by the time Frank had poured a few drinks we were getting on like we'd known each other all our lives. Vivie and Billie knew a lot of people in common, and by the end of the evening they had their arms round each other like sisters. Frank was delighted."

"Yes, I'm sure he was."

"What's that supposed to mean, Mitch?"

"Well, it sounds as if he planned all this very carefully. Making you part of the family, binding you closer to him. That suited his purposes nicely."

"If you're suggesting that Frank was the one who did all the running, you're wrong. I was just as bad as he was. I wanted him all the time. I would have taken stupid risks just to spend time alone with him—he was always the one who advised caution. I was head over heels. God, it was mad—really, it was like a form of madness. The more I saw him, the more I wanted him. It wasn't just the way he made me feel when we were in bed together, although that was a big part of it. It's the way he made me feel as a man—he was so confident, so clever, so experienced, and that's how I started to feel. He cared about me, and he wanted me to do well. He taught me things. I've never felt so...so cared for."

I knew that Morgan's relationship with his own father had been chilly and distant, without much love on either side. I didn't wish to sound like some kind of crazy trick cyclist, so I said nothing—but this sounded like a mixed-up Oedipus complex to me.

"So what happened?"

"We carried on like that for months. It seems like a dream, or a nightmare, to me now. I suppose what really snapped me out of it was when Teddy was born. Suddenly I couldn't just leave home at the drop of a hat. I had responsibilities, I had a loving, beautiful wife and two children who needed a father. I tried to talk to Frank."

"And he didn't want to hear it?"

"On the contrary," said Morgan. "He was very under-standing. He said that my duty was with my family, and that he didn't expect to see so much of me. And he was as good as his word. I didn't see him for a couple of weeks, then a couple more, then a month. I couldn't stand it, Mitch. I couldn't sleep. I wasn't eating. Billie didn't notice much because she was preoccupied with the children, and to be honest it wasn't easy to sleep through the night even without Frank on my mind. But eventually I couldn't stand it anymore. I had to arrange a meeting with him at the bank anyway, and afterwards I told him that we were going out for dinner. I couldn't stand being without him anymore."

"And he would have known that, Morgan."

"What? Maybe. Perhaps it was all part of his plan. I don't know."

"And what happened that night?"

"We had dinner at his club. It was all very civilized. I tried to touch him under the table, like I had before, but he very discreetly moved my hand away. He said we needed to talk about business."

"Really? At a time like that? What was so important?"

"He had an offer to make me. He said he realized that, with a growing family, my salary was pretty stretched. He seemed to know exactly how much I earned, and exactly what my outgoings were. I don't know if he'd been prying, or if it was just a shrewd guess; like I say, he was a brilliant businessman. And it was true—the money didn't go as far as I'd have liked. We were still living in the old house in town at this time, of course, and with two children on the go there just wasn't enough room. We didn't want to bring them up in town, we wanted to move out somewhere with more space and fresh air. Like this."

"I see."

"He must have read my mind. Because he said that he'd like to offer me a helping hand."

"A loan?"

"Not a loan, exactly."

"A gift?"

"I suppose so. That's not exactly how he put it. He said he'd be prepared to put down a deposit on a house of my choosing."

"Oh, Morgan. How could you be so stupid?"

"It was just until we got ourselves on our feet. He said that I'd be promoted by the end of the year, my salary would go up—he'd talked to my boss at the bank, and it was as good as done. He said he just wanted the best for Belinda and Margaret and Edward—that they had become like his own family, his and Vivie's. They both wanted to help us. And so—I said yes. What else could I do? It was a dream come true. We'd never have been able to afford the house without him. It was no skin off his nose, he said, and it would mean so much to him to see us better provided for."

"What did you tell Belinda?"

"I told her we'd had some good luck on the stock market."

"You lied."

"Frank thought it would be better to keep the details to ourselves."

"How much did he give you?"

"I say, old man, I'd rather not—"

"Morgan," I said, turning toward him, "I don't wish to speak ill of the dead, but are you one hundred percent certain that your Frank Bartlett was on the level? Because from what I could read between the lines of what friend Godley was saying, there's more than a whiff of embezzlement here."

"Don't be daft."

"Then what, Morgan? Why else would a man like Frank Bartlett kill himself?"

"Because," said Morgan, staring out across the Common, "I tried to finish with him."

# Chapter Three

THE COMMON WAS STARTING TO GET BUSY WITH NANNIES pushing prams, workers on an early lunch break, and the leisured classes taking a preprandial stroll. Morgan got up, stretched his legs, and headed back to the house. "Just in case the police need me," he said. "I suppose it wouldn't look good if they thought I'd run away."

I glanced up at him, hoping to see a smile on his face. It wasn't there. "You weren't thinking of doing that, were you, Morgan?"

"Not really," he said, in a dreamy voice, as if that's exactly what he wanted above all else. "It's just…" He sighed, then sounded more like himself. "Of course not. I'm ready to face the music, and all that. It's just I can't stand those coppers looking at me as if I'd done something."

"That's their job."

"What—making innocent men feel guilty? Is that what we pay their wages for?"

Better let him blow off some steam, I thought, so I listened to his rantings until we were safely back indoors.

Sometimes Morgan sounded like the crustiest colonel in the stuffiest club in the whole of the British Empire. It was one of the contradictions in his character that I found charming; he could switch in a moment to the sparkling-eyed, mischievous boy who couldn't wait to get my dick in his mouth.

I was hungry by the time we got in, and rustled up some sandwiches, which we ate in the kitchen while Morgan continued to talk.

"The whole thing was becoming too much for me, Mitch. The money for the house, the time we spent together, the hiding and sneaking around—it was wearing me out. I wanted to get back to how I was, to being a proper husband to Billie and a proper father to the children. But every time I struggled, the bonds seemed to get tighter. He never said as much, but Frank Bartlett was determined to keep me, and nothing that I said convinced him that I wanted to break with him."

"Perhaps you just weren't very convincing. Did you really want to finish it?"

"I did and I didn't. That's the truth. Part of me dreaded seeing him, but part of me wanted him more than ever."

"I know which part that was."

"Yes, well, you understand." He was embarrassed by such direct references. "Anyway, it got to the stage that I couldn't very well finish with him, because he'd done so much for us. He lent us that money, and I knew perfectly well that he didn't expect to get it back. He even helped us to find this house. It belonged to an old client of his who sold it for a song when he went bust. Bartlett made sure we got first dibs. Belinda was thrilled—it's just the sort of house she always wanted to live in."

"It's a very nice house."

"I hate it now."

"Come on, Morgan. Don't be ridiculous."

"It feels like a trap."

"You'd better not tell that to the police."

"There's a lot I'm not going to tell the police, Mitch." He looked at me across the kitchen table. "But you... Well, I'm rather hoping that if I tell you everything, you might be able to find a way out of this—" He waved his hands in front of his face, as if brushing away cobwebs. "This muddle."

Only an Englishman of Morgan's class could call a queer suicide with overtones of financial wrongdoing a "muddle."

"Go ahead," I said.

"The first time I told him that we ought to stop, he just wouldn't listen. He told me I was confused, that I didn't have enough experience to judge these things rightly, and that was that. The next thing I knew, the boss called me in to say how pleased he was with my work on the Bartlett and Ross account, that he was giving me a raise, and that Mr. Bartlett wanted me to take over a much larger investment portfolio now that his partner, Ross, was moving towards retirement."

"A honey trap," I said. Morgan nodded.

"So I had to spend even more time at Bartlett's office, and my life was even more intimately tied up with his. I was working almost exclusively on his business; the bank was so happy to have this important client that they didn't want me to be distracted by other matters. If I'd tried to break with Bartlett, I'd have had a lot of explaining to do. I owed him my house, and now I owed him my job."

"If you'd really wanted to break with him, Morgan, you could have done so."

"Maybe. Is that what you'd have done, Mitch?"

"I don't know."

"You see? It's not always black and white. Anyway, I was happy. I put all the worries out of my mind and concentrated on the good things. The house was fine, work was successful, and I really enjoyed being part of Bartlett and Ross. It was a privilege to work there. Walter Ross is a fine man, Mitch. He made a great deal of money, and he was planning to spend the rest of his life enjoying it. He was always laughing at

Bartlett and me, calling us worker ants, saying that we should stop slaving away and start enjoying life—if only he knew! We were still together at every opportunity, and it seemed that any time we had a break, we came back even stronger than ever. The personal side of things was... Well, I'll spare your blushes, old man. You don't want to hear me talking about all that."

He was right, there. However exciting it was to think about Morgan being fucked by a powerful, athletic older man in principle, in practice it hurt me, right in the gut.

"I was spending more time at B and R than I was at the bank. There was so much stuff to go through—they had their fingers in a lot of pies, and part of my job was to consolidate all their investments into a streamlined, efficient portfolio that would carry on making them lots of money without them having to lift a finger. That meant shifting things around, buying this, selling that, like an enormous juggling act. Bartlett did what he could, but he had clients to work with. Thank God they had an efficient office manager. Tippett, his name was. One of the best damn men I've ever had the pleasure of working with. He came from a very humble background, did Tippett, but he'd done well for himself just through brainpower. Not like me. Good education and a bit of charm gets me a long way, but next to Tippett, I'm as thick as two short planks."

I was about to say something unkind, but I held my peace. This degree of self-knowledge was a new development. Perhaps Bartlett had been a good influence after all.

"Anyway, thanks to Tippett I got everything shipshape, Bartlett was pleased, the bank was pleased, old man Ross was bloody delighted, and swanned off on an extended holiday in Italy as soon as he knew the money was in the right place. I got all the glory, but to be honest with you, Mitch, it was Tippett who deserved the credit. He was brilliant—he knew every shortcut in the book, how to make the most of money, how to work just within the rules. I could see why Bartlett relied on him so heavily. You wouldn't have thought it to look at him, but Tippett had a mind like a steel trap."

"What is he like?" I asked, envisaging some shaky, thin-legged man in late middle age, hunched from years of bending over a ledger.

"Oh, not much older than you and me," said Morgan. "Slight little chap—quite short—slim as a whippet. Dark hair. Nice looking, once you really look at him—but not the sort of man you'd ever pick out in a crowd. Tends to sort of blend in with the background. Self...self... What's the word, Mitch?"

"Self-effacing?"

"That's the feller. Self-effacing. Bit self-conscious, I suppose. Grew up in Kent, or Essex, or somewhere like that. His people were shopkeepers. I suppose that's where he learnt the tricks of the trade. Dragged himself up by his bootstraps, put himself through night school to qualify as an accountant, got a job at Bartlett and Ross as little more than an office boy, and he's been there ever since. Frank's right-hand man, you might say."

"Were they—?"

"Certainly not." Morgan scratched his chin. "At least, I don't think so. God, Mitch, you've got a dirty mind sometimes. That had never occurred to me."

"And did you have a go?"

"No, I didn't," he said, "although I wouldn't have said no. I saw how he looked at me sometimes. Nice little arse," he said, kneading it in the air, "and I bet he'd know what to do with it."

I made a mental note to meet Mr. Tippett, the organizational paragon with the promising rear end.

"Tippett took care of a lot of Frank's more delicate business dealings," said Morgan. "For instance, after I'd made one final attempt to cool things down between us, Tippett

43

happened to mention that Frank had transferred some stock into my name, 'for tax purposes,' he said, but I knew that this was yet another gift. If Frank had given it to me himself, I'd have turned it down—maybe. But if it came through Tippett, if it was presented as nothing more than a business arrangement, it was so much easier to accept."

"Did Tippett know about you and Bartlett? Did he suspect?"

"I don't think so. He never said anything."

"You don't always notice these things, Boy. Sometimes you have to be hit over the head."

"Well, if he did have his suspicions, he kept them to himself. He wasn't married or anything; I think he lives with his mother, or an aunt or older sister or something—in any case, he's the confirmed bachelor type. I wouldn't be at all surprised if he was like...you."

I raised an eyebrow, but said nothing.

"Anyway, after that I didn't even try to get out of the affair. It just seemed to make things worse, and I was worried that Bartlett would do something really compromising. So we carried on as we were, seeing each other most days at work, several times a month at each other's houses when we entertained, and then sneaking off to hotels or empty houses to be together. I kept waiting for him to tire of me, but he never did. He was just as passionate as he was that first night. And—well, I have to be honest with you, Mitch. He made me feel the same way. The things he did to me... I don't know. It was like electricity." He shuddered. "God, it was wonderful. And now I'll never feel that again."

Did I never make you feel that way?

Poor Morgan—he was deeply distressed, and there was no one he could tell but me. But something was nagging at my brain. What was it? I held his hand while he struggled to compose himself—and then it came to me.

"Morgan—earlier on you said that you thought you

knew why Frank Bartlett killed himself."

"Did I?"

"You said you tried to finish with him. What did you mean?"

"We had a big row."

"When?"

"Yesterday. No—when was it? My God, yes, it was yesterday. It seems like a lifetime ago."

"What happened?"

"He came here so full of beans. I think he'd been looking forward to this weekend more than anything else in his life—to have me to himself for two whole nights, in the home that he'd bought for me, without having to make do with hotel rooms, without hiding and lying and sordid arrangements. And he was being very mysterious—he said he'd done something special for me, but he wouldn't say what. Something to show me how much he cared. I knew exactly what it would be—another of these damned awkward cash gifts. I told him I couldn't accept it, that he was making things difficult for me, and we ended up fighting. God, it was awful. Like two—well, like a man and his mistress. I felt so ashamed. And the worst thing was, the servants must have heard."

"The servants? I thought they had the weekend off."

"They did. They do. But they were still here when Frank arrived, they were clearing up after lunch. We were in the living room with coffee. They must have heard. It's so...so bloody awkward."

"And you said things that might have driven him to... you know?"

"I don't know. Maybe. Yes, I think I did. I said that this couldn't go on, that we would have to finish. I lost my temper, Mitch. I felt trapped, and I hate feeling trapped. I loved him in a way, but at times I hated him. My life had been jogging along quite nicely before I met Frank Bartlett, and suddenly it was all tied in knots. I told him we should stop, and he said he couldn't. He said he couldn't do without me. That I was his whole life. That's when we both realized that we were not alone in the house. We heard the front door closing very quietly; it must have been cook or the maid letting themselves out."

"And do you really think that's why he killed himself? Because you'd told him that you were through? Because he was overheard saying something compromising by a servant girl?"

"I don't know, Mitch. What am I supposed to think? I can't ask Frank. He's dead."

It was obviously too soon to ask Morgan exactly what happened last night to precipitate the crisis, so I turned back the clock. "So you and Frank had been happy together up to that point?"

"As happy as we could be, knowing that we were both living a lie. Sometimes Frank was moody and irritable. He'd cancel arrangements at the last moment, or he'd snap at me, say something unkind just to upset me. I was confused. I asked him what was wrong, and he'd either pretend that nothing had happened, or he'd just wave me away as if I was some little clerk who was badgering him at the wrong time. He could be cruel when he wanted to be; he knew how hard it was for me, how much I was compromising myself to keep him happy, and it wasn't easy to put up with this kind of treatment."

"What was going on, then?"

"I don't know. He never told me. I thought at first that it was business trouble—but of course it couldn't be, because I knew as much about the business as Bartlett himself. I made a few discreet inquiries, and Tippett assured me that B and R had never done better—they had bigger clients and more money than ever before. Bartlett was the most respected man in his field—and he should have been happy."

"So why wasn't he?"

"I've thought about nothing else, Mitch, and I don't know."

"Was there...anyone else?"

"It occurred to me. But I don't think there was. I mean, I knew him well—really well—and I do not believe that he could have done what he did to me if he was giving it to someone else as well. He was in his mid-forties, Mitch. I mean, even men as fit as Frank Bartlett slow down a bit in their mid-forties."

"You drained him dry."

"Something like that. And I never got the impression that he was—you know. Playing around."

Did Belinda ever get that impression, I wondered? Does Vince?

"Sometimes he was just like his old, cheerful self—especially when we were with the girls, and particularly if the children were around. He doted on those kids, Mitch. He always had a little present for them, and he seemed to take real delight in playing with them. He talked to them as if they were equals—none of that silly baby talk that so many people go in for. And they adored him. Margaret called him Uncle Frank, and even Teddy would smile and hold out his arms when he walked into the room. It was such a shame he never had any of his own."

He'd have had to fuck his wife first, I thought.

"But more and more of the time that we were together, he was miserable and distant. I tried to reach out to him—and sometimes, when we were making love, he came back to me, and it was just like before. But things were getting worse in every other way. He started talking about ending it all. I thought he meant us—ending the affair. Now I realize that's not what he meant at all."

"But this weekend? You said he was happy when he arrived."

"He was. It was strange, now that I think about it. In the

last few weeks, he's been so gloomy. But then suddenly he changed—he invited Belinda and the children down to Teddington to stay with Vivie, and he brought himself up here to be with me, and he was full of the joys of spring. Until we had…words…"

"Why the sudden change?"

"It was as if a huge weight had lifted off his shoulders. But I was too bloody stupid to see that, wasn't I? I was only thinking about myself. Whatever had happened to make him change like that, I just didn't want to know. God, what a fool I've been."

"He didn't say anything that might help us to figure it out?"

"No. Just what I told you before. That he'd done something special for me. And I threw it back in his face."

"But he didn't just rush out of the room and cut his wrists then and there, did he? You had the argument after lunch, you said, before the servants left. You didn't find him until early this morning. What happened in between?"

"We went for a walk."

"A walk?"

"On the Common."

"You went for…" I was starting to sound like an irritating parrot, but suddenly I understood. "Wimbledon Common has a certain reputation, doesn't it, Morgan? Especially after dark."

"I…"

"It's a place where unspeakable vice takes place, I believe. That's what I read in the Sunday newspapers, at any rate."

"Hmmm."

"And did you and Bartlett by any chance…stumble upon some?"

"It's a long story," he said.

"I'm all ears."

# Chapter Four

"WE'D BEEN SITTING IN DIFFERENT ROOMS, SULKING like bears, which was ridiculous—we were supposed to be having the time of our lives, and we were both perfectly miserable. In the end, I couldn't stand it anymore, and neither could Frank—he came out of the living room, I came out of the dining room, both at the same time, and we met in the hall. The situation struck me as so ridiculous that I burst out laughing, and that broke the mood. He smiled, thank God—I hated seeing him so gloomy—and put an arm around my shoulder. 'Let's get out of here,' he said, 'and go for a drink.'

"It was way too early for the pubs to be open, so we went for a long ramble on the Common. It wasn't a bad day yesterday—the sun was doing its best to break through, and it wasn't too cold, and we walked for ages, talking about this and that."

"Did he say anything that seems significant, in retrospect?"

"No, Mitch. I've been racking my brains, honestly I have,

but he seemed completely normal. Too normal, if anything; that's all I can put my finger on."

"What do you mean?"

"Well, considering what we'd just been through—and all that the weekend meant to him, all the planning it had taken, all the ups and downs of his moods—I'd have expected him to say something a bit more...you know. About 'us.' But he didn't. We talked about business, we talked about the children, politics, banking, even the weather—but we didn't touch on anything remotely sensitive. I'd seen him like this many times before, usually when we were with the girls, charming, bluff, not a care in the world. You'd never think that there's another side to him. The side that I knew so well."

"And that struck you as odd?"

"To be honest I was so relieved to have got off difficult subjects that I was quite happy to make small talk. You know what it's like, Mitch—you can jabber away without really thinking, and all the while you're going over things in your mind that don't come out of your mouth. I certainly was—I was wondering where the hell this thing was going, what the 'surprise' was, why his moods were so unpredictable. Finally, the light started fading, and when I looked at my watch it was gone five o'clock. The pubs down in the village would be opening soon, so we turned back that way. I'd noticed a few chaps coming onto the Common in ones and twos, strolling around, glancing at each other and at us, but I hadn't really paid them much attention. Just as we were getting close to the streets, a fellow in a cloth cap and a shabby old jacket stopped and asked us for a light; Frank gave him a box of matches, and we went on our way."

"To the pub?"

"Yes. There's a pub right on the edge of the Common called the White Bear, which I'd never been into, but Frank liked the look of it, so in we went. Perfectly decent place, a bit rough and ready but none the worse for that. There was a public bar and a lounge bar, and somewhat to my surprise Frank headed for the public bar. It was a big square room with a bare floor, wooden chairs, and a few shabby old stools along the bar. It was pretty empty, because the landlord was only just opening up, but the place already stank of beer and fags from lunchtime. Frank ordered two pints of bitter and we sat at a table in the corner where we could watch the door. He seemed... I don't know. Distracted. We were still making small talk, but he had one eye on the door all the time. Whenever someone walked in, he gave them a real once-over, as if he expected to recognize them."

"And did he?"

"Not at first. I asked him what he was up to, and he just laughed and said that he liked the look of some of the fellows that came to pubs like this—working types. It was the first time he'd ever talked like that about other blokes, and I was a bit shocked. I thought he was so wrapped up in me that he never looked at anyone else."

"You know what men are like, Boy," I said. "We can be head over heels in love, but we'll still keep an eye out."

"Yes, I suppose so. I mean, I notice a nice-looking girl, even when I'm out with Belinda, pushing the pram around. She doesn't mind."

No, I thought, it probably reassures her.

"Anyway, by the time we'd finished our pints, the pub was getting fairly full, and I thought we'd just push off home and get down to business, as it were. But Frank wanted to stay, and so we got another. He said he liked the atmosphere, it cheered him up—and if it kept Frank cheerful, I was all in favor. The beer seemed to have raised his spirits as well."

"Yes, it does have that effect."

"It was halfway through the second pint that I started to notice something rather peculiar about the place. Now, you know I'm not always that quick on the uptake, Mitch, and I'm sure you'd have twigged the moment you walked in, but it dawned on me that there were absolutely no women in the place whatsoever."

"That's not unusual, in a public bar."

"No, I suppose not, but—there was something about the atmosphere that made it particularly obvious. The way people were looking at each other."

"Oh. I see."

"And it was quieter than a normal pub. You'd expect men who came straight in from work to let off a bit of steam, but this lot were very hush-hush. There were a few conversations going on, but none of the shouting and laughter that you'd expect in that class of place. People were arriving alone, for the most part, or in pairs; there were none of those big groups of lads that you'd expect. And then I noticed the funniest thing of all."

"What was that?"

"They kept going in and out of the toilets."

"Ah."

"There was one chap in particular—great big bruiser of a man, looked like a navvy—and he came and went about five times. I was thinking 'poor fellow, must have a weak bladder'—but then when I had to go myself, he was standing at the urinal with his prick in his hand, wanking away, having a good look at whatever was on either side of him."

"And did you—"

"Most certainly not. I finished off and buttoned up and got out of there as fast as I could. I don't mind a bit of fun and games in private, but I'm not going to take a chance like that in public. At least, not just down the road from my own home. When I told Frank about it, he just laughed and said it took all sorts to make a world. As his beer went down, he was paying less attention to me, and more attention to the comings and goings in the pub. I was starting to feel quite uneasy. And then he came in."

"Who?"

"The chap we'd seen earlier on the Common, the one who asked us for a light. At least, I'm pretty sure it was him. Cloth cap, jacket, scarf tied round his neck. Before I even saw him, I felt Frank somehow stiffen beside me; his body went tense, and he was staring towards the door. I looked over, and this bloke gave a bit of a nod in our direction. He was very ordinary looking—not much older than me, I'd have said. Well built. Manual laborer, I thought. Anyway, he must have recognized us from the Common. He went to the bar, sat on a stool, and drank a half. Then, when Frank got up to go to the loo, he followed him. Not right away, mind you. He waited for a good minute or so. It could have just been a coincidence."

"Or not."

"So I sat there for a while on my own, sipping my pint and feeling like a lemon, wondering where the hell Frank had got to, and, to be honest, wondering what he was up to in the loo. I was just about to go and look for him when the navvy with the weak bladder came and parked himself next to me. 'On your own?' he said. 'No, I'm just waiting for my friend.' Then he asked me if I'd had my dinner, and I said no, I'd be eating later. Then he said the most extraordinary thing."

"What?"

"He said, 'I've got a nice big juicy sausage for you.' Just like that."

"Ah. The direct approach."

"I must have blushed like a schoolgirl, because he suddenly started apologizing and backing away from me. Perhaps he thought I was a policeman or something. It would have been funny if it hadn't been so damned awkward. And it was just then that Frank came back from the toilet, with that other fellow hanging around behind him. 'Finish up your drink, Harry,' he said, 'and let's go.' I was only too pleased to get out of there, so I swallowed the rest of my pint and we left—all three of us. 'What's he doing?' I said to Frank, and he just said, 'He's coming with us.' "

"Good grief. What was he thinking?"

"That's what I wanted to know. I asked him who this person was, and he said he was a friend of his. A friend! They'd only just met! And I asked him what the idea was, bringing that sort back to my house, and do you know what he said?"

"No."

"He said, 'I want to show you that I'm not the possessive type. I want you to have some fun.' "

I whistled.

"I tried to tell him that he'd got the wrong end of the stick—the very last thing I wanted was someone else in on the act. But he seemed to think that I'd been unhappy because I felt I was 'tied' to him, and that it was only fair if I had a chance to play the field a bit. I said I had no desire whatsoever to play the field. Then he said he wanted to see me with another man, that it would give him pleasure. In the end, he begged me to let this bloke come home with us, that it was the one thing in all the world he most wanted to do. So of course, like an idiot, I went along with it."

"And what was the other guy doing all this time?"

"He was walking a few paces behind us, with his hands stuck in his pockets, whistling. I glanced over my shoulder a couple of times, and he gave me a wink and a cheeky grin. He wasn't bad looking, actually, and by the time we got to my house I thought, Oh well, in for a penny, in for a pound. If anyone saw him coming in with us, they'd just think he was a tradesman or a plumber or something."

"You should have sent him around to the back door," I said.

"Well, there was no one around. It was pretty dark by that time. It must have been—what, seven o'clock, or near enough. We got indoors, and he was walking around the hall looking at everything. For a moment I wondered if he was planning to burgle us. He had that look on his face as if he knew the value of everything. In the end he just said, 'Nice place you got here,' and his accent was the broadest Irish you've ever heard."

I have a weakness for British regional accents, and had already pictured his rough Irish laborer as a pale-skinned, brown-haired, blue-eyed sex machine.

"Frank took him into the living room and poured us all a large whiskey, and we sat down making small talk. You should have seen us, Mitch! It was like a vicarage tea party. We all knew why we were there, and we were all waiting for someone to make the first move. Damned if I was going to do it—this was Frank's fantasy, and he was going to have to manage it."

"Did you even know the guy's name?"

"Oh, that's it. Frank said, 'Harry Morgan, this is Sean Durran. Mr. Durran, Mr. Morgan,' and we shook hands. He had big, strong hands, and I noticed they were dusted with plaster and paint—he must have been a builder or a decorator or something. He looked me straight in the eye and said 'Hello, Mr. Morgan, pleased to meet you,' and he grinned and winked again."

"What color eyes did he have?"

"God, I don't know, Mitch. I don't notice things like that."

"You don't notice enough, Morgan. Could you pick him out in a crowd?"

" 'Course I could. Anyway, he was holding on to my paw for a bit longer than was absolutely necessary, then Frank came up behind him and said something like 'Can I take your jacket, Sean?' and he said 'Take anything you like, mister.' And that's how it started."

"What started?"

"You know." Morgan smiled. "Monkey business."

"Tell me everything."

"Oh come on, Mitch. You can imagine, can't you? There's only so many things that three men can get up to in an evening. Work it out for yourself."

"If you think that I want to know for my own prurient enjoyment, you're very wrong. I just think there might be a few things that you—overlooked, in the heat of the moment, that might help us to understand why Frank Bartlett took his life."

"Must I?"

"Yes. You don't have to be shy with me, of all people."

"Oh God, all right, then. Do you mind if we go upstairs, though? It seems wrong to be talking about this in the kitchen, somehow. You know what I mean."

I didn't, exactly, but I guessed it was something to do with Belinda—the kitchen, after all, was her province. We hurried upstairs, trying not to shudder as we passed the locked bathroom door with its star of shattered glass, and the horror within. Morgan's study was on the second floor, a pleasant room with a view over the garden and, I noticed without much surprise, not a lot of books in it. I suspect that the "studying" he did in this room was mostly of the racing pages. But it was, at least, a conspicuously masculine room, with sporting prints on the wall and none of the pleasant feminine touches that distinguished the rest of the house. It put me in mind of Mr. Jarndyce's growlery, and I imagined this was where Morgan came to escape from the demands of his children. He threw himself down on an old leather Chesterfield that I remembered well from his rooms in Cambridge; I sat on a swiveling wooden chair at the desk.

"I don't know where to begin," said Morgan, idly picking at the front of his pants. I guessed he had a pretty good idea.

"Bartlett took Durran's jacket off."

"Right. Yes. He reached round from behind him and unbuttoned it, then pulled it off him and threw it down on a chair. I was still standing right in front of Durran, just as when we'd shaken hands. Then Frank untied Durran's scarf and wound it off his neck. Durran was looking at me all the while with a funny, laughing look in his eyes, as if this was exactly what he'd expected. I don't know what I looked like—my mouth must have been hanging open or something. I should have stopped it, shouldn't I?"

"I wouldn't have."

"No. You wouldn't. Then Frank started undoing Durran's shirt—it was a white, collarless shirt, a bit frayed but quite clean. Frank's hands were shaking slightly, with excitement I suppose. Durran had a nice body—quite heavyset, but not fat; you could tell that he did a lot of hard work. Finally Frank got down to the last button and pulled the whole thing over Durran's head—it was one of those things that doesn't unbutton all the way down. So he was standing there half naked, Frank behind him, me in front of him, and he still had his cap on. That struck me as ridiculous, so I took it off his head—and he kissed me. Just like that. Full on the mouth. He tasted of beer and tobacco. He was unshaven, and I remember how sharp that felt, like sandpaper on my chin. I was taken by surprise at first, but then—well, Mitch, you know what it's like. Something just clicks inside you, and suddenly you want it."

"I know."

"We were kissing, and my hands were all over his body— he had very smooth skin, considering he was a workingman, pale as milk except round his neck and on his forearms, which were burnt to freckles by the sun. He had lovely tits, Mitch—like little pink rosebuds. When I found them, he went weak at the knees, literally—Frank had to hold him under the armpits, because his legs were giving way. I started sucking one of his tits, and Frank was kissing him on the neck, and Durran's hands were in my hair, pressing me into his chest."

Morgan was rubbing himself through his pants, enjoying the memory. I, needless to say, was hard, and wanted to do something about it, but tried to concentrate on Morgan's story. There must be something in there—some little detail that would help us.

"When I came up for air, Frank was undoing Durran's belt, then unbuttoning his trousers, and it was pretty clear that there was something in there that wanted to get out. I knelt in front of him and helped, and in a few moments his pants were round his ankles and there was a great big hard cock staring me in the face. God, it was huge, Mitch! I mean, you're big, but this one—"

"Thanks, Morgan. Spare me the measurements. What did you do?"

"I did what anyone would have done under the circumstances," said Morgan. "I started sucking it."

Try telling that to the judge.

"Frank was still up top, kissing him, grinding his hips into Durran's bum, and I was down below, getting as much of him down my throat as I could without gagging. I suppose I'd forgotten what a damn peculiar setup this was—I just thought, Good old Frank, he's surprised me again, this is exactly what I fancied doing and I didn't even know it. It was like that with Frank; he knew what I wanted before I did."

"And where did it go from there?"

"Well, I could tell that Durran was close, and I didn't think Frank would want him to finish quite so soon, so I got up and took my clothes off."

Good old Morgan, I thought, always ready to strip at the drop of a hat.

"What was Bartlett doing?"

"Watching. He seemed to be absolutely transfixed by

the whole thing. And, you know, it must have looked pretty good. Durran was sitting down on the floor, unlacing his boots, and he ended up rolling over on his back, sticking his foot up at me and getting me to pull his socks off. Then, when his feet were bare, he started playing with my cock. He got it between the balls of his feet and started wanking me. Extraordinary. Never even occurred to me to do that before."

"Me, neither." I thought I'd done most things, but foot jobs? I made a mental note to try it.

"Made me feel randy as hell, him lying there with his legs in the air, looking up at me, and...doing what he was doing. Frank sat down on the sofa and lit a cigar—a cigar! Exactly as if he was in a box at the theater, enjoying a show. So I thought—right, you bastard, if that's what you want, I'll give you a show. And I did."

"What did you do?"

"First of all, I gave that cheeky little bugger Sean Durran what he was asking for. I knelt down, held his knees up and fucked him, right there on the rug. He was hot as hell, Mitch, and he knew exactly what he was doing. There was no difficulty; I got right up him in one. Almost as if his arse was all greased up and ready."

"Be prepared," I muttered. I'm not sure if Morgan heard me.

"He was a bloody good fuck. He didn't just lie there— he was squirming around so much I felt like I had to nail him to the floor with my prick, and every time he moved or struggled it made me want to fuck him even harder. And he was hard the whole time. You know how sometimes you go soft when someone's fucking you? Well, Durran didn't. That great big dick of his stayed up like a flagpole the whole time. He was pushing it forward between his legs, making sure I could see it. Well, I did more than look at it. I grabbed it and gave it a good squeeze, and that really made his arse tighten up round me. I looked up, and Frank had his cock out as well, lying back on the sofa, cigar in one hand, cock in the other, and a strange smile on his face, a look I'd never seen before. Maybe he did this sort of thing all the time. Maybe he'd been testing me, seeing if I was willing to go this next step with him."

"Sounds like you were more than willing."

"I was thinking with my prick, Mitch. You know what that's like."

"Yup."

"I was getting close to shooting up Durran's arse, so I pulled out for a while and kissed him on the mouth. Then Frank got up and said, 'Gentlemen, shall we retire to the bathroom?' He led the way upstairs, holding Durran by the cock, Durran holding me by the cock, like we were doing some kind of dance. As soon as we were in the bathroom, Frank turned the taps on and started filling the tub, and then he undressed. We were all stark naked, all hard, and all up for anything. I think Durran was the first one who said that he needed to piss."

"Oh yes."

"I mean, we'd been drinking beer and whiskey, and I'd been fucking him, and that always makes me want to go. So he stood at the loo, pointing that great big hose at the bowl, but of course he was too hard to do anything. Frank wasn't helping, caressing Durran's arse, and so on, but eventually he managed to close his eyes and concentrate, his cock softened a bit, and he started pissing, a great big thick stream of the stuff that made a hell of a noise when it hit the water. Frank grabbed my hand and brought it down to hold Durran's cock, and I could feel the piss passing through it.

" 'Your turn,' said Durran when he'd finished, and before he'd shaken off the last drops, Frank was down on his knees, sucking him. So I stepped up, and after a bit of an effort I managed to get a few squirts out, then a bit more, then I was pissing away like a carthorse. Durran put his hand in the stream and then brought his fingers up to his mouth, sucking the piss off them. God, Mitch, I'd never seen anyone do that before."

"It was a day of firsts for you, wasn't it?"

"Then he started kissing me again, while I was still pissing, Frank still sucking his cock, and I could taste it in his mouth—salty and bitter. I suppose I should have been disgusted, but I wasn't. It made me feel—I don't know. Wild. Mad. Dirty. Like I didn't care about anything."

"That's a dangerous way to feel, Morgan."

"Hmmm." He stopped talking for a while, and lay quietly, his eyes half closed, rubbing his hard cock. I wanted to leap onto him and do all the things he'd been talking about, but I crossed my legs and stayed safely in the swivel chair.

"The bath was half full by this time," he continued, "and Frank told us to get in it. There was just about room, if we wound our legs around each other, for Durran and me to fit in, but the water came right up to the rim and started gurgling down the overflow. Then Frank stood over us, pointing his cock at us, and he... Well..."

"He relieved himself."

"Yes. All over us."

"Wow."

"God, Mitch. Have I really sunk this low? Picking up some stranger in a pub and—now this?"

"Go on. It's okay."

"When he'd finished, we took it in turns to suck him. He had a hand on each of our heads, and he pulled us on and off him just as he pleased. I was wanking Durran, Durran was wanking me, we were both sucking Frank..."

"Mmmm..."

"And then Frank did something rather peculiar."

"Some people would say he already had."

"Yes. But this... I remember thinking at the time it was

a curious thing to do with someone that you really didn't know. You remember I told you about how he'd shaved me that time?"

"Oh yes." Another item on my list of things to do to Morgan when this is all sorted out.

"Well, he said he was going to shave Durran. Durran looked puzzled—a bit worried, I suppose, as well he might, because Frank got his razor from his room and started stropping it. A great big old-fashioned cutthroat razor. If I'd been in Durran's shoes, I'd have shat myself."

"He didn't, did he?"

"No, thank God, considering I was in the bath with him. But Frank put him at his ease, and lathered his face up, and got to work on him, wiping the foam and the bristle off the blade with a towel. Durran was excited, and so was I—it was wonderful to watch Frank concentrating so hard, doing such a neat, careful job. Durran's head was thrown back, his eyes were closed, and his throat was exposed. Frank could have killed him in a split second, but Durran trusted him. Then Frank handed me the razor and said, 'You finish him off, Morgan.' There was just a little patch of lather on the side of his face, and I think he wanted to see me do it. I was all fingers and thumbs—when I took the razor from Frank, I fumbled it a bit, and almost dropped it, and cut my finger. Look."

He held out the index finger of his left hand—there was a small nick between the first and second knuckle, about a quarter of an inch long, and not very deep, but enough to have drawn blood.

"Durran looked worried then, and well he might—I was sucking my finger, and my hands were shaking, and I don't think he wanted me waving a razor in his face. So Frank took it back and finished the job himself. Durran washed his face, and then got back to sucking Frank's cock. After a while, Durran and I got out of the tub and dried each other, while Frank had a quick splash around, and then—well, we finished off."

"How, exactly?"

"I was down on my knees sucking Frank's cock, when I felt Durran's fingers at my rear end. So I hoisted my bum up in the air like a dog, and he fucked me. God, Mitch, I like a good fucking—nobody knows that better than you—but that thing was enormous. I felt like he was stretching me."

That explained why Morgan had afforded such easy entry this morning.

"But once he was in, and I'd got used to him, it was fine. I had Frank down my throat and Durran up my arse, and I just let myself go. I don't know who came first. I wasn't even aware that I'd come at all, until we were wiping up afterwards and I noticed that there was spunk all over the floor underneath me. I'd lost all track of the world—all I could think about was cock."

He sighed.

"And then Durran left?"

"After a while. I went downstairs to get my clothes, because I was cold. When I went back up, Durran was on his way down. He slapped me on the arse and told me I was a lovely ride, or something like that. Then he went down to get dressed, and I went to see what Frank was doing. He was in the bathroom with a towel wrapped round his waist, standing at the sink cleaning his teeth. It was his normal ritual after sex—he'd brush his teeth, he'd go over them with a toothpick, he'd gargle with that infernal bloody mouthwash of his, and I knew better than to interrupt him. I stood in the doorway for a while watching him, thinking how little I really knew him, wondering what surprises he had in store for me."

"Did you speak?"

"No. Not really. Maybe a few words. 'You all right?' 'I'm fine,' that sort of thing. Then I heard Durran moving around downstairs and I thought, hang on, there's a strange man in my house and he could be helping himself to the family silver. So I popped downstairs and he was waiting in the hallway with his cap in his hand, looking a bit awkward, like a schoolboy who's been called up to see the head. He lit up when he saw me, and said all sorts of thanks, and asked if he could come round again, and I said no, that wouldn't be convenient—I was dreading that he would try to blackmail me, or something. But he said he understood, he was a married man himself, and he wished me all the best and said that if I ever wanted to see him again, he could often be found down at such and such a pub in Clapham or Tooting or somewhere. And then he put his cap on and tied his scarf round his neck, and shook my hand as if he'd just been round to fix a leak in the roof or something, and we said good night."

"What time was it by now?"

"About nine. No, later than that. Nearer ten."

"You'd been at it for a long time."

"I suppose so. You know what it's like."

"Did you see a clock? Or look at your watch?"

"No, I can't honestly say I did. But it must have been pretty late, because I was dog tired."

"I'm not surprised, after all that."

"And I thought—well, time to turn in. I needed a bit of shut-eye. Up I went again, and Frank was still in the bathroom, only now the door was locked. I told him to hurry up, and he said he wouldn't be a minute. He must have been having a crafty smoke in there—he was partial to a smoke after you-know-what—because I could smell it coming out from under the door. I said I'd be waiting for him in bed, and I was looking forward to talking it all over with him—everything we'd just done, and all the things we could do in the future. I felt quite excited, really. It was like I'd been given a wonderful new toy. God, how selfish of me. How stupid, how bloody stupid and selfish."

"And that was—?"

"Yes. That was the last time I spoke to him. I undressed and got into bed, then I had a brainwave—I'd better just mess up the bed in the guest room a bit, just in case the servants came back unexpectedly, or, God forbid, Belinda. If anyone came in, we'd hear them, and Frank could run back to his room and no one would be any the wiser. I checked that all the lights were off downstairs, I crossed the landing back to my bedroom, and I yelled out one more time, 'Hurry up, Frank.' "

"Did he respond?"

"Yes, I think so. He said something indistinct—I just assumed that he was cleaning his bloody teeth again. I was used to his ways, and I thought nothing of it. And as soon as I lay down in bed and closed my eyes, I started thinking about all the things we'd done, and I drifted off to sleep."

"And when you woke up?"

"I told you. He wasn't there."

# Chapter Five

I HAD A THOUSAND QUESTIONS TO ASK MORGAN. WHAT kind of mood was Bartlett in when last they spoke? Why would Bartlett, who had set such store by getting Morgan alone for the weekend, suddenly decide to pick up a piece of rough trade at a notorious pub? Why would he put so much at risk—his marriage, his professional reputation, not to mention his friendship with Morgan—for the uncertain pleasures of a casual encounter? And, above all, what had happened after the wild enjoyments of the bathroom to pitch Frank Bartlett into suicidal despair? Morgan isn't the most sensitive of souls, but even he would have noticed something that dramatic.

But, as it was, there were no witnesses. At the time of his death, Bartlett was alone in a locked room without other means of access. Nobody could have spoken to him after Durran left, after his last indistinct communication with Morgan. Certainly, nobody could have snuck into the bathroom and murdered him. It was suicide, all right—but why? The obvious interpretation, and the one the police would surely jump to if they even sniffed the truth, was that Bartlett had killed himself out of remorse for his shameful, unnatural actions. But that was not consistent with the behavior of a man who introduced his male lover to his wife, who made extravagant monetary gifts, who cheerfully picked up Sean Durran in a pub and enjoyed him so fully. A remorseful man wouldn't indulge in shaving and pissing and sharing his boyfriend, as Bartlett had done. He would be furtive and hectic in his behavior: I should know, I'd fucked the type often enough. So what secret had driven Bartlett to this ghastly death?

I wanted to ask Morgan a lot of questions—and I wasn't the only one. The doorbell rang, and I looked out the landing window.

"It's the police, Morgan."

Sergeant Godley was back, with his handsome young blond sidekick, PC Knight, and this time they were accompanied by a man in a well-cut suit and a brown herringbone overcoat.

"You answer it. I need to—you know."

If ever a man looked as if he had something to hide, it was Boy Morgan at that moment. He was pale, his eyes red and shifty, and for a second I wondered if he'd told me everything. Well, it was too late now—the cops were back, this time with a detective, and they meant business. I'd have to make the best of what I'd got. I went down to let them in.

Godley looked at me as if I were something he'd just stepped in; he may not have liked Americans, plenty don't, but I wondered if there was something else behind his obvious hostility.

"This is Detective Sergeant Weston," said Godley. The plainclothes officer took off his hat, observed me coolly, but at least shook my hand. He looked like a university man, the type of highflier one encountered at Cambridge or Harvard, clean cut, bespectacled, hair neatly parted, a glint of icy intelligence belying the rather eager-beaver manner. He must have been in his mid-30s, his hair slightly receding at the temples, the parting a little wider than it might once have been.

"Is Mr. Morgan at home?" he said in a friendly tone, as if his call were purely social.

"I'll get him."

I showed them into the dining room; Godley and Weston sat, while Knight, once again, stood sentry by the door. I looked back at him as I ran up the stairs, and found myself wondering if, somehow, I could get him alone.

But there were more important matters than satisfying my taste for uniformed junior police officers. Morgan was standing on the landing looking as if he'd just shit in his pants.

"What do they want?"

"For God's sake, Morgan, pull yourself together! They just need to ask you some more questions. It would help if you could try looking a bit less guilty."

"Guilty?" said Morgan. "Guilty of what?"

"Hey! Calm down!" Something was wrong, and I think if Morgan could have shinnied down the drainpipe without being caught, he would have done it. "They're taking it seriously. It's a good thing. They want to get to the bottom of this as much as you do." I bit my tongue; that wasn't the most sensitive way of putting it, given what Morgan had just been telling me. I took him by the shoulders, forced him to look at me. "Come on, Boy. I'm with you. There's nothing to worry about. Just answer their questions."

"If I do that, I'll be the one in prison."

So that's what this was about; he thought they'd come to arrest him on a buggery charge.

"Look, Morgan, they're investigating a murder. Even in the Metropolitan Police, that's more important than prosecuting queers." I hoped that sounded convincing; I was far from believing it myself. "Let's go downstairs. It won't look good to keep them waiting. Just pretend they've come to the bank to ask for an overdraft. Breathe deeply. Good boy."

The color returned to his cheeks, and he was the charming Boy Morgan once again.

"Mr. Morgan." Weston stood up, shook hands, and set Morgan at his ease. He was definitely "our class," unlike the somewhat boorish Godley.

"What can I do for you? Awful business," said Morgan. "I wish to God I knew what had got into Bartlett's head."

"Please, sit down," said Weston, gesturing toward a chair. I could see Morgan's jaw muscles working—he would not like being invited to sit down in his own home. But he kept calm. "We have a few more questions, that's all."

"Fire away."

"What brand of cigarettes did Mr. Bartlett smoke?" asked Weston.

"Gosh, I don't know. I've never noticed. Turkish, I think. He always carried them in a cigarette case."

"Would you recognize the smell of his regular brand?"

"I suppose so," said Morgan. "I never gave it much thought. Bartlett wasn't a particularly heavy smoker."

"When did you last notice him smoking, Mr. Morgan?"

"Good Lord, you can't expect me to remember a thing like that!" I caught Morgan's eye and raised my eyebrow; it was enough to calm him. "Sorry, officer," he said. "I'm still terribly upset. Now, let me think. I suppose he must have been smoking last night when we were working."

"What time did you retire last night, sir?"

This seemed to be taking us onto dangerous ground, but Morgan kept his cool. "About ten, ten-thirty, I suppose."

"And did Mr. Bartlett go to bed before you, or after you?"

Surely they weren't trying to trick him into saying "with me," were they?

"After. He was finishing work when I went to clean my teeth, and then he was in the bathroom after me. I vaguely remember thinking that he was taking a long time about it, but then I dropped off."

"Was Mr. Bartlett a fastidious man, would you say?"

"Come again?"

"Particular in his personal habits."

"Oh, golly, yes. A great one for dental hygiene and all that malarkey."

Weston nodded, perhaps wondering how Morgan knew so much about the deceased's bathroom behavior. "I see. And you say he was not a heavy smoker."

"That's right."

"We found ash in the bathroom, sir."

"Ash?"

"Do you smoke in the bathroom?"

"Certainly not. Disgusting thing to do."

"Would you have expected Mr. Bartlett to do so?"

"No, but now you come to mention it, I did smell smoke. I was just telling Mitch."

"Ah." Weston looked at me, the light from the window reflecting in his glasses. It was hard to read his expression. "Mr. Mitchell. You weren't here last night, were you sir?"

"No, sir," I said.

"When was the bathroom last cleaned, Mr. Morgan?"

"Yesterday morning. The maid does it every morning, I believe."

"And neither you nor your wife—"

"I can assure you that Mrs. Morgan is not in the habit of smoking in the bathroom. Nor, indeed, anywhere else."

"Of course, of course," said Weston. "I am simply trying to be methodical, sir. Does it strike you as unusual that a man of Bartlett's high personal standards would smoke in the bathroom?"

"Yes, it's odd," said Morgan. "Seems out of character.

That said, though, we had been working jolly hard. Maybe he just fancied a quick puff to calm himself down."

"Perhaps," said Weston, nodding at Godley, who was taking notes. "Mr. Bartlett was in the habit of using mouthwash, was he not?"

"Good grief, I don't know," said Morgan.

But you do know, I thought. Why are you lying?

"We removed a bottle of mouthwash from the bathroom this morning. I assume it was his."

"I suppose so."

"You don't use it yourself?"

"No."

"Are you familiar with a brand called Fresh-O?"

"I told you, I don't use the stuff."

"Very good, sir. Finally, just one more thing. Did you have any reason to borrow Mr. Bartlett's razor?"

"His—razor?"

"Yes. The one he—the one we removed from the bathroom this morning."

"Certainly not. I would never use another chap's things like that."

"Could anyone else have used it?"

"How on earth would I know? What are you driving at, man?"

"There were several different sets of fingerprints on it, sir."

"Well? What's that got to do with me?"

"I'm just curious to know whether you had…moved it, or handled it, perhaps?"

"No. I don't even remember seeing it before this morning."

You're lying again.

"I see." Weston nodded, Godley scribbled.

"Is that all?" asked Morgan, putting his hands on the arms of the chair as if he were about to get up.

"I think so," said Weston, pushing his chair back. "Oh—a moment, Mr. Morgan. There is one more question."

"Yes?" Morgan stopped, halfway between sitting and standing.

"Did anyone else come to the house yesterday evening?"

"Anyone...else?"

"Yes, sir. Any callers at all?"

"I... I don't think..."

"You and Mr. Bartlett were alone in the house all evening, were you?"

Morgan was darting glances at me, but Godley was watching us closely. I could do nothing to help.

"Yes. Yes we were."

"Nobody could have found their way into Mr. Bartlett's things, then? Nobody would have gone near the guestroom or the bathroom other than you and Mr. Bartlett."

"That's right," said Morgan.

"In that case, Mr. Morgan," said Weston, standing up and motioning to his sergeant to do likewise, "I'm going to have to ask you to accompany us to the station."

"I say," said Morgan, "what's this all about?"

"Just a few more things we need to ask you."

"Am I under arrest?"

"No, sir. But it would help matters considerably if—"

"Mitch?" Morgan looked terrified.

"It's okay, Morgan," I said. "I'm sure it's just a matter of routine. I'll come with you if you like."

"That will not be necessary," said Godley. No "sir" for me, I noticed.

Morgan put on his coat and hat in a daze, and left in the back of the police car with Godley at the wheel and Weston in the passenger seat.

Young Constable Knight remained standing at the gate.

We were in trouble.

This was the third time I'd been involved in a mysterious death. Three years ago, during a long hot weekend that I spent with Morgan at Belinda's parents' place, Drekeham Hall, a dead body came tumbling out of the closet—and with it a few family skeletons. The year before last, I got caught up with that murky business at the Rookery Club after a bumpy ride on the Flying Scotsman and a close brush with the British royal family. And in both of those adventures, Boy Morgan had been at my side, the one person I could trust when everyone else was acting suspiciously. He wasn't always the brightest of sidekicks, but then again, neither were Dr. Watson or Captain Hastings. It was Morgan's dogged honesty that I could rely on—that, and his eager readiness to jump into the sack whenever the opportunity arose.

But now things had changed. Everything was in place— a dead body, a heap of unanswered questions and sexual secrets, even a fresh-faced, broad-shouldered young copper who, with a bit of persuasion, might soon be wrapping his cherry lips around my hard dick. Everything but the one thing I needed above all: Morgan at my side. Without him, I was working alone, in the dark, with one hand tied behind my back.

It wasn't so much that I relied on Morgan for practical help—it was more that I needed a friend, a pal, some kind of moral absolute in a world where evil so often gets the upper hand. And now not only was Morgan at the police station, but I had the distinct impression that he was keeping something from me. He'd been frank enough about the sexual side of his relationship with Bartlett, but on the subject of their friendship, I wondered if he was telling me the whole truth. If they were such close friends, surely Bartlett would have confided in Morgan before slashing his wrists. I already suspected that there was a piece of the jigsaw missing before the police arrived with their questions about cigarettes and mouthwash, and now I was sure of it.

Cigarettes.

Mouthwash.

Fingerprints on the razor.

A third party visiting the house—which Morgan denied.

All of these things pointed to foul play rather than suicide. They had not gone so far as to arrest Morgan, let alone charge him with anything, but they clearly had enough doubt about the appearance of Bartlett's death to take no chances. If Morgan was the last one to see Bartlett alive, to speak to him, then, reasoned the police, he was the one with the key to the mystery.

But what was the mystery?

Cigarettes.

Mouthwash.

They suspected something, and that something sounded a lot like poison. But Bartlett cut his wrists with a razor. The evidence was splashed all over the bathroom, according to Morgan.

According to Morgan, who had lied to the police and who might be lying to me.

Wait a minute, I thought: this is Morgan we're talking about, the most honest man I've ever met, a man who makes me look like the father of lies. If he's lying to the police, it's only because he's frightened that they might find out about his secret life. He's muddled. It's the first time he's ever had to confront the reality of what he does—of what he is—the fact that the fun and games we have when no one else is around makes him a criminal in the eyes of the law. And now it's not just me—it's Bartlett as well, and now Sean Durran. Morgan's up to his neck in it, and he's scared.

But lying to me? His best friend, almost his brother?

Well, said a cold little voice in the back of my mind, he's been cheating on you. Why shouldn't he start lying to you as well? He lies to Belinda.

No—that's not how our friendship works. We have no

hold on each other. We are not tied. I have Vince, he has Belinda, we both have fun when the opportunity arises—God knows I do. Just because he's been seeing Bartlett on a regular basis.

*He feels more for him than he ever felt for you.*

My head felt full of clouds. I couldn't think straight. No—if Morgan is a liar, then nothing in the world makes sense anymore. I can't let sexual jealousy turn me into a cynic. Okay, so he's been fucking Bartlett—I'd have done the same thing. An older man, experienced, wealthy, who takes an interest in you, befriends your family, helps you out financially, and has a big dick that he wants to stick up your ass? Who am I to say that Morgan shouldn't have done it? I'd have done it. Hell, I'd have seduced Bartlett even if he hadn't been interested. Morgan was flesh and blood, as I knew only too well.

I took a deep breath to clear my head.

If Morgan really was in trouble, then I had to help him. And in order to help him, I had to find out why he had been taken to the police station. And in order to do that, I had to speak to a policeman.

And, as luck would have it, there was a very fine specimen of the force standing at the gate.

At times such as these, one really can combine duty and pleasure.

I sauntered out the front door, being careful not to let it close behind me; Morgan had left in a hurry, and I wasn't sure where he kept his keys. It was a pleasant afternoon on a pleasant street. The only false note was the uniformed policeman. Well, that would give the neighbors something to gossip about.

PC Knight was standing in classic cop position, feet apart, hands clasped behind his back, facing out into the street. I had a moment in which to survey him from the rear—the golden stubble on the back of his neck, catching the sun and shining like straw, the broad shoulders and narrow waist accentuated by the tapered cut of his tunic, the strong legs curving up to a nicely rounded ass. And all topped off with a helmet.

He heard me and turned around, touched two fingers to his brow.

"Sir."

"Knight, isn't it?"

"Sir."

"Left you to keep an eye on the place, have they?"

"Sir."

They obviously don't teach the art of conversation at police training college. I would have to ask a more open-ended question.

"Why have they taken Mr. Morgan to the station, Knight?"

"I'm not at liberty to discuss that, sir."

Not much better—but enough to establish that he had a London accent, and a pleasant, deep voice that worked well with his boyish blond looks.

"Poor guy looked terrified. I would be as well. Not only does he discover a business colleague bleeding to death in his bathroom, he then gets hauled off and treated like a suspect."

"Sir."

The only monosyllables I wanted to hear from PC Knight were "yes" and "God" when I fucked him. Well, he could call me "sir" then too, if he wanted to. I wouldn't object.

"Did they give you any lunch, Knight?"

"Yes, sir."

"Can I make you a cup of tea? Or would that be inappropriate?" I could see that he was gasping for a cup of tea, but he couldn't leave his post. "I'll bring it out."

"Very kind of you, sir. I won't say no."

I already had plans for Knight—but first, I needed information. The rest would have to wait. I brought him his tea, well sugared, and the moment he had his hands around the cup he relaxed.

"Nasty business, this."

"Yes," I said. "You can say that again."

We then went through the usual dialogue in which the English workingman expresses his delight at meeting a real, live American, and I play up the accent for maximum effect. It's been an invaluable weapon in my arsenal of seduction; I've found that most Brits are willing to do things with a foreigner that they wouldn't consider with their own countrymen. There's also the abiding myth that all Yanks are filthy rich—and I never let them down until afterward.

We chatted about life across the Atlantic, and by the time I'd spun a few yarns about skyscrapers and fast cars, jazz clubs and movie stars, he was putty in my hands.

"That boss of yours is a prick," I said, apropos of nothing.

"Who, sir?"

"Sergeant Godley. Rude bastard."

Knight blushed and half smiled.

"It's okay, pal," I said, "you don't have to say anything. But I don't like the way he barged in here and treated Morgan and me as if we'd done something wrong."

"Well, sir, we have certain procedures that we have to follow in cases like this."

"Like what?"

"Well, if there's a reasonable suspicion of foul play—"

He must have seen my eyes widen, because he stopped in midsentence. I thought it better not to push the point; I didn't want us to get back to one-word responses. Still, I smelled a rat, and I intended to flush it out.

"Poor old Morgan, he's half crazy with worry. His wife and kids are staying with Mrs. Bartlett at the moment. I mean, if they keep him in, what is poor Belinda going to do?

That's Morgan's wife. Belinda. Lovely girl."

"I'm sure that he won't be away for long."

"Are they questioning him?"

"Yes, sir."

"What about?"

"A few things that came up this morning."

"You mean evidence?"

"Yes, from the lab." He was warming up now, not thinking so carefully about his answers.

"Ah, right. Scientific stuff. Well, that's important, of course. I'm a doctor myself."

That surprised you, I thought. Suddenly, Knight's manner was more respectful.

"A real doctor, sir? Like a medical doctor?"

"Exactly so." And I wouldn't mind giving you a thorough physical, copper.

"Well, then, you'll understand. They weren't satisfied with the corpse."

"What do you mean?"

"I'm not sure exactly. Something about inconsistencies."

"You mean they didn't tell you."

"No, but I can figure it out for myself. They sent stuff off for tests."

"Stuff they took from here?"

"Yeah. The mouthwash from Mr. Bartlett's room."

"I see. And what did it come back with?"

Knight drew breath to answer, but then stopped himself. Damn—he'd remembered just in time that I was Morgan's friend, possibly an accessory to a crime.

"I don't know, sir. Thanks for the tea."

He tried to get away from me.

"Listen, Knight," I said, taking his arm and turning him back toward me. "Have you ever had a buddy? Not just a friend or a mate, but a really good buddy? Someone you would do anything for?"

"Sir?"

"Is that a yes or a no, damn it?"

"Yes, sir, but—"

"Well then, you'll understand what I'm about to say. Morgan is my buddy, see? We've been friends since we were kids." This wasn't strictly true, but I didn't mind lying; I could see from Knight's pretty, open face that it was working. "And there's nothing I wouldn't do for that guy. I'd walk through fire for him. He's like a brother to me. And if he's done anything wrong—well, I just won't believe it until I've seen the evidence. And even then I won't believe it. So I might as well tell you, Knight, that I'm going to do anything in my power to make things right for Morgan." He looked ready to crumble. One more turn of the screw. "And for his wife and kids."

That did it. The blue eyes turned to me, the rose-pink lips parted.

"Don't tell anyone I told you this, sir."

"It's okay, Knight. You can trust me." I almost added "I'm a doctor."

"The thing is... I mean, Mr. Morgan's really lucky to have a friend like you."

"Damn right."

"I've had a friend like that myself."

Oh yes? I would have to find out more about this mystery friend—later. "I bet. You're the kind of guy any decent fellow would want to—help."

"Thank you, sir."

"My pleasure." This was developing nicely; should I ask him in for a further discussion of Anglo-American relations?

"And I'd hate to see an innocent man go to the gallows."

The gallows? Fuck, that took the wind out of my sails. But I kept a poker face and said, "You're right, there, Knight."

"The weird thing is, sir—I mean, it was Mr. Bartlett's, wasn't it? It's not like it was something that Mr. Morgan had given him."

"What was?"

"The mouthwash."

"What about the mouthwash? Spit it out."

"That's what they sent to the lab, you see."

"Bartlett's mouthwash? Why the hell would they—"

"And when the lab called back at lunchtime, that's when Sergeant Godley contacted DS Weston, and—"

"What the hell did they find?"

"I shouldn't tell you this, sir, but—" He leaned close; I could feel his breath on my cheek. "Strychnine."

Holy shit. Strychnine.

"And do they think—"

"I don't know, sir." He was closing down, aware that he'd said too much. But the damage was done.

"Do you have any idea what strychnine does to a man?"

"Kills him, sir."

"Yes, Knight, kills him—eventually. But first it causes agonizing convulsions, starting with the head and neck, then moving through the body until, finally, the backbone is arching continually and uncontrollably. What kills you isn't the poison itself—it's exhaustion or asphyxiation. It's the most horrible way to die."

Knight was pale. "Right." He ran a finger inside his collar. "I see."

"And don't you think that if Mr. Bartlett had died of strychnine poisoning, then Morgan would have heard something? He'd have been thrashing around on that bathroom floor like a landed fish. Morgan's a heavy sleeper—trust me, we used to share rooms at Cambridge, and he could sleep through a lot. But I think he might have heard a man dying of strychnine poisoning in his bathroom, don't you?"

"I suppose so."

"And how do you explain the razor cuts?"

"I don't—"

"Surely Godley doesn't think that Bartlett attempted to shave after taking strychnine, and the razor got out of control and accidentally slashed his wrists?"

"I couldn't—"

"Why are you looking for a secondary cause when it's clear that Bartlett bled to death?"

Knight was gaping, and looking puzzled; this one would never get beyond the rank of sergeant, I thought. But it wasn't his intellect that attracted me. I needed help, and I wanted to fuck him. Not a bad basis for a beautiful friendship.

"Another cup of tea?"

"What I really need is a drink," he said, clearly rattled by my melodramatic account of strychnine poisoning, something I've never actually witnessed, thank God, but have read about in medical textbooks, not to mention Conan Doyle.

"A brandy?"

He frowned. "I'm on duty."

"You won't be for much longer if you don't pull yourself together. You look as if you're going to faint. What is it? The idea of the razor slashing into the flesh, the blood spurting out of the wound, or the horror of the convulsions?"

That did the trick. "Perhaps just a very small one."

"You'd better come inside. It wouldn't do for anyone to see you drinking out on the street. Come on. It won't take a moment."

He followed me down to the kitchen with uncertain footsteps, like a stray dog that can't quite believe it's been adopted. I wasn't going to pounce; I know enough about the male mentality to realize that a precipitate move can spoil any hope of winning the ultimate prize. But to have him alone in the house, with a drink in his hand, was a big step. He'd disobeyed two important orders in order to please me;

I'm a great believer in starting at the thin end of the wedge and working my way in.

The brandy worked its magic, and two spots of red appeared in his cheeks. That English coloring always appeals to me. I'd make that flush spread all over his face, down his neck, onto his chest—

"Good stuff, huh?"

"Yeah. That's better. Sorry about that, sir, I felt a bit—"

"Call me Mitch, please." I gave him a hand. "Dr. Edward Mitchell to my enemies, but Mitch to my friends."

"Mitch." I could see that he liked the Americanness of the name. "Right." He finished his brandy at a swig and looked toward the door, eager to get back to his post. This I could not allow.

"So what are these 'inconsistencies' they're talking about?"

"I don't know, Mitch."

"I think I do. There's poison in the mouthwash, but that's not what killed Bartlett, right?" I poured Knight another cup of tea; he took it without thinking. "There's an indication of foul play, but no actual evidence. The strychnine did not enter Bartlett's body."

"Maybe." He frowned over his teacup.

"So they're thinking—suicide, or murder? Looks like suicide—locked door, slashed wrists, razor. But they don't want that, do they? You cops want an arrest and a conviction and a nice neat line drawn under it. Case closed."

"I don't think that's—"

"So you're looking for ways to implicate Morgan. You've ruled out the obvious theory, the 'mystery intruder'—because nobody entered the house. So now you're suggesting that Morgan's prints are on the razor, or he put poison in Bartlett's mouthwash. In short, you're trying to frame him."

"No!"

"And why? Why not just let it be what it appears to be— suicide? Because if a prominent man like Bartlett commits suicide, then a lot of unpleasant questions will be asked. Who knows what will come out? No—easier to close ranks, find a culprit, and be done with it. What are they doing now? Trying to scare Morgan into a confession?"

"I don't know." Poor Knight looked close to tears—just as I meant him to.

"I bet you'll find they're all Freemasons," I continued, warming to my theme. "They're covering up for a brother in trouble, so Morgan gets the chop. It's wrong, Knight. It's evil."

Knight's voice was shaky. "I need the toilet." He stood up, and headed for the stairs.

"Not that way. The upstairs bathroom is locked—and covered in blood."

He stopped in his tracks, his face pale. I took him by the shoulders and steered him to the scullery. "There's one in there, for the staff, I guess."

"Thanks, Mitch."

"That's okay, Knight. Hey—that's not fair. What's your first name?"

"Stan."

"Go ahead, Stan." I opened the lavatory door. "All yours. Though, now that we're here, I need to go, myself." I started unbuttoning. "You don't really believe this was murder anymore than I do, do you, Stan?" I started pissing. "Come on, step up. There's room for two."

His bladder got the better of his scruples—that's tea and brandy for you—and he took his place beside me. "No, I don't." He pulled out a nice-looking piece, very pale against the dark material of his uniform, fringed with a little golden fuzz.

"And if it was suicide," I said, in midflow, "there was a reason for it."

"Must have been." He was pissing too, our streams mixing.

"And it's up to us to discover the reason, and save Morgan from the gallows." I looked him in the eye. "Isn't it, Stan?"

Silence for a while, broken only by our liquid duet.

"Isn't it, Stan?"

"Yes, Mitch."

"And how are we going to do that?"

He thought for a while, as our streams ran dry. Would he break all the rules in the police book, and help me with my investigation? Or would his training win the day?

I needed leverage. So, instead of putting my cock away, I kept shaking it until it started to grow.

Stan did not look away.

# Chapter Six

I HAD A POWERFUL SENSE OF DÉJÀ VU—ME, A YOUNG policeman, a pissoir... Were all my encounters with the forces of law and order destined to be played out against the tinkle of urine on porcelain? Well, there has to be some excuse for these boys to expose their private parts, and what could be more natural and explicable than airing your hose in order to pass water?

But now—well, there was no need for both of us to be standing in the pisser with our dicks hanging out, mine half hard, his stirring.

I had to get him over to my side before he had a chance to think about the step he was taking.

"Looks like you needed that," I said—a totally fatuous remark, but it did the trick.

"Yeah."

I swung my hips from side to side, making my cock wave and rise. "Hey—wanna fight?"

"What?"

"A cock fight."

"You mad?"

"We do this all the time in America." That seemed to persuade him, and he stepped up to face me. "Yeah—looks like you're nearly ready."

His cock was fully hard now, and he blushed again.

"Two out of three?"

He had no more idea what I was talking about than I did, but he understood enough. We stood a foot apart, hands on hips, waving at each other. It took a bit of coordination, but then—baff!—my cock hit his, broadside. After that it was easy to make it happen again and again, until we slipped into a rhythm, swaying our bodies, our cocks getting stiffer with every contact. He was grinning like a kid with a brand-new toy, and would have continued with this "traditional American" game if I had let him. But I decided it was time to make the rules a bit clearer, and, as our cocks collided once again, I reached down and grabbed them both in one hand, pressing them together so he could be in no doubt that one was just as hard as the other.

"Looks like I win," I said. "You have to do a forfeit."

He didn't ask by what recondite scoring I'd "won," but just said, "What?"

"The loser has to kiss the winner."

"Kiss?"

I pointed down. "Yeah. There."

"On the…"

"Exactly." I mashed our pricks together again, then stroked the two shafts. "Go on."

I let him go, and he knelt, just as obedient as I could wish. I must write a letter of commendation to the Police Training College.

"You want me to…kiss it?"

"That's the rules, Stan."

"Where?"

"Doesn't matter."

He frowned, as if deciding whether to plant his lips on the flower or the stem—and then, some decision obviously reached, he pouted his mouth into a small O and placed it right on the end of my cock. It fitted neatly into the little pucker of his lips, until his lips parted in a kissing noise, and he drew back. But now we were joined by a thin, glistening string of precum that hung for a moment like a skipping rope, then snapped, leaving viscous drops on his mouth.

"How was that, Mitch?"

"That was good."

"Want me to do it again?"

"Sure. It's all yours."

This time it was an open-mouthed kiss, and my cock, touching for the first time the wet, firm softness of his tongue, forged ahead. I rested a hand on Stan's bristly blond head, feeling the warmth of his scalp, and gently drew him in. He looked up for reassurance, his bright blue eyes troubled, as young men's eyes so often are at the first taste of penis. I smiled back down.

"That feels good, Stan. Really good."

That did the trick; he closed his eyes, and concentrated on the new sensation of cock in his mouth. It's a long time since my lips first parted to admit a man, but I still remember the shock of the size, the stiffness, the salty taste, the strangeness of taking one body part into another. I looked below Stan's head to see if he was enjoying this as much as I was. He was.

After sucking ineptly on my cock for a while, Stan came up for air with a look on his face that clearly said *What now?* This is always a difficult question for me, especially when faced with the prospect of a handsome young convert to whom I want to do everything in a limited time. Top of my list was fucking him, but it was a high-risk strategy—I didn't want to send my new friend running, or rather hobbling, back to the station and busting me in a fit of postcoital remorse. I had to keep this first encounter lighthearted and, above all, pleasant. So I cupped his chin in my hand, feeling the wetness of his saliva where it had smeared against his handsomely molded chin, and raised him to his feet. His cock was as hard as it could be. It was time for a little reciprocation.

I took him in my hand and jerked him off slowly; he let out a loud sigh, and for a moment I thought he'd come. I had to check my hand for sticky evidence to make sure he hadn't. I maneuvered him to the toilet and sat him down, taking care to lower the seat first. Then I dropped to my knees between his spread legs and got to work. My hands felt firm, muscular, football player's thighs through the rough blue material of his uniform pants, and my tongue tasted a fresh, hard cock. I gave one good, slow lick along the underside of his shaft and then, when I reached the top, opened up and swallowed him whole. He groaned as if someone had winded him, and his hips bucked upward, leaving the seat and allowing me to slip my hands around and cup his ass. So PC Stan Knight got his first blow job, and I could tell by the rigidity of his cock and the way his fingers clamped down into my hair that he'd be back for more.

I wanted to see him naked, but this would have to wait. In order to get his pants off I'd have to unlace and remove his boots; as for his shirt, first there was the nightmare of buckles and buttons on his tunic. So I contented myself with lowering his pants halfway down his thighs and pulling his shirt up to his belly button—enough to expose the whole of his midsection, and more than enough to see that Stan Knight was pale-skinned and smooth, except around his cock and ass, where blond hair formed a thick bush. I licked all around his balls, which were already getting tight; it wouldn't be long before he was coming in my mouth, and that was just as well. There was work to be done, mysteries to be solved, friends to save...

And a very nice cock to be sucked. First things first.

I took him back into my mouth and moved my lips down to the base, and soon I had a good rhythm going. With one hand I stroked his stomach, feeling the muscles working underneath the tight skin; with the other, I worked my way beneath his balls and around to his ass. Stan was so caught up in what was happening to his dick that he didn't really notice the added attention I was paying to his ass—all he knew was that he was easing into that final rapid downhill slide toward orgasm. If he hadn't been so far gone, he might have steered me away from that taboo area; as it was, he allowed my fingers to rub his ass lips and push a little way into the hole. And, when I judged the time was right—when his abdominal muscles tensed, and his cock stiffened in my mouth—I slipped one into him, just to the first knuckle.

His climax hit him like a wave breaking over a seawall, and he was helpless, holding on to my head, pumping his cock into my mouth, unloading his balls, unable to think of what he was doing, let alone analyze the fact that he was having sex with a man who had just digitally penetrated him. I took care to slip that finger out in plenty of time, before he came to his senses. Next time—oh yes, there would be a next time—he'd have an empty feeling in his ass and he wouldn't know why. He'd just want me to fill it.

I swallowed his spunk, and let him soften a little in my mouth. My own cock was hard as hell, of course, but I had no urgent need to come; it wasn't long since the last time, and though my powers of recovery have been met with disbelief on occasion, I was content to save myself for later. What mattered was not that I shot a load over the young copper's boots, or into his handsome, flushed face, but that I had got myself a sidekick. And a very useful, decorative one at that. So I pushed my cock back into my pants—Stan gave it a lingering glance, already looking forward to his next taste—and buttoned myself up.

Would he make his excuses and leave? Would he arrest me? Or did he realize what I intended him to realize—that we were now partners in crime as well as in pleasure, and that it would be definitely in his interest to help me out? I would never willingly stoop to threats or blackmail, but when Morgan's life was in danger, morals took second place.

Happily for both of us, PC Stan Knight showed no remorse, nor any urgent inclination to leave. Instead, he wiped himself up with a bit of toilet tissue, splashed water on his face, and rearranged his clothing.

"You—" he started, then stopped. There was a mischievous smile on his face.

"What?"

"You swallowed it."

"Yup. Rude not to."

At this he threw back his head and laughed long and loud, his Adam's apple working in his throat. I had a terrible desire to kiss him—but he'd keep.

"Right, Mitch," he said, when he was once again a respectable, properly dressed young copper on duty, "what next?"

"You'd better get back outside. I don't want Godley or Weston turning up and finding that you've deserted your post. As for me, I've got a lot of questions and I need some answers."

"What sort of questions?"

How much could I tell him? I decided on the bold course of action. After what had just happened, he could hardly cause me problems. "There was someone else here last night."

"Mr. Morgan never mentioned him."

"No. He wouldn't. He wasn't the sort of person that a gentleman—ought to be entertaining at home."

"I see."

"Do you?"

"I'm not stupid, Mitch. I mean, Mr. Morgan is...like you, right?"

Like us, I wanted to say. "Yes. Sometimes."

"And he and Bartlett..."

"Yes. They were friends."

"Hmmmm. I see. So would I be right in thinking that this third party who visited the house last night was also...that way?"

"Ten out of ten. Top score."

"So who was he?"

"They met him in a pub."

"What sort of pub?"

"You tell me," I said, holding the front door open; now that I'd thought of Godley and Weston, I wanted to get Stan back to his post as quickly as possible. "Where do men of that sort go around here?"

"There's the White Bear, just across the Common."

"That's the one. How do I get there?"

He gave me directions.

"Any others?"

"Why? You planning a pub crawl?"

"Maybe. Wanna come with me?"

"I don't get off till seven." It was now just after four.

"Okay. Pick me up at seven-thirty. You can show me around."

"There's quite a few of 'em," said Stan, counting on his fingers. "The White Bear in Wimbledon, the Ship in Tooting, the Ring of Bells in Balham, the Queen's Head in Clapham High Street—"

"You seem to know a lot about it."

"Yeah. First job they gave me when I started was that beat. Going round the queer pubs, looking out for any funny business."

"Did you find any?"

"Nah. Copper turns up in uniform, they're all good as

gold, aren't they? Doesn't do any harm to let 'em know we've got an eye out."

"Right." Little bastard, I thought—I'll fuck you extra hard for that when I have you at my mercy. "Bet you never thought you'd be visiting them undercover, did you?"

"I wouldn't go in any of 'em on my own, not without the uniform. But I'll be safe with you, won't I?"

"Yes," I lied, setting myself a challenge of breaching his virgin ass with my dick within the next 24 hours. "Safe as Fort Knox, Stan. See you later."

I went back inside.

Just over three hours before I had any chance of finding the mysterious Sean Durran—the last person, apart from Morgan, to see Frank Bartlett alive. He, surely, held the key to the mystery. What had he said to Bartlett? What had happened to turn him from a happy, horny husband into a suicidal wreck? Was Durran what he appeared to be—a casual encounter? Or was there some missing piece to the puzzle? Was Durran a killer? You heard such things whispered among friends, or you read between the lines of the crime reports—men killed in hotel rooms, or in parks late at night, a guardsman arrested, or a laborer, or unemployed. Was Bartlett simply unlucky in his choice of playmates? Was Durran a lunatic with a hard cock and a guilty conscience?

It was an attractive idea, in many ways: at least then we'd be talking about a straightforward murder, a crazed killer, an unlucky victim. I pictured Durran to myself—attractive, hot-eyed, mad with lust, madder with remorse, picking up the very instrument with which he had been given such exquisite pleasure just a short while before—Bartlett's razor—and using it to blot out the unthinkable fact of what he'd just enjoyed.

I got carried away with the notion and even started composing the speech I would give to Sean Durran when I trapped him—pompous nonsense about justice and honesty and self-respect. But suddenly the cold water of reason quenched my ardent fantasy. Was I not falling into the same trap I'd warned Stan Knight about? Pinning the death on some sinister intruder—not, admittedly, the burglar or tramp of popular imagination, but just as convenient. The fact that Durran had been invited into the house, and had joined Morgan and Bartlett in the bathroom, did not alter the fact that he was an outsider. He was not "one of us," at least in terms of his class, even if other aspects of his nature made him a brother. The police would happily pin the crime on the likes of Sean Durran—a working-class idler, obviously of Irish descent, an habitué of the pubs, shiftless, dishonest, immoral. And I was doing exactly the same thing myself.

Worse, I was admitting to myself that I did not believe Morgan's account of what had happened the night before. Durran had left the house—Morgan himself saw him off the premises. Bartlett was still alive at that time—when Morgan met Durran coming down the stairs, Bartlett was in the bathroom brushing his teeth. They had spoken; Bartlett had been his normal self. Durran left, Morgan went to bed, leaving Bartlett in the bathroom, the door now locked—from the inside. There was no one else in the house, no other means of access to the bathroom—it did not communicate with any other rooms. True, there was an external window, but that was closed from the inside when Bartlett was found, and it would have taken a long ladder to reach it. Morgan went to bed, got up again, mussed up the guest bed, told Bartlett to hurry up, and heard an indistinct mumbling from the bathroom. All this was long after Durran had left. He could not possibly have killed Bartlett. Poison was a possibility—but what of the razor cuts? It did not make sense. It had to be suicide—but why?

I felt helpless, trapped in the silent house. Morgan was at the police station, saying God knows what, Belinda and the children were with poor Vivien Bartlett—what a miserable time they would be having!—and the servants were out, little knowing the mess to which they would return. The house in uproar, muddy footprints—Durran's, the police's—up and down the stairs and, worst of all, the sealed-off bathroom. Someone was going to have to clean it up sooner or later, and even I, hardened by years in operating theaters, blanched at the thought of that job. The thought of scrubbing up all that blood, the water in the bucket turning red, the smell...

I was standing in the hall, my brain stuck in a cycle of horror and confusion, staring vacantly at the floor—the tiles—a stain on the tiles—a stain in the shape of a leaf.

Blood.

The blood I had noticed before.

Why is there blood on the hall floor?

There was on obvious explanation—it had dripped from the dead body of Frank Bartlett as the police removed him from the house. That's what Morgan had said, and it was entirely possible. But what if that blood was telling a different story? Durran lashing out with a knife, right here in the hallway? Or, worse still, Morgan? Or a game that had gone wrong—the razor, the cut on Morgan's finger, an accident covered up by Morgan to look like suicide. Or no suicide at all, but a way out of a tricky situation.

Damn that spot of blood! I had a good mind to fetch a brush and pail and scrub it away myself.

I needed to get out of the house and clear my head. Every avenue of thought led to the horrible possibility that Morgan had lied to me, and once that thought took hold, others followed like links in a chain. He has lied to me—he lies to Belinda—he lies to the police—he lies to Bartlett. Links in a chain that drags our friendship into the abyss, that binds Morgan on his way to the scaffold.

Sherlock Holmes never has these moments of intense confusion and distress; his mind cuts through every tangle like Alexander's sword through the Gordian knot. Hercule

Poirot simply sits in a chair, his fingertips touching, his eyes closed, and thinks it through until he reaches that eureka moment and denounces the killer in a pleasant drawing room, amid potted palms and cups of tea. Mitch Mitchell, however, was far too close to his mystery, far too emotionally and physically involved than those two cold fish—and, while I don't think I'm a bad doctor, I've never regarded myself as a great detective. Those mysteries that I've managed to "solve" in the past have become clear more through luck than judgment, by blundering across the truth when I was looking for something else—usually cock. Now I felt like running away from the whole horrible mess, racing to Victoria to get the boat train to Paris, forgetting it all in the certainties of Vince's embraces—and I would have, were it not for the thought of Morgan, alone and afraid in a police cell, digging himself into a hole by lies and prevarications, going to his death because I, his best friend, had been too scared and confused to wear out a little shoe leather in pursuit of the truth.

I scribbled a hasty note to the effect that I'd gone to get some air—I didn't want the servants, the police, or Belinda to know what I was up to, if they got back to the house before Morgan did. I closed the front door behind me, realizing as I did so that there might be no one to let me in when I returned. No matter; I had everything I needed. I had over three hours to kill before my rendezvous with Stan Knight. What could I do on a Sunday afternoon in southwest London that could possibly be of use? Under normal circumstances, I'd head for the nearest public baths or fleapit movie house and hope to find a pleasant way to pass the time—but under the present circumstances that would not do.

What I needed more than anything was to find out all that I could about Frank Bartlett—what kind of man he was, what had happened in the days and weeks before his death, what possible motive he could have for suicide. Or, if not suicide—if this was the cleverest, most dastardly murder of all time—then who were his enemies? I couldn't ask Morgan, and I definitely couldn't go to Bartlett's home and start pestering his widow. Who else knew him? If it were a weekday I'd go to Bartlett and Ross's office, perhaps posing as a wealthy American investor—all Brits believe that Americans are loaded, and I grew up around enough rich folk back home in Boston to do a pretty good impression of the type. But it was a Sunday, and the office would be closed. Unless, for some reason—what was the name of that paragon of efficiency Morgan had mentioned, the industrious, selfless drone who kept B and R's business afloat? Topper? Tiptree? Maybe, just maybe, his life was so empty that he would spend his day of rest at the office. It was a long shot, but what did I have to lose? Only the price of a phone call.

There was a pay phone at the end of Morgan's street, and within moments I was dropping coins into the slot and being connected to the City office of Bartlett and Ross. It rang, and rang, and rang. Of course there was no one there. Now I had to think of some other way to—

"Bartlett and Ross, good afternoon."

A man's voice, soft, hesitant.

"Hi." Did I sound rich enough? "This is Edward Mitchell. Who am I speaking to?"

"Arthur Tippett."

Tippett! Of course! With the brown hair and the promising ass. "Tippett. Working on a Sunday? Good man. Frank told me you were conscientious."

"I try to—"

"Listen, Tippett. I've been talking to old Frank about some investments."

"Yes, sir?"

I listened hard for any inflection in his voice that suggested a knowledge of his boss's recent demise, and detected nothing. "Would you mind if I came by with some papers?

I won't be in town after tonight and I wanted Frank to look them over."

"Of course, sir. What time may I expect you?"

"I'll be there in an hour. That suit you?"

"I'll be here, sir."

"All work and no play makes Jack a dull boy, Tippett. I can put 'em through the letterbox if you want to get off."

"No trouble, sir. I have no plans."

"Good. See you soon, Tippett."

"Very well, Mr. Mitchell."

Sherlock Holmes would summon a cab, and Poirot would get Hastings to drive him to the City in a sporty little car, but I, with neither the resources nor the wheels, was obliged to wait for a train.

The City on a Sunday afternoon is like a ghost town. Streets that in a few hours' time would be crowded with bankers and clerks, errand boys, and secretaries were now eerily quiet. An occasional car or horse-drawn cart broke the silence, and here and there you saw the City's hidden population, the beggars and down-and-outs who eke out a miserable existence cheek by jowl with the richest in the land. But for the most part, it was just me, the dust, and the sparrows.

Bartlett and Ross set up shop on Cheapside, just up the street from St. Paul's Cathedral. I could happily spend the afternoon poking around that historic quarter, visiting the birthplace of Milton, brushing against the shades of Chaucer and Dickens—and I might have, if Morgan's life were not in peril. I looked up Newgate Street, once the home of the most notorious prison in England, toward the Old Bailey, with its figure of Blind Justice, and shuddered. Would Morgan be caught in the jaws of that implacable machine?

The B and R office was in a handsome red-brick building with bright brass plaques on the door and windows that were clearly cleaned every day. The place shone like a jewel among the dusty facades on either side, proclaiming its prosperity. I rang the bell and waited.

But not for long.

"Come in, Mr. Mitchell."

Tippett was short and slight, the sort of build that you'd expect in a runner, light on his feet, making me feel heavy and clumsy in comparison. His wrists were thin, his hands long, and there might have been something effeminate about him were it not for the strength of his jaw and the darkness of his brow. He wore his hair in the approved City style, long on the top, short at the back and sides, parted on the left and combed back, glossy with brilliantine. His clothes were impeccable. Since it was Sunday, he had allowed himself some relaxation from the weekday uniform of collar and tie, but even in an open-necked shirt, conservatively cut gray tweed trousers, and a sleeveless argyle sweater—the only hint of color in an otherwise drab wardrobe—he looked every inch the humble clerk.

"Tippett?" I took his hand and pumped it hard, keeping up my role of the bluff, loaded Yank with money to burn. "Good to meet you. Bartlett speaks very highly of you."

"Thank you, sir." I watched his eyes, but there was no flicker of reaction; clearly news of Frank Bartlett's death had not yet reached him.

"Will you come through?"

I followed him into the main office. Papers were stacked in careful piles on his desk, with ink and pen ranged neatly around them. The place reeked of method and order—things I wish I had a little more of. Perhaps I could learn something from Tippett, with that look of keen intelligence that belied his meek demeanor.

"Damn it," I said, stopping in my tracks and slapping my forehead. "I've left the papers back at my rooms. Hell's bells!"

"Would you like to come back later, sir?"

"No, it's okay. I guess you can tell me everything I need to know."

"What was the nature of the investments?"

"Stocks and bonds." I was improvising wildly; I have little head for finances, and leave that side of things to Vince. "My folks have been investing heavily in African copper, and it's been doing pretty well."

"Yes. The Kenyan mines are providing a good return."

"Now we're thinking of going into rubber."

"Rubber, sir?"

"Yes. There's an operation in—er..."

"Malaysia?"

"That's the place. Know it?"

"I know something about it."

"Good. Knew you would. Now, Frank said that we should look into the legal side of things before we—you know. Took the plunge."

"Ah. I see."

"That something you could do for me, Tippett?"

"We do a good deal of commercial law, of course. Shipping, commodities, sale of goods, and so on."

"Could you run a check on things?"

"If it's for a friend of Mr. Bartlett's—"

"Yes. I don't like to impose, but Frank did say he'd help me out. He's a good man, Frank."

"Yes, sir. Mr. Bartlett is a wonderful man."

This was the turn I hoped the conversation would take—just as well, as my improvisational powers were running dry. "He sure is. He's been a true friend to my family."

"I don't think you're one of our clients, sir?"

"No. It's always been a friendly relationship. Bartlett went to law school with my dad."

"Ah. I see."

"Has he never mentioned Jack Mitchell of Boston?"

"Not to me."

"Well, he's a busy man. Fingers in many pies, I guess."

"Yes."

"So, how's business?"

"Very good."

"Glad to hear it. Last time I was over, Frank said that things were a bit tight."

"When was that?"

"Oh—last fall." This was a stab in the dark if ever there was one, but I figured that if there were any hidden problems behind the prosperous facade of Bartlett and Ross, this might flush them out.

"I believe Mr. Bartlett had some personal financial issues at that time which have since been resolved."

"Great, great. Well, listen Tippett, I'd love to spend the afternoon chatting, but I guess I'd better get back to the hotel and pick up those papers. Unless you'd like to swing by yourself when you finish up here?"

One eyebrow lifted an inch, and there was a twinkle of interest in his eyes. "Where are you staying, sir?"

I was staying in the staff quarters at Middlesex Hospital, where visiting doctors could usually find a berth—hardly the most impressive address, and difficult to pass off as the "hotel" of a wealthy Boston businessman. It was only a place to store a suitcase; when I arrived, I had hoped to spend the weekend with Morgan. How wrong that plan had gone. Still, the room had a door and a bed, and if I was going to get anything out of—or into—Arthur Tippett, then both would be necessary.

But first, charm. "In the West End. Say, why don't we get a drink? You look like you're finishing up here." I gestured to the tidy piles of papers on the desk. "You can't spend your whole life in the office. Let me buy you a pint."

"I'm afraid the pubs will be shut at present."

I played dumb. "You're kidding! Wow, your laws are crazy. Well, how 'bout you take me to some bar or club."

"I'm afraid I don't know of any such places, sir. We could have a cup of tea—"

"Tea? Damn it, Arthur, you've been at work all day, and I bet you were here yesterday too. You need a man's drink. Not a cup of tea." I simpered as I said it, raising my little finger and wrinkling my nose like a fussy old lady. "Don't tell me you're a prohibitionist. We have enough trouble with them back home."

"No, sir. I like a drink now and again."

"Good man. Tell you what. I've got a bottle of scotch in my room."

"Oh. Well, I don't know. I told Mother I'd be back at—"

"Hey!" I held up my hand. "I swear, I won't tell Mother."

That made him laugh, and when Tippett laughed he was a much more likable man. Creases appeared around his eyes, and he lost the look of a disappointed vicar.

"Let's walk." I opened the office door.

"I just need to—"

"No, you don't." I took a jacket off a peg and handed it to him. "You're all done here. Come on, Tippett. How often do you get a rich American offering you hard liquor in his room on a Sunday afternoon?"

"Rarely."

"See? Make hay while the sun shines. Carpe diem, and all that jazz. Let's go."

I stood in the doorway, gesturing to the world beyond. In order to get past, he had to squeeze. I put a hand on his upper arm and guided him through. I liked what I felt.

# Chapter Seven

OUT OF THE OFFICE, ARTHUR TIPPETT SEEMED TO BLOSSOM, to expand. He reminded me of Vince—when I first met him, an underpaid secretary to a rich, secretive man, oppressed by his employer's knowledge of his true nature, waiting only for an understanding friend to come along and set him free. As soon as we were in the open air, Tippett breathed deeply, shook off his servile professional manner, and, apparently, grew an inch or so in height. We walked along Ludgate Hill and Fleet Street, through the Inns of Court, all of them deserted but for the birds and the bees that reclaimed them at the weekend. By the time we reached St. Giles, Tippett had a spring in his step. He chatted about this and that— new buildings, politics, the latest books and shows—and I found myself enjoying his company. He was a nice-looking guy—a bit on the slight side for my liking, but personality could go a long way toward making up for any lack of bulk. Soon I forgot that I was luring him to my room in order to pump him for information about the late Frank Bartlett; I could think only of pumping him, period.

He took an interest in me, asking about my work, my circumstances, and I had to think on my feet: if, as I pretended, I was the scion of a wealthy New England family with money to invest, what was I doing in humble medical quarters?

"My folks insist that I get a professional qualification," I said, "and medicine seemed the best bet. I was never going to make it in the law—not smart enough." He accepted this with a deferential nod of the head. "As for the church—well, they would never have me. Too much of a hell-raiser."

"Indeed?"

"Yeah. I could never do all that chastity stuff. Could you?"

"I've never thought about it," said Tippett, avoiding my sideways glance as we walked along Oxford Street.

"I hope you're not going without, Tippett."

"I don't have much time for that sort of thing. And I certainly can't afford to marry."

"Who said anything about marriage? A man doesn't need a wife to enjoy himself."

"I suppose not. But even the most casual enjoyments cost money."

"They don't have to." We'd reached the hospital, and I held the door open. "The best things in life are free, Tippett. After you."

My room was on the top floor of the building, at the end of a long corridor, far from the wards, if not quite out of range of the pervasive smell of disinfectant. It was quiet up there—a few doctors sleeping off night duty, perhaps, but otherwise everyone was at work. We would not be interrupted.

"Come on in. It's not exactly a palace, but it's enough."

Tippett walked in, and I closed the door behind us.

"It's bigger than my room at home."

"You should get Frank Bartlett to give you a raise. Get a place of your own."

"I manage." He took his jacket off and handed it to me. His shirt was immaculate; the collar and cuffs looked brand-new. I found his pride in his appearance curiously touching. I hung the jacket on the back of the door, feeling for a moment the heat of his body trapped in the fabric.

"Sit down." I gestured to the bed, which, thank God, I'd made before I went out in the morning. The armchair was covered in clothes and books; I took the only other seat, a hardwood chair, and, turning it around, sat down *à cheval*, my legs wide apart. Tippett made himself comfortable, but the mattress was saggy, bringing his face almost to the level of my crotch. The furniture was on my side.

"So, Arthur... I can call you Arthur, can't I, now that you're in my room?"

"Of course, er..."

"Mitch. Drink?"

"Well, maybe just a small one."

"No chance. With me, you'll always get a big one." I swung a leg over the back of the chair, and found the bottle and a couple of glasses. He was watching me—not staring with that hungry look that betrays so many, but with a cool, appraising air. I think he liked what he saw.

"Here's to new friendships." We clinked glasses, and drank. The color rose in his cheeks immediately.

"So, old Frank's doing great business, by the look of things. Very prosperous."

"Mmmm."

"Knows how to make money, and knows how to spend it, of course. Expensive tastes, he has." Again, I was making wild guesses, hoping to elicit something from Tippett about Bartlett's personal circumstances.

"Ah," he said. "He told you, then."

"Wha—oh, yes. You mean about the..." I rolled my eyes and tried to look knowing. "He didn't tell me in so many words, but I guessed." I didn't have a clue what I was supposed to guess, but it seemed that Tippett was eager to tell me. Perhaps being out of the office made him reckless— or was it the whiskey? Or the treats to come (which I was pressing into a gap between the struts of the chair back)?

"I hope it's all cleared up now," said Tippett. "We so wanted to avoid getting the police involved, and of course Mr. Bartlett didn't want Mr. Ross to know anything. I was happy to help in any way I could."

This sounded murky, so I made encouraging noises. "Right. I mean that sort of thing—the police never really understand, do they?"

"They understand, all right," said Tippett, sounding suddenly bitter. "All too well, most of the time. We're completely unprotected. Some type wants to extort money with threats—a gentleman like Mr. Bartlett is a sitting duck." His voice sounded shaky, as if he were about to cry.

"So I was right," I said. "He was being blackmailed."

Tippett glanced around the room like a frightened rabbit.

"It's okay, Arthur. No one can hear us. You must have had a hell of a time keeping a lid on this. Why don't you tell me about it?"

"I can't—"

"You can." I sat beside him on the bed; the mattress did its work, sagging so much that I was leaning against him. "You'll feel better if you do. Don't worry. I'm not going to tell anyone. We're all in the same boat, aren't we?"

"Are we?"

I put an arm around his shoulders. "You bet we are."

He sighed, sagging forward. "Oh, thank God. I wondered, when you walked into the office, if you...you might... understand."

"I understand, all right, Arthur." I rubbed his neck. "Go ahead."

He turned to face me, and I thought for a moment that we were going to fuck first, talk later. I didn't object to that order of play—I was hard in my pants, and I wanted to get up his ass. But instead of leaning in for a kiss, he took a deep breath and began.

"It's been so hard," he said, with no trace of a double meaning. "Keeping Mr. Bartlett's affairs under control. Making sure that Mr. Ross doesn't suspect anything. Dealing with certain undesirable...customers. You know what I mean."

"No, Arthur, I'm not sure that I do. You're going to have to spell it out."

"You were right," he said at length. "Mr. Bartlett was being blackmailed."

"Who by?"

"I never knew the person's real name. He operated through intermediaries, people who delivered letters and collected money."

"At the office?"

"Yes. Messengers are in and out all the time. That's one of the reasons why I go in at weekends—it's the only way I can get any peace and quiet. During the week, it's nonstop comings and goings. It could have been anybody."

"When did this start?"

"About a year ago, maybe a bit more. I'd have to look in the ledgers."

"You mean you kept a record of everything?"

"Yes. At Mr. Bartlett's orders. Of course, all the payments were put down as legitimate business expenses, but he was most insistent that I should keep a record. I suppose he was thinking of going to the police."

"And did he?"

"Not as far as I know. At least, the demands kept coming in, and the money kept going out. Sometimes he started to speak to me about it—I suppose he needed to confide in somebody. But then he'd just stop. Poor man—he must be going through hell."

Well, he was at peace now—but I didn't tell Tippett that.

"Did you get any idea of the nature of the blackmail?"

"I was never certain—but there are some things that you can work out for yourself. If it had been a legal matter, Mr. Bartlett would have stood up to it. I honestly can't think of a more honest, upright man. If he had done something wrong in his professional life, it would have been a mistake, and he'd have been the first person to own up to it. So we can rule that out."

"He wouldn't have taken bribes, or fixed a case?"

"Definitely not. I know what you're thinking, and one hears of these things all the time, but not Mr. Bartlett."

"Fair enough. Go on."

"Then I wondered if there was some financial problem—whether, perhaps, he'd been obliged to borrow money from the company which he was unable to pay back. It's possible that someone at the bank might have found out about it, I suppose."

The bank? Morgan?

"And maybe if they were covering up for Mr. Bartlett," continued Tippett, "or somehow creaming off a percentage for themselves, then that might explain it."

"What made you think that Bartlett might have gotten into financial difficulty?"

"He's been investing heavily in property, and I think he ended up spending more than he intended."

Morgan's house...

"And then there was the matter of his will."

"What about it?"

"He made a new will just a few days ago. I don't know the exact details, I've not seen it—but just before he made it, he moved a great deal of money across from the business account to his private account. If Mr. Bartlett was a family man, I'd think that he was putting money into trust for his children. But as he and Mrs. Bartlett have no children—well, it just seemed strange."

"Did he say anything about it to you? For instance, why he chose to rewrite his will just at this time? Had his circumstances changed?"

"No. Nothing that I know of. But then, I'm only a clerk. I'm not party to the private affairs of my superiors."

"But you have ways of finding out, I guess."

"Well, one hears things."

"And?"

"There was talk of some kind of trouble at home."

"With his wife?"

"Quite."

"An affair?"

"Perhaps."

"Who?" Morgan thought they had been so discreet—but of course word was out.

"I couldn't say. But that's what made me wonder about the third possibility. That this wasn't a professional matter, or a financial matter, but blackmail of a much more basic and brutal sort."

"You mean Bartlett had been doing something else that's illegal."

"Precisely."

"Fucking another man."

Tippett flinched and looked at the floor. "Yes. If you must put it so crudely."

"How would you put it, Arthur?"

"It's none of my business what Mr. Bartlett does in his private life, and it's nobody else's business either. Why must people be so quick to judge? How could it possibly affect his standing as a lawyer if he chooses to…fall in love with someone of the same…"

"Sex?"

"Yes. It's so unfair."

"Indeed it is, Arthur. But you know that already. Life isn't fair for people like us, is it?"

"No. But we try. Mr. Bartlett is very happily married."

"To all appearances, yes. And you, Arthur Tippett? What about you?"

"I live with my mother."

"Yes. And what about…"

"I am a devoted son and a dutiful employee. I don't have time for…"

"Fun?"

"Quite."

"You don't have time, or you don't have the guts?"

"Both, perhaps. I certainly don't have the money to pay off blackmailers."

"So you keep to yourself, because you're too scared of what would happen if you got caught."

Tippett stood up; I'd gone too far. Vince tells me off for bullying people, and I suppose that's just what I was doing to Tippett.

"If I may say so, sir,"—I was "sir" again now, not "Mitch"—"you and I come from very different backgrounds with very different expectations. I don't know what it's like in America, but I imagine in the social circles to which you belong, such things can be easily arranged. But for those of us who have to work for a living, who are dependent on the good opinion of our neighbors and employers, I'm afraid discretion is necessary."

"I wonder if that's what you'll say on your deathbed, Arthur? 'I didn't have any love in my life, but at least I was discreet.' "

"Perhaps I will. Love is a luxury I can ill afford."

"Love is free, Arthur." I lay back on the bed, opening my legs—I certainly wasn't planning to charge for it. "You just have to reach out and take it."

"Playing with fire…" he murmured, half turning to face me.

"So? Get burned." I reached down and pressed into my

groin with the heel of my hand. It certainly felt hot down there.

"I can't..."

"When did you last suck a cock, Arthur?"

"I..."

"Come on. What's stopping you?"

"I'm..."

Afraid. He's afraid.

I unbuttoned the waistband of my pants, the top two buttons of my fly. "Come here."

"No, I mustn't..."

The poor guy was shaking. Under such circumstances, I would have to remove the possibility of choice. The nervous need to feel that they have no control over what happens to them, that they have been seduced, that it is someone else's fault. I clicked my fingers, pointed to the floor beneath my feet. "Get down on your knees, Tippett."

He stepped forward; this was better.

"Now!" I raised my voice, and he obeyed, dropping to the ground like a poleaxed ox. I undid two more buttons. A bulging mountain of stretched white cotton filled the V-shaped gap at my fly. Tippett knelt and stared, his hands fussing together, each trying to stop the other from reaching out and taking what it wanted.

I sat up, grabbed his wrist and placed a hand on my groin. "Take it. It's yours."

He made a strange, half-sobbed "Oh" as his hand cupped my stuffed package; even now he might spring to his feet and run. I caressed the back of his neck, drawing him inward. Finally his resistance evaporated, and with a look of resignation, almost regret, he buried his face in my crotch. I pressed him down, relishing the warmth, bucking my hips up, mashing his nose and mouth with my cock.

I don't know what it was—the heat of the moment, the scent that Tippett was inhaling with every lungful, the caressing pressure of my hands on his neck and head—but, suddenly, something in him changed, as if a switch had been flicked. Where before there had been a timid clerk, suddenly there was a wildcat. He looked up, eyes wet and shining, cheeks flushed, his hair, normally so carefully parted and combed back, falling into his eyes. One hand grasped the elastic of my underwear and yanked. My cock sprang out, bounced once in the air and then fell back onto my belly with a smack. Tippett gripped it and started licking and slurping like a dog with a bone; I guess it really was a long time since he had a cock to play with other than his own, and he was determined to make the most of it. I lay back and enjoyed the ride—and when his lips opened and admitted the head into his mouth, I knew I was in for a good time. Tippett may not have had much practice, but he took to cocksucking like a duck to water. After a few false starts, some choking and gagging, he took me into his throat and started sucking like a pro.

He came up for air, his lips swollen, his chin wet with spit. I like to kiss a man when he's been sucking me, so I pulled Tippett onto the bed beside me and thrust my tongue between his lips. With Tippett reclining beside me, I could let my hands run over his body, admiring its leanness and grace. I wanted to see him naked, to feel his flesh against mine, but for now I was content with a clothed embrace, my exposed cock making a mess on his pants leg. He surrendered absolutely to the moment—a far cry from the nervous, shaking young man of a few minutes ago. His hands ran up and down my back, clutching my ass and pulling me into him; it didn't take too much intuition to guess what he wanted.

"Strip," I said.

"Really?"

"Yes. I want to see you."

He stood up, pulled off his sweater, unbuttoned his shirt. His torso, when it was revealed, was beautiful—pale and smooth, graceful rather than strong, the body of a dancer or a gymnast rather than a football player.

"Now the rest."

He turned around, either out of embarrassment or because he wanted to present me with my ultimate goal, a very shapely ass that would not have been out of place in the sculpture galleries of the British Museum.

"Very nice, Arthur," I said. "I bet a lot of men have wanted to get into that."

He was struggling with his shoelaces and socks, and I was getting impatient. As he bent over, I came up behind him and pressed my rigid dick between his buttocks. He almost pitched over onto the floor, and braced himself on his fingertips, like a runner on his marks, keeping his ass as high as possible. I pushed my pants and underpants down and pulled my shirt over my head. The position was too good to waste. Grabbing Tippett by the hips, I pulled him back against me, pressing my cockhead against his hole. His face, what I could see of it, was red, a thick vein standing out in his neck, his eyes shut tight. Perhaps he had never been fucked before. Perhaps this was going to be difficult. Was that going to stop me?

I pressed harder; Tippett moaned, and pushed back. If he could have taken me dry, I think he would have—the pain would not have spoiled his pleasure, might even have enhanced it. I've often found that men who habitually deny themselves enjoyment welcome a bit of discomfort, in the same way that simpler mortals enjoy mustard with a sausage. I'm a doctor of the body, not of the mind, so I make no great claims to understanding, but Tippett was definitely of this type. I knew exactly how to treat him.

Since we were *chez moi*, so to speak, there was lubricant within easy reach—a trusty jar of Vaseline in my toilet kit. So, unwilling to break the contact, I pushed Tippett across the floor with my cock. We would have appeared comical to any onlooker, like contestants in a depraved variation of the three-legged race, my ankles hobbled by my pants, Tippett trailing clothes behind him, one shoe off, the other still on, his nose nearly touching the carpet. But we weren't laughing; we just shuffled toward the washbasin, and I found what I was looking for. I unscrewed the lid and took a small gob; I wanted this fuck to be possible, but not easy.

It didn't take long before I was inside him, and God, his ass was tight. He was making noises as if he were in pain, but at the same time he was reaching around, grabbing me, pulling me in. I steadied myself, bent my knees for extra stability, and forged ahead. Soon I was buried up to the hilt, the dark hair around my cock pressing against Tippett's lily-white ass cheeks. I gave one last shove, and suddenly he shut up, as if he were holding his breath. Give him a moment to get used to it, I thought, and then fuck the living daylights out of him.

Which is precisely what I did. It was just as well that my fellow residents were either at work or fast asleep; anyone nearby and awake would have had no trouble identifying the nature of the rhythmic thumping that came from my room. Tippett braced himself against the oversize wardrobe, which banged against the wall. There was a dirty, somewhat decayed mirror on one of the doors, which afforded me an excellent view of what I was doing—and just how much Tippett was enjoying it. His face, so close to the glass that his breath was misting it, expressed nothing short of rapture.

He was close, and I wanted to finish with us both naked in bed. To that end I withdrew, raised him to a standing position—he was a little shaky on his legs, just as he should have been—and kicked off my shoes. He followed my lead, and soon we stood naked, facing each other, both stiff, both breathing heavily. Tippett made the first move, pressing himself against me, rubbing the hair on my chest and stomach, kissing my neck. We walked, almost waltzed, to the bed, and I laid him down. He knew what he wanted, whether by instinct or experience, and drew his knees up to his chest. After a minute of shifting and thrusting, I was back inside him, delivering the final movement of this sexual symphony. Tippett's eyes were open, but how much he saw, I do not know. I fucked him deep, slow, and hard for a while, and then, feeling my orgasm approaching, I lifted myself onto my toes, put my whole body weight onto the fulcrum of my prick, and pounded him like a jackhammer. His hand stole to his groin, working in between my thrusts, and he started tugging. It did not take long before he was thrashing around underneath me, but I knew how to hold him in place, fucking him through his climax, knowing that the last few merciless thrusts up his tender ass would stay with him for many days to come.

And then, I passed the point of no return. I thrust once, twice—and here it was, that feeling of panic and release and violence and tenderness, all shooting out of my cock and deep into Tippett's guts.

We stayed locked together for a while, his feet around my back, my face buried in the pillow, until finally I rolled off, my softening cock, wet with spunk, slipping out of him. He hissed a sharp intake of breath as I left him; he would be sore, but he would like it. I kissed him on the mouth and stopped him from getting up. I didn't want this to be a quick rinse and goodbye; I still had things to ask him.

"No regrets?"

"None."

"You should do that more often, Arthur. You're very good at it."

"Thank you." He smiled.

"I think you've found your true vocation."

"I'm not sure how to take that."

"Take it as a compliment. And in half an hour or so, take it again."

"If you like." He was putting his manners back on, if not his clothes. I found the contrast exciting; just minutes ago, he was writhing underneath me like a stuck pig, not caring what came out of his mouth; now he was weighing his words again. I savored the sense of power that gave me, of control.

"So," I said, putting my arms around him, holding him tight, "what were you saying about Bartlett? You think he's been doing what we've just been doing?"

"I'm sure of it."

"Why?"

"Because—I just know."

"Nobody 'just knows,' Arthur. Come on. Maybe I can help him." I knew perfectly well that Bartlett was past helping, but it sounded plausible.

"I saw one of the letters."

"The blackmail notes?"

"Yes. And it made it fairly clear."

"Did it mention any names?"

"I'm not sure that I should say."

"Don't you trust me, Arthur? All I want is what's best for Bartlett. And what's best for you." I hugged him, and his ass pressed back against me. We might be ready in less than half an hour, at this rate.

"What's the point in telling you? What can any of us do? We'll just incriminate ourselves. It's hopeless."

"Nothing's as bad as it seems. Who was telling me, just twenty minutes ago, that he would never have any fun with his body?"

"I know, but—"

"No buts. You may not believe it, but I've gotten out of some pretty tricky situations in the past. Nothing is ever as bad as it seems. You just have to use your head."

"That sounds good."

Ah! The first double entendre! He was a fast learner.

"All in good time, Arthur. If you want this"—I brought his hand to my prick—"then I want some information. Who was Bartlett being blackmailed by?"

"I honestly don't know."

"But you said—"

"All I know is what they were accusing him of. Buggery. Sodomy. Unnatural vice. All that sort of thing."

"But names, Arthur. I need names."

"The blackmailer made it pretty clear that he knew who Mr. Bartlett had been seeing. Who he had been seen with. He hadn't been...careful."

Neither had we, really—if any of the Middlesex staff had a mind to bust us, we'd have spent the night in a police cell. There was only the flimsiest of locks on the door; one swift kick from a boot was all that stood between us and two years' hard labor. But now was not the time to remind Tippett of this. He was comfortable in my bed, with my arms around him, with his hand cupping my balls. I had won his trust.

"It was a young man from the bank that handles B and R's investments."

My blood ran cold—did he feel it?

"Really? Who's that?"

"London Imperial. A Mr. Morgan."

"I see. What do you know about him?"

"Not much. Nice fellow. Married, with two young children. Mr. Ross thinks very highly of him. And Mr. Bartlett—well, Mr. Bartlett was smitten the moment he walked into the office."

"Really?" That gnawing jealousy again, even as I held Tippett against me.

"If it had been a man and a woman, you'd have called it love at first sight. *L'amour fou.* Mr. Bartlett was...well, he was not himself. You could tell. He started making mistakes, and I had to cover up for him. After a while, he recovered, and he was his old, reliable self again—and by that time I knew that he and Mr. Morgan were..."

"Yes, I understand," I said. "No need to elaborate. So this...Morgan, is it? He's the one Bartlett's been giving money to?"

"Exactly," said Tippett. "And more than that."

"What do you mean?"

"The will."

"The—oh. My God." I remembered Morgan's account of the evening before Bartlett had died, those crazy statements that led to the argument, the "something special" that Bartlett had done for Morgan, the "surprise" he had in store.

He'd rewritten his will—in Morgan's favor.

Morgan, of course, would not know about it. They had never gotten around to discussing it.

Had they?

Bartlett's death would make Morgan a very rich man— and then the story of the strychnine in the mouthwash, the mystery of Bartlett's apparently impossible murder or improbable suicide, suddenly admitted a very different interpretation.

An interpretation that the police would be only too glad to jump to.

"Who knows about the will, Arthur?"

"Nobody. Mr. Bartlett's solicitor, I suppose."

"And who is that?"

Tippett laughed. "Why, it's Mr. Ross, of course. They keep all their business in the firm."

"And would Mr. Ross—"

Tippett rolled around to face me. "Look, Mitch. I've got to get home to my mother."

"No, don't go yet."

"I have no intention of going yet. I have about an hour. And, if you don't mind, I'd like to spend all sixty of those minutes with your cock inside me."

Matching his actions to his words, he slid down my body and took my still soft prick in his mouth, sucking and licking until it started to harden again. And as worried as I was about Morgan and the horrible suggestiveness of Bartlett's changed will, I soon found that my mind was cleared of everything but sensation.

# Chapter Eight

I RAN OUT OF THE HOSPITAL WITH MY HAT IN MY HAND, MY
shirt buttoned wrongly, my shoelaces in knots that I was too
flustered to untie, and hurried to the station. As the train
trundled out through the suburbs, I tried to clear my mind
of the poisonous idea that Tippett had planted there—that
Morgan, my best friend, the man I had always regarded as
a paragon of honesty and decency, was somehow implicated
in the death of Frank Bartlett, his lover, benefactor, and pro-
tector. Death—by suicide, or by murder? And if by suicide,
why? Driven to it—by blackmail? And who had more reason to blackmail him than a man whom he had seduced,
who had so clearly benefited from his victim's generosity—a
new house, gifts of money, and now, finally, the change of
will? Perhaps these gifts, as Morgan had described them—
lavish, embarrassing, even unwelcome gifts—were not given
so freely after all. Perhaps Morgan had asked for money,
and when he realized how easy it was to persuade Bartlett to
be generous, he'd asked for more—a house, a bequest. And
then he got greedy, too greedy to wait for Bartlett's natural

death, too eager to get his hands on money that should, by rights, have gone to his widow.

No—this was insane. This was Boy Morgan we were talking about, not some sleazy blackmailer, some confidence trickster, some low-life murderous scum. And yet I knew all too well that blackmailers and even murderers were seldom if ever the Bill Sykes type of the popular imagination. Killers were nearly always known to their victims, and blackmailers were often to be found within the intimate family circle. If I have learned anything from my voracious reading of detective fiction, it's that the most obvious person is usually the culprit, however many red herrings are thrown in to distract us. I thought of Morgan as honest, decent, and true, but what did I really know about him? How much of his life did he keep from me? He lied to his wife, and he lied to me; for all I knew, he was lying to his employers, using his position in the bank to feather his own nest and then, knowing only too well how attractive he was to men of a certain type, identifying the one man who was best situated to help him.

Morgan had always been ambitious—his marriage to Belinda Eagle proved that. She was his social superior, and would have brought a great deal of money into the Morgan household, were it not for the unfortunate fact that her parents had themselves been ruined and incarcerated after a messy murder. That must have been a great disappointment to Morgan—and when he saw a chance to better himself, when the money was handed to him on a plate, he grabbed it. Impatient as ever, he'd killed the goose that laid the golden egg. The money was as good as his. Once probate had been attended to, Morgan would be a rich man. Perhaps the will would be contested by Bartlett's widow, but what could she do? Morgan had her, fair and square. Nobody would speak out. Any witnesses, such as Tippett, were so terrified of being implicated in a queer scandal that they would keep their mouths shut. Nobody would state the obvious fact that Morgan had obtained Bartlett's trust through a sexual relationship, and then exploited him and finally driven him to his grave.

It was with a heavy heart that I walked up the street I had positively skipped along earlier that morning. The house, which once promised a weekend of fun and fucking, now looked like a mausoleum—paid for by Bartlett. Bought in blood.

The only ray of sunshine was the open, smiling face of PC Stan Knight, back at his post, stamping his feet with impatience, looking up and down the street for my approach, grinning the moment he caught sight of me. Well, that did me good. At least there was some honesty in the world. Perhaps my grim misgivings about Morgan were all wrong.

"Thought you weren't coming back, Mitch," said Knight.

"Am I late? Sorry. I've been up to town."

"Find anything?"

"Yes." I gave him a highly edited version of what Tippett had told me, leaving Morgan's name out of the picture. No doubt his superiors at the station had already formed their own conclusions—and, despite my suspicions, I had no desire to add fuel to that particular fire.

Out of uniform, Stan Knight looked like exactly the sort of young man a mother would like her daughter to bring home: clean, neatly barbered, well proportioned without being unnecessarily attractive. He was wearing a tweed jacket, a white shirt with a knit tie, carefully polished brogues, and dark-blue trousers—possibly part of his uniform, which I found rather touching. Police pay obviously didn't go as far as a young man like Knight wished it might. I would have to see if I could help out in that area, I thought, forgetting for a moment that I was not actually a wealthy New England playboy.

121

"How are things going back at the station?" I asked, as casually as possible.

"Hard to say," said Knight, as we walked side by side along the street. "They're still questioning your friend."

"I'm sure he's helping them as much as he can."

"Yes." He looked down at his feet; this was enough to tell me that things were not going well for Morgan. I felt a tightness around my heart. God, I had been ready to find him guilty myself, to execute the sentence—and I was supposed to be his friend. I had a sudden urge to save him, and felt ashamed of what I had allowed myself to think. That was not the action of a friend. Morgan would have sworn to my innocence and knocked down anyone who accused me, even if I'd been found covered in blood with the razor in my hand, such was his faith in me. And I'd been ready to condemn him on nothing more than hearsay.

It felt good to be doing something, at least. "So, where are you taking me?"

"First stop, Clapham High Street." Knight grabbed my arm and ran. "Come on! That's our bus!"

Twenty minutes later we were seated in the saloon bar of a tiny little pub under the railway bridge at the north end of Clapham High Street, rather ambitiously named the Queen's Head. Less regal premises it was hard to imagine, though judging by the number of soft felt hats, suede shoes, and colored scarves in the lounge bar, it was possibly not to the royal variety that the name alluded. As for the head— well, there was a silhouette of Victoria on the sign above the door, but I could think of other meanings, and remembered with pleasure the taste of PC Knight's spunk in my mouth a few hours before. He was eager for a return engagement, that was obvious—but he'd have to wait awhile. Tippett had drained me dry, and I would have nothing for my sexy little copper until bedtime at the earliest. I wondered where I would end up sleeping—my room at the Middlesex, Morgan's sad, blighted house, or—where did Stan Knight live?

We had a pint and watched the comings and goings, but there was nobody in the Queen's Head resembling Morgan's description of Sean Durran, and by half past eight I was getting anxious. We were wasting time. The clientele of the Queen's Head, at least tonight, looked more like out-of-work chorus boys and window dressers than rough trade. A cursory glimpse into the public bar told me that I would find nothing to my advantage in there—the hostile glances, the loud, braying conversations, showed that this was not a sympathetic environment.

Next stop, the Ring of Bells in Balham, another short bus ride away. Stan was an efficient little Virgil in this trip through south London's underworld. "We raided this a few months ago," he said cheerfully, as we pushed through the swinging doors. "All sorts goes on here. A regular brothel, it was."

"And now?"

"It's been quiet for a while, but they'll soon get going again. Landlord pays us off, I reckon. That's how it usually works."

"Nasty business."

"Way of the world, I'm afraid. Come on."

Two more pints were ordered and drunk; Stan was slightly merry now, and let his knee touch mine rather more often than was necessary.

"That him?" he asked, nodding toward a handsome brute in the corner, his hands dirty from a day's manual labor.

"Could be."

"Shall I ask him?"

He seemed eager, perhaps thinking of what he, I, and the dirty-handed brute in the corner got behind closed doors.

"All right. But be tactful. Don't mention—"

"I'm not going to ask him if he knows anything about

the death of Frank Bartlett," he said. "I'm trained in these matters. Leave it to me."

I watched the two of them chatting, occasionally looking over to me; when the laborer sized me up, I raised my glass and jerked a thumb at the bar. He nodded slowly, so I ordered another pint.

"Says he knows Sean," said Stan when I delivered the beer.

"Oh yeah? Good. Know him well?"

"Well enough," said the man. "He drinks here and at the Bear."

"That's the White Bear in Wimbledon," said Stan. "You know."

"Ah." I wondered if this was the big brute who had so scared Morgan in the White Bear's urinals. "Any idea where he is tonight?"

"Sunday? At home, if he's got any sense." He took a swig of beer, wiped his mouth on the back of his hand, grimaced. "Waste of time being out tonight."

"Too quiet for you?"

"Yeah. Even here."

"What about the Ship?" asked Knight. "Think he might be there?"

"Could be. That's his manor." The laborer thought for a while, drank off half his pint, and smacked his lips. "That's better. Gets the plaster dust out of a man's throat. Not good, working on a Sunday. Still, needs must." He drained his glass and placed it carefully on a beer mat.

"Another?"

"Wouldn't say no."

"What's your name?"

"Bert."

I gave money to Knight. "Three more pints, Stan, if you would."

"He your bit of stuff?" asked Bert, when Stan was standing at the bar. "Nice arse. Bet he's a good ride. Not seen you round here before."

"I'm not from around here."

"Right." I expected the usual dialogue about Americans, but instead Bert said "North London, I suppose," as if that were just as remote as Massachusetts. "Come down south for a bit of trade?" He let his huge hand dangle in front of his crotch.

"That sort of thing."

"I know Sean. Nice lad. He been recommended to you?"

"Yes, in a way. Friend of mine—"

"Yeah, very popular is Sean. Should be. I broke him in. Trained him to the work, if you like."

"I see."

"Met him on a building site. Arse like that, boy, I said, money in the bank. And he likes it, too. They're always the best, them that actually likes it. He's a good fuck, my Sean." He sighed. "Would have kept him for myself, if I had the readies."

"And what about you, Bert? Do you like it?"

"Yeah." His eyes shone, and his face opened up into a smile, huge creases appearing along his cheeks. "I love it. But that's not what gents want from me, is it? It's this." He gave his cock a squeeze. "So that's what I give 'em. Don't like to disappoint by rolling over and sticking me arse in the air, do I?"

"I don't know that you should be telling me this, Bert. Suppose I was thinking of…using you."

"Don't get me wrong. I like giving it as well as taking it. And I give satisfaction. I've got a lot to give, if you know what I mean."

I thought I probably did.

"But once in a while it would be nice to…you know."

"Roll over."

"Yeah." Stan brought the drinks, and half of Bert's disappeared immediately.

"I'd be more than happy to oblige," I said; I like nothing better than turning the tables on men who are bigger and stronger than me. Fucking slim lads like Tippett, or eager young puppies like Stan, is one of life's greatest pleasures, but slipping it to a caveman like Bert would delight the true connoisseur.

"But first," I said, "I need to find Sean."

"Why?" Bert's eyes narrowed. "Is he in trouble?"

"No. But I think he knows something about a friend of mine who is."

"You ain't been to the cops." It wasn't a question.

"Of course not," I said, hoping that none of the patrons of the Ring of Bells recognized Stan Knight out of his uniform. "This is a...private matter."

"All right. Look for Sean at the Ship. If you don't find him there, come back, and I'll get a message to him."

"Thanks."

"But promise me one thing."

I saw his eyes glancing down at my crotch, and I thought I could guess what that one thing was.

"Bert," I said, "I'll be happy to fuck you all night long, in any position you like, as often as you want, if Sean can help my friend."

"Good." He finished his pint, shifted around in his seat—he obviously had a hard-on, and if it was as large as he said, it must have been causing him some discomfort. "Now drink up. Let's go."

"You're—"

"Yeah. I'm coming with you." He leaned toward me and whispered in my ear; I could smell the beer on his breath. "There are rooms upstairs at the Ship, and I've got my own key."

And so we were a party of three taking the bus further

south to Tooting Broadway. Bert was well known at the Ship, dispensing handshakes and backslaps and greetings on all sides, and, as his guests, we were made welcome too.

"Sean in?" he asked the landlord, a short, balding, pointy-featured man with a sandy moustache.

"In and out."

"Working?"

The landlord shrugged and continued to polish glasses.

"He won't be long," said Bert. "While we wait, we'll have three pints and three whiskey chasers. On the house, eh?"

The landlord nodded. " 'Course, Bert."

"I'll take a rain check on the whiskey," I said; I'd already had too much beer, not to mention the scotch I'd drunk with Tippett earlier in the afternoon. "I don't want to disappoint you." I winked.

We made ourselves comfortable at a corner table, and surveyed the room. The customers here were a rougher bunch than in Clapham and Balham—much more to my taste. A casual visitor might have mistaken this for any other workingman's pub, the air thick with tobacco smoke, the tables covered in sticky rings and puddles of beer, the voices thick and deep. But to the practiced eye—and my eyes were just as practiced as my other organs—it was clear that this was a specialized hostelry. Men were standing a little too close at the bar, their legs touching, hands dangling into crotches. Every so often, a better-dressed customer would arrive, to be greeted with a lot of jostling and posing—not the exaggerated preening of the boys in the West End, but recognizable as a rougher, more masculine form of display. The men who visited the Ship were hunting different game.

We watched as two or three men—city workers, perhaps, or civil servants, doctors, lawyers, maybe even vicars far from their parish—came in, took their pick of the men at the bar, bought drinks, and retired to tables to discuss the issues of the day. Some of them disappeared into the toilets, where,

Bert informed us, the cubicles were large and the lighting was low. Others left the Ship together, bound for flats or hotels. The upper rooms, Bert told me, were out of bounds to all but regulars, of which he was obviously one.

So it looked as if my berth for the night was secure—and, of course, it would be so much more convenient to Morgan's house than my room in town.

Stan was enjoying his night out more than circumstances justified; I think he was just as eager to get into my pants as Bert was, and the idea of having both of them begging for my cock was extremely agreeable. When Bert suggested that we might repair to the bathroom for a little preview—well, that's not exactly how he put it, he actually said, "Give us a taste while we're waiting"—I was quick to agree. That's how seriously I was taking my investigative work. My advice to any would-be detectives would be: avoid strong drink, big men, and low dives, in any combination. The three of them together, with my little tame cop Stan Knight as the cherry on the cake, had almost driven Morgan out of my mind.

We left our drinks unfinished and hurried into the toilet, making no attempt to disguise the fact that we were going together; the landlord must have felt very confident that he was not currently under police observation. Little did he know what Stan did for a living.

No sooner had the door swung shut behind us than Bert was on his knees in front of me, heedless of the dirt on the floor, unbuttoning me with his huge, dirty fingers, leaving chalky traces over the front of my pants. His skin, when it came into contact with my cock, felt rough, and there were big calluses on his hands; whatever else he did to earn a living, Bert was no stranger to manual labor. He was no stranger to cocksucking either, judging by the ease with which he took me down his throat. I wasn't yet fully hard—there had been no preamble before he swallowed me—but even at this halfway stage I was big enough to make most men gag.

But when I hit the back of Bert's mouth, he just opened up and admitted me, running his lips down to form a tight seal around the base of my cock. I rubbed his head; his hair was thinning, close-cropped around the back and sides, with a tuft at the front that was now marooned as the rest receded around it. Seeing him like this, this huge brute of a man on his knees sucking me, was enough to bring me quickly to maximum hardness. In fact, if I hadn't been so efficiently drained by Tippett, I might have spewed a load down Bert's throat there and then. The fact that Stan was beside me, his arm around my waist, watching the show, added greatly to my enjoyment. I was tempted to abandon the chase and take advantage of Bert's private key. And I might have, if the door hadn't opened and a rough voice which I recognized as the landlord's said, "Sean's in."

Bert mumbled some sort of reply and kept sucking; now that he had me, he was reluctant to let go, and it took all my willpower to step back and button up. "Now you know what you've got to look forward to. Get up, Bert. Don't waste it."

He growled and grumbled, but did as he was told. "Come on, then," he said, sounding like a sulky child. "Let's go and find out what all the fuss is about." He held the door open for me. "You will fuck me later, won't you?"

"I promise."

"All right." We went back to the bar. "You're worth it."

I almost said "thank you," but I didn't think this was meant as a compliment.

Sean Durran was better looking than Morgan had led me to believe—but then his idea of beauty was well biased toward the feminine, and he would never have thought of a man in terms of his looks, only in terms of what he could do for him. Morgan had never told me he found me attractive, only that he liked how my dick, ass, mouth, or hands were making him feel. Durran was no movie star, true, but he had the kind of man-boy looks that I find irresistible. He was sitting on his own, his hands clasped between his knees, looking around expectantly—in fact, he looked as nervous as a kitten. This was not the swaggering cocksman I'd been led to expect. He had dark rings around his eyes—which, on closer inspection, were bloodshot. He looked like a man who hadn't gotten much sleep. He looked like a man with something on his conscience.

"Sean Durran?" We shook hands. "I'm Edward Mitchell. Dr. Edward Mitchell." There was a certain amount of back-straightening from Bert and Sean; that title does come in useful now and again.

"What can I do for you, sir?"

"Plenty, from what I've heard."

He relaxed, slouched back in his seat, and opened his legs. "What's Bert been telling you?"

"He says you're a good fuck."

"Yeah. I am."

"In fact, everyone I speak to tells me you're a good fuck."

His brows contracted, and he looked suspicious. "Who's been talking? Who's this?" He nodded toward Stan, who was standing behind me.

"Don't worry. We're friends. I hope we're going to be good friends."

"He's all right, Sean," said Bert, pulling up a tiny stool and planting his huge, solid backside on it; I expected it to be reduced to matchwood. "We've been...chatting."

"Where were you last night, Sean?" No point in beating around the bush; I needed to get this investigation back on track.

"With some pals."

"Where?"

"Here and there."

"Do you ever take a walk on Wimbledon Common, Sean?"

"Maybe."

I took my wallet out of my jacket; fortunately, I was well provided with cash. I pulled out a pound note. Durran's eyes widened.

"Yes. I was on the Common last night."

I put the money on the table and set a beer glass on top of it. "There's more where that came from if you want it," I said. "It all depends on whether you tell me the truth."

"He's an honest boy, is Sean," said Bert, eager to get his hands on some of the loot as well—though possibly not as eager as he was to get his hands on my dick.

"Can we talk somewhere in private?"

Bert and Sean exchanged a glance, and Bert nodded. "Upstairs," he said.

"Ah. The famous upper story. Okay. Lead the way. But remember: I want answers, and I want the truth."

Bert had a quick, muttered conversation with the landlord, who gave him a candle. The stairs were dark, the carpet worn and torn, and it was hard, by that guttering light, not to trip and fall. We ascended to an *L*-shaped landing, the floor covered in dirty brown linoleum; it may not have originally been brown, but it certainly was now. There were six doors, all of them a sickly green.

"Number four is the biggest," said Bert. "Two beds. We should manage."

"There will plenty of time for that," I said, "if I get the answers I'm looking for."

"I'll vouch for Sean," said Bert. "He's honest."

An honest whore—the oldest cliché in the book. Well, we'd see. Lucky for me that the big man was so eager to get fucked; perhaps we would ensure that his protégé gave me what I wanted first.

The room was long, with low ceilings and two windows that presumably looked onto the street, but had long since been covered over with sacking that was tacked to the frames. Daylight and a view, even of Tooting Broadway, were obviously not important to the many hundreds of men who had been in this room before us.

We sat on the beds, Stan and I on one, Sean and Bert on the other. The springs were predictably creaky, the mattress lumpy as hell, but that would not matter; there was plenty of room on the floor, and enough old rugs to protect our elbows, knees, and backsides from splinters.

"Can't we just—" began Bert.

"No." My voice sounded harsh in that drab room. I softened it. "Sean, tell me about last night."

He looked to Bert for permission.

"Go on, son. He's all right."

"I met a couple of gents in the White Bear." So far, so truthful, I thought.

"Did you get their names?"

"Ah, come on now, sir. We don't give names."

"Then I'm sorry." I stood up. Bert glared at Sean.

"Frank, one of them was. The other was something like… I dunno. What was it? Morden."

"Morgan?"

"That's it. Morgan. Or Harry, he called him."

"How did you meet them?"

"I was out walking on the Common earlier and I noticed them. They kind of…looked at me. You know the way some gents do? So when I saw them later in the pub, well, I thought I'd go over and have a chat."

"You thought they'd be interested?"

"Yes. And they were."

"Is it usual for men of that kind to hunt in pairs?"

"Not particularly, but I've had it before. You know, them that wants to add a bit of variety. Posh blokes, mostly, like them two. They like a bit of rough."

"And where did you go?"

"House just off the Common. Nice place. Couldn't tell

you the address, honest I couldn't."

"All right, Sean. I believe you. And you're absolutely sure that you'd never seen either of them before?"

"Only like I said, on the Common."

"You didn't know anything about them?"

"No."

"The one named Frank—you'd never met him before?"

"I swear, sir. He was just another gentleman."

"He's telling the truth, Doc," said Bert. "Honest he is."

You'd swear black was white if it would get a cock up your ass, I thought.

"Right. So you and the two men had—"

"A bit of how's your father. Yeah." Durran smiled for the first time; obviously it had been every bit as wild as Morgan had described it. "In the bath. All sorts of monkey business."

"Anything unusual?"

"Yeah. He shaved me."

The story matched in every particular.

"And you liked that?"

"Very much." He stroked his chin. "Did a good job, too. Better than I can do it."

"And then you left?"

"When we'd finished, the bloke called Morgan went out for a while, and the other one gave me some money."

"How much?"

"A couple of quid."

"Not bad for an evening's work."

"No more than I usually get. And I don't normally have to work so hard for it."

"Sounds like it was more play than work."

"I never said I didn't enjoy it." Durran had a shifty look about his eyes, and kept glancing at Bert for reassurance.

"So," I said, trying to lighten the tone, "you took the money and said good night and left."

"Where's this going?" said Durran, still on the defensive.

"Has something happened?"

Ah—at last the light was dawning. Bert was so consumed with lust that he hadn't thought to question my interest in Sean Durran beyond the obvious; Durran, though younger, was obviously the more inquisitive.

"Yes," I said. "Something has happened. Something bad."

"I didn't do nothing." Durran's face was set, his eyes hooded, hard to read.

"Nobody's accusing you. I'm just trying to figure out—"

"Who is this geezer, Bert?"

"Calm down," said Bert, rubbing Sean's back. "He's a friend."

"Just 'cos you want him to fuck you—"

"Oi," said Bert, gripping Durran's neck. "That's enough. Answer the gentleman's questions. You've got nothing to worry about."

Again—that sideways glance.

"You hiding something, boy?" Bert's grip on Durran's neck tightened.

"I done nothing!" Durran's voice was higher now, and he tried to knock Bert's hand away.

"You better be telling me the truth, Sean. I warned you—"

"All right!" Durran sprang to his feet, and for a moment I thought he was going to make a run for it. Stan thought likewise, and positioned himself in front of the door, his feet braced a yard apart. He couldn't have advertised his true profession any more clearly.

"Sit down, Mr. Durran," I said. "If you have something on your mind, it would be much better if you told us."

"Why should I?" Durran's arms hung by his side, his fists bunching, as if he were ready for a fight.

"Because it will be a lot easier than explaining yourself to the police."

That took the wind out of his sails. His hands relaxed,

and he let out a great sigh. "If I tell you something," he said, "do you promise that I won't get into trouble?"

"I promise nothing, Durran, except that if you don't tell me, you're in shit up to your eyes."

He sat down, put his head in his hands, and grabbed his hair. Bert looked worried, stricken, almost paternal.

"What's up, Sean? What have you gone and done?"

"I don't know, exactly," said Durran. "I was only doing what the other bloke told me."

Bert put an arm around his shoulders.

Durran looked me steadily in the eye, took a deep breath, and started talking.

# Chapter Nine

"I NEEDED THE MONEY," SAID DURRAN, IN A PLEADING, self-pitying tone of voice. "You got to understand. The landlord's going to throw us out on the street. We're behind with the rent."

"Just tell us what happened."

"I don't know where to start."

"What about the money?"

"Right." He cleared his throat and began. "I expect Bert's told you that I make a bit of a living out of…gentlemen like yourself."

"Yes. I gather you're much in demand."

"I wouldn't say that, exactly, but I have a few regulars that seem to like what I've got. It all helps. Money's hard to come by. I can work a full week on the roads and the building sites to make what a gent will give me for a couple of hours."

"I can see that it's very tempting."

"Don't get me wrong. I'm not one of them that makes it a way of life. Not like some that you see up in town, waltzing up and down the Dilly in makeup and perfume and that."

The only difference is the outfit, I thought, but I said nothing. If Durran wanted to play the man, let him.

"I've got responsibilities, see? I've got a wife and a kid and another on the way."

"Expensive business, having a family."

"Yeah, it is." I wondered if Mrs. Durran knew how her resourceful husband was putting bread on the table.

"So, like I say, if a chap comes along and wants to have a bit of fun, and he's got money to burn, then I'm not going to turn it down."

Like many men of his class, Durran would never have considered himself queer—what he did he did out of necessity, it meant nothing, he was doing it for his family, the usual justifications. This was better than going off with another woman. Sex with another man was just for laughs and money. I'd heard it all before.

"What happened this time? Was there something different?"

"The bloke... Well, it was a lot of money."

"How much?"

"Ten quid."

Bert whistled.

"Frank Bartlett gave you ten pounds?"

"No, not him. The other fellow."

"Morgan?"

"No."

"Then who? I think you'd better go back to the beginning."

"All right. I was in here one night last week. Tuesday it must have been, when her mum came round for tea and I said I was slipping out for a pint. They don't mind. Glad to see the back of me, I expect. Her mum loves running me down. She doesn't know how bloody hard I work to look after her daughter and granddaughter."

"You were in the Ship." I had no desire to hear about Sean Durran's mother-in-law.

"Yeah. It was quiet, but I saw one of my regulars come in. He's the timid type, won't come straight over and buy you a drink, you have to get chatting to him first, talk about the weather and what's in the newspapers and so on, then he might suggest that you go for a walk. As if we haven't been through the same rigmarole a dozen times before. Anyway, he was standing at the bar, looking over at me, all nervous he was, and I was biding my time, finishing my pint. That's how it works with them types. Take it slow, reel 'em in. And I was just about to go over to him when in comes this other bloke. Never seen him before in my life. Walks in the pub, takes a look around, sees me sitting there, and comes right over. The other feller was right pissed off."

"What did he look like, this stranger?"

"Tall. Let me think. Taller than me. Very handsome. Real Douglas Fairbanks type. Well dressed, suit and tie, shiny shoes. Every head in the place turned when he walked in, and they were all spitting tacks when he came over to me. Straight to me he came. Never looked at nobody else."

Durran sounded so proud—much more so than a normal family man would be expected to.

"Did he introduce himself?"

"Let me think. No, I'm not sure that he did. He asked if I was Sean Durran, and when I said I was he shook my hand and sat down beside me. Very cocky, I thought he was, but I didn't mind because he looked like he had money. Didn't even offer to buy me a drink, which I get most of 'em to do, the price of beer being what it is."

"And what did he say?"

"Said he had a business proposal to make. I thought it was going to be the usual—come home with me, screw my wife while I watch, come up to my hotel and fuck me or let me fuck you, come into the bog for a quick suck.

Could have knocked me down when he pulls a fiver out of his wallet and tells me that there's another where that came from if we can find a quiet place to talk. So we come up here."

"It all happens up here, doesn't it?"

"And what did he do, Sean?" asked Bert, eager for the juicy details.

"Nothing." Durran looked disappointed. "Just talked."

"I know the type," said Bert.

"Yeah, but not like that. He said there was a job needed doing and I was the right man for it if I could keep my mouth shut and follow orders."

"I see. So it was something he wanted to be kept secret?"

"It always is, ain't it? That's the name of the game. You don't get very far in this business if you start shooting your mouth off."

"Shooting off in your mouth's what most of 'em want," said Bert, rubbing himself. Of all of us, he was the only one still anticipating an orgy.

"Anyway, he says there's a delivery that needs to be made. What sort of delivery, I says, no funny business I hope, I don't want to get into trouble with the police. No, he says, just a letter. A letter, I says, yes a letter, he says."

Durran's narrative style was, to say the least, elliptical, but I gathered that his Douglas Fairbanks look-alike had told him to deliver a package to a gentleman he would find in the Wimbledon area, that he would have him pointed out to him, and that he had to "make friends" and "win his trust," and so on—all of them euphemisms for what Durran, Morgan, and Bartlett had spent last night doing. Then, when he had Bartlett alone, he was to deliver a package and a simple verbal message: "Don't forget."

"And that was all?"

"I swear. I've done nothing wrong."

"Apart from buggery, gross indecency, soliciting for an immoral purpose, and living off immoral earnings," said Stan, still standing by the door.

"And blackmail," I added.

That was the only thing that Durran took the trouble to deny. "I never blackmailed no one! I fucking hate them bastards! I wouldn't. Never. Tell him, Bert. I wouldn't." He sounded close to tears.

"Honest, Mitch," said Bert, his voice trembling with concern, "he's not like that. If he's done wrong, he never meant to."

"What was in this package?"

"I don't know."

"A letter?"

"S'pose so."

"Did Bartlett open it?"

"Not while I was there."

"Did he seem surprised when you gave it to him?"

"Not 'specially."

"He didn't say anything? Ask anything?"

"No. He just said thanks, or something like that, and he gave me some money like I said, then I says good night, and he says good night, and I go downstairs to get my clothes."

"So your clothes were downstairs but you had the letter with you upstairs."

"Yes. Took it with me. Didn't want to forget."

"I see. You planned it."

"Look, sir," said Durran, a belligerent gleam in his eye, "ten quid probably means nothing to you, but it means a lot to the likes of us. I don't know what you think I've done. Your little friend over there sounds like he's ready to lock me up and throw away the key. But when you're poor, and someone offers you that kind of money, you don't ask too many questions."

"I understand. And believe me, I wouldn't say no to an

140

extra tenner myself. Did you ever see the man in the pub again? Douglas Fairbanks?"

"Yes. Just now."

"Tonight?"

"Yeah. Up in town. Gave me another five quid for a job well done, he said."

"You'd arranged to meet him?"

"Told me to come to such and such an address at such and such a time and tell him what happened. So I did."

"Where?"

"Lyons Corner House on Tottenham Court Road."

"And he still didn't tell you his name."

"No. But at least he bought me a cup of tea this time."

"Sounds like you did very well out of this little arrangement, Durran. You got ten, no, fifteen pounds, you got good and fucked, you got the best shave you've ever had in your life, and you even got a cup of tea."

"Are you taking the piss?"

I was familiar with the expression; this wasn't an offer, but an accusation. Durran thought I was making fun of him. "Not me. It was you who took the piss, I understand. You and Morgan. In the bath. Ring any bells?"

"Hey," said Bert. "What's your game? You seem to know a lot about this all of a sudden."

"I certainly do," I said, "and so does my friend Stan. I'm not sure that I introduced you properly, did I? This is PC Stanley Knight of the Metropolitan Police."

"You fucking bastards!" Durran jumped to his feet. "This is a put-up job! You fucking framed me! I deny it all! I made it all up!"

"Calm down, Durran. Nobody's going to arrest you. This is all strictly off the record. Look—you've been honest with me, so in return I'm going to be honest with you. Harry Morgan, whom you met last night with Frank Bartlett, is a good friend of mine. He's in trouble, and I'm trying to help

141

him. Stan, here, is trying to help me. So we're all in the same boat, right?"

"Why should I believe you?"

"I'm not asking you to believe me. The choice is yours, Durran. We can work together to try to right a great wrong, or we can work against each other. In which case, you're back in the shit."

"So, your friend's in trouble. What's that to me? If he's done something—"

"He hasn't."

"Then he's got nothing to worry about, has he? Posh blokes like him always get off the hook."

"I appreciate your confidence, Durran. But when I said that a great wrong has been done, that's not what I was talking about."

"Oh? What then? A couple of queers pick up a bit of rough and it doesn't work out the way they planned. What's the matter? You had a quarrel with your mate? Is that what this is all about?"

I kept calm. "Oh no, Mr. Durran. This goes far beyond my hurt feelings, or even my concern for my friend."

"Go on." Durran was getting cocky again. It was time to take the wind out of his sails.

"Frank Bartlett is dead."

Job done. He opened his mouth to speak, stopped in midbreath, and turned as white as a sheet.

"Dead?" asked Bert. "What the fuck—"

"He was found in the bathroom in the early hours of this morning."

"The bathroom?" said Durran. "The bathroom where—"

"Yes. The bathroom where you had sex last night. The bathroom where you gave Bartlett the letter."

"What happened?"

"That's what I'm trying to find out. And that's what the police are trying to find out too."

"You're not going to pin anything on me. I didn't do nothing. I gave him the letter. That's all, I swear. On my baby's life, I swear."

"Nobody thinks you killed him. Morgan was the last person to see him alive—after you left the house. Unless, of course, you got back in after you left."

I was testing him, pushing him—but I wanted to see how observant he'd been. If he came up with a glib excuse, an explanation, I might suspect him. "I didn't. I swear I didn't. I left. I went home. Straight home. Ask my missus."

Good—nothing about routes of access to the house, windows in the bathroom, and so on. He didn't have a ready-made story. I was glad—for his sake. But in the pit of my stomach, a cold feeling told me that this was one more link in the chain that led Morgan to the scaffold. Unless...

"We have to find out who gave you that letter," I said, "and what it contained. That's the key to the mystery."

There was a knock on the door. Had we been over-heard?

"It's all right," said Bert, noting my alarm. "It's Vinnie. The landlord. Open the door."

Stan let the foxy little man in. He was wringing his hands nervously. "I'm closing up, gentlemen," he said. "Are you going to be much longer? It's gone eleven."

"We're staying," said Bert, decisively.

"All of you?"

"All of us." He didn't consult.

"Well, I don't know," said Vinnie. "I shouldn't really leave the place unattended..."

"Don't worry about us," said Durran, digging in his pockets and producing, to my astonishment, a ten-shilling note. "We'll keep an eye on things."

"Well, as it's you, I suppose it's all right."

"And no peeping," said Bert. "I know what you're like."

"Me?" said Vinnie, backing out of the room with the

ten-shilling note clutched in his skinny paw. "I never—"

"Get out of it," said Bert. "If we need anything, we'll help ourselves."

The door closed, and we heard the landlord descending the stairs.

"Dirty old bastard," said Bert. "He's one of them as likes to watch. Doesn't get much himself. Doesn't want it, from what I can make out, 'cos there's plenty that would give it in exchange for free beer. He's a whatchamacallit."

"A voyeur?"

"Yeah. And a wankeur an' all." Bert got up and bolted the door. "Now we won't be disturbed," he said. "I think it's time for bed."

"But Morgan—"

"Look, Mitch," said Bert, "there's nothing we can do before morning. Your friend will spend the night in the cells, even if there's the slightest suspicion that he's done something wrong. Eh, copper? I'm right, aren't I?"

"He's right," said Stan.

"And there's not much we can do to find Sean's mystery man until tomorrow, is there?"

"I suppose not. But I still want to know—"

Bert stepped toward me and held a finger to my lips. "You've talked enough, mate. We've all talked enough. Now it's time to fuck."

I couldn't fault his reasoning, and I liked the directness of approach. We were four horny men in a room with two beds, a couple of chairs, and ample floor space, and the hours of darkness ahead of us. Such a God-given opportunity was not to be missed. It was a Sunday night. Anything that could be done had been done. I had tracked down my star witness, hadn't I? I'd found out all I could about Bartlett from the man who knew him best. I'd even enlisted the unofficial assistance of a young police constable, who at this moment was licking his lips, blushing like a virgin bride, and wondering which of us three was going to fuck him first.

I was wondering the same thing. Did I want to take his cherry? Or did I want to watch as Bert shoved his mammoth meat up Stan's tight white ass? I was spoiled with choice, like a hungry man in an expensive restaurant. I wanted everything on the menu. Every dish looked delicious, and though I'd eaten well, even excessively, in the last 12 hours, I was hungry again.

Not as hungry as Bert, however, who wasted no time in getting to the hors d'oeuvres. He knelt at my feet, placed a hand on each of my thighs, and started caressing me, feeling the muscles through my black pants. I leaned back on my elbows and let him set the pace. He buried his face in my crotch, breathing deeply, sucking at my fly—if he could have drawn me out by suction alone, he would have. I was quickly hard, and Bert could feel it, rubbing the sides of his face against the stiffening length, his stubble making a rasping noise as it sandpapered the wool. Sean watched, squeezing his groin, while Stan looked anxious, thinking that the prize he'd waited for was going to be snatched from him.

"Don't worry, Stan," I said. "There's plenty for everyone. Why don't you help Sean get undressed while you're waiting?" I had a sudden desire to get everyone naked—we were behind closed doors, and there was no need for anything other than complete nudity.

Bert wasted no time in getting me back down his throat, picking up exactly where we'd left off when we were interrupted in the toilet. His interest in helping me help Morgan was entirely self-serving, but that didn't worry me—especially as the great lunk was such an accomplished cocksucker. He made none of the mistakes of the novice, instead shielding his teeth with his lips, keeping his mouth wet, applying just enough suction to bring me to full hardness but not so much that I thought he was trying to suck my brains out through my dick. I've had a lot of mouths on my penis over the years, and of all the common errors in cocksucking that I've encountered, I'd say that overenthusiasm is the worst. A blow job should be a pleasure, not a contest of wills. It should certainly not resemble some kind of industrial process. Bert struck exactly the right balance between smoothness and firmness. I wanted to tell him so, but the most I could manage was a hoarse "Suck it." That was all the encouragement he wanted, and he went down as far as he could, tightening his lips around the base of my shaft and holding me in his throat for 20 seconds, until he had to come up for air.

Stan was making a good start on Durran, who seemed very content to be undressed. He lay back on the other bed, his hands behind his head, while Stan unbuttoned his shirt and unbuckled his belt. The body that was revealed was fine, the skin pale, a little fan of hair on the top of the chest, a pair of rosy pink nipples that I couldn't wait to pinch. His underpants were frayed and worn, but clean. His cock was stretching them, sticking straight up toward the ceiling. Stan, unlike Bert, was uncertain how to proceed.

"Get his boots off, boy," I said. "I want him naked."

"Right."

"And then you."

"Yes."

"And then," I said, grabbing Bert's ears and pulling him down on my cock, "you." He didn't, in fact he couldn't, say much in reply, but sort of nodded.

"And then I'm going to fuck all three of you."

"Yes," they chorused as one. Bert even stopped sucking me for long enough to speak. And only long enough.

Stan was making good progress with Durran's bootlaces, and it excited me to see the little blond cop kneeling before an arrogant thug like Durran, digging himself deeper and deeper into trouble, and all because he trusted me. I am not, generally speaking, the sort of man who abuses the trust of others, and I had no intention of landing Stan Knight in trouble with his superiors—provided he played the game in the morning. If he started to have second thoughts, a hint in that direction should be enough to set him back on track. One of Durran's boots was off now, revealing a thick woolen sock, and Stan got to work on the other. I couldn't resist poking him in the ass with my foot and toppling him over, which gave me a clear view of the firm, meaty buttocks I intended very soon to pry apart.

Bert was in a world of his own, sucking away like a baby on a pacifier, and even though I'd come so often in the last 24 hours, I didn't want to shoot down his throat when there was so much ass to be fucked, so I pushed him off and told him to strip as well. He was quick about it, revealing a huge, solid body, thighs as thick as Stan's waist, and the ludicrously big cock that I'd already heard about from Morgan. I shed my own clothes as quickly as I could; the floor of the room was starting to look like the aftermath of a yard sale. Stan had succeeded in getting every stitch off Durran, and all that remained was for the three of us to gang up on the little blond cop. Bert grabbed him from behind, pinning his arms, while Durran and I tore his clothes from his tight body. He wriggled and struggled, but as soon as his pants were down Bert's great log of a cock made contact with his ass, and that seemed to calm him, whether through excitement or fear I'm not sure. Soon he was naked, his arms still held, his cock sticking straight out from its bed of blond fuzz.

The most accurate description I can give of what happened over the next three hours in the squalid room above a deserted public house in Tooting Broadway is not verbal but mathematical:

0.333 recurring.

That is to say: one into three will go. Repeatedly, in different ways, but you get the picture.

My cock has never been so much in demand. Durran, as

I had been led to believe, was a very accomplished fuck, doing most of the work himself, squeezing and loosening his anal muscles, sucking me in and pushing me out; all I had to do was stay hard, and leave the rest to him. Stan, on the other hand, was delightfully fresh to the sport, his eyes widening as I entered him. I made sure he was on his back when I did so; I wanted to read every sensation in his face—he was surprised by the pain, even more surprised by the pleasure that followed in its wake, ricocheting between the two sensations as I drove into him. And then there was Bert, the sort of man who looked as if he'd rather kill you with one swipe of his mighty fist than allow you anywhere near his puckered fuckhole. Bert was the greediest of all, backing into me, throwing himself onto his back, and, on one rather alarming occasion, straddling me and lowering his full weight onto my cock. Fortunately for me, he had good, strong thigh muscles, and supported himself for the rest of the ride, otherwise there was a very real danger that he might have snapped me off at the base. I don't think he would have minded, as long as I stayed inside him.

Without wishing to brag, I made all three of them come while fucking them. Stan remained on his back, and came over his tight, ridged stomach, the spunk forming a pretty fan pattern over his muscles.

Durran came while straddling me, performing an extraordinary corkscrew motion, holding his cock like a garden hose and aiming it toward my face, which he hit.

Bert came while he was on his knees on the floor, his face buried in the mattress, for which I was grateful: even though the pub was empty, his unstifled bellows would have been heard several streets away. Throughout the fuck, he'd kept his prick pushed back between his thighs, so I could see how hard he was, I suppose; when he started shooting, his spunk hit the dusty floorboards, where it sat for a moment like a handful of large baroque pearls before being soaked into the wood. I imagine much had preceded it.

They were all ready for Round Two, but it was the most I could do to produce one decent orgasm after the exertions of the day. I lay back on the bed, jerking myself off while Stan—who was a quick study—sucked and licked my balls. Durran and Bert stood at either side of my head like guardian angels, watching and jacking off, and when they judged that I was ready, they increased their rate so that both of them shot into my open mouth as I came over my hairy stomach. That left only Stan with a hard-on. He lay beside me on the bed while Bert licked his ass, Durran sucked his cock, and I put my arms around him and kissed him.

And then, as dawn broke, we slept, Stan and I in one bed, Bert and Durran in the other. I felt sorry for Durran, sharing that narrow mattress with such a huge man; at least my companion was built on more compact lines. But somehow we won a few hours' respite from the hurly-burly of sleuthing and fucking, and when I opened my eyes and looked at my watch is was seven o'clock on Monday morning. Stan lay warm and peaceful in my arms, his blond hair sticking up on top of his head. Bert lay on his back, one arm flung across his eyes, the other hanging down to the floor, like a resting giant.

Durran had gone.

"He has to work," said Bert. "Starts at six. Building trade, you know. Job over in west London today. He'll have walked it, to save a few pennies."

"I didn't hear him leave."

"He's light on his feet, is Sean Durran. Comes and goes as he pleases. Comes—and goes." Bert climbed out of bed and stepped into his trousers, chuckling at his own pleasantry, but I had a twinge of misgiving. And then Stan woke up and put my hand on his morning hard-on, and my mind turned to other matters.

# Chapter Ten

I don't often regret things I've done—if I regret anything, it's what I haven't done. So when I left that dingy south London pub and said farewell to my companions of the night, I experienced a slight pang over the fact that I hadn't yet managed to get Bert the laborer's massive prick inside me. I'd spent the whole time satisfying three very hungry asses. Stan, once he'd gotten used to being fucked, was a natural, and took everything I could give him. Bert and Sean, more at home in Sodom than the newly arrived young cop, were even more eager. But I couldn't stop thinking, every time I saw the huge telegraph pole that stood out between Bert's sturdy, hairy thighs, that I would like to feel it inside me, pinning me down with his weight, fucking me into that state of trance that only a really big cock can achieve.

My friends and regular readers will know that, on the whole, I tend to take the active role in these encounters—partly, I suppose, through personal preference, but also because most men, in my experience, are so eager to take what they're not used to being given that I have very little

choice in the matter. Nature has equipped me for the job—
I've got plenty to go around, and enough stamina to keep
up with demand, even when, as in the last 24 hours, men
were lining up with their asses open. But there comes a time
in every man's life when he wants nothing more than to lie
on his back with his legs in the air and take an enormous
hard prick up his rectum, and that time had come for me.
I felt an unscratchable itch in my rear parts—no, not the
onset of hemorrhoids, but something much more welcome.
If I didn't get fucked soon, I wouldn't be able to concentrate on the important business of getting Morgan out of
trouble. A huge cock pounding in and out of your guts has
a way of focusing the attention; as far as I'm concerned,
it's a more effective path to enlightenment than some of the
Eastern philosophies currently advocated by sandal-wearing
vegetarians in Bloomsbury.

It was a nice morning, so I walked from Tooting down to
Wimbledon, hoping that I didn't smell too obviously of sex;
the washing facilities at the Ship were, to say the least, rudi-
mentary, and I was convinced that anyone passing within a
few feet of me would have detected the musky waft of cock
and ass.

Morgan's house was quiet, with another police officer
at the gate—this one responded to my friendly greeting
only with a surly grunt. I rang the doorbell, not at all sure
whether I would gain admittance, but within a moment the
pale, round face of the maid appeared, looking frankly terrified.

"My name is Edward Mitchell. I've been visiting Mr.
Morgan. Is he at home?"

"No, sir. He never came back last night. Missus tele-
phoned. She told us you were coming. Oh dear, sir, whatever
is going on?"

"Everything's under control," I said, thinking the opposite. "No need to worry."

She let me in, thank God—the copper at the gate was starting to give me dirty looks, as if I were some muckraking journalist sniffing around the scent of blood. Blood! That reminded me—the bathroom! I hoped, for the maid's sake, that it was still locked.

"Did Mrs. Morgan tell you anything?"

"No, sir. Just that we were to let you in and give you anything you needed."

"That's all?"

She frowned and bit a nail. "Oh, yes. I'm not to do the bathroom today. It's to be kept locked. Broken glass in there, I suppose. One of the panes is smashed. Has there been an accident, sir?"

"That's it. Nasty accident with the glass. Someone cut themselves." I thought I had better mention the possibility of blood, knowing that the maid would almost certainly have peeked through the broken pane and may have seen some stomach-turning evidence of self-slaughter.

"Nasty stuff, broken glass," she said, looking far from harrowed. Perhaps her curiosity was not as great as I imagined. "Cook's downstairs in the kitchen, sir, if you require any refreshment."

I was starving, having skipped dinner last night and spent a considerable amount of energy satisfying three greedy asses, and the thought of a proper English breakfast was very appealing. The maid trotted downstairs to convey my request for eggs, bacon, toast, marmalade, and coffee.

I was halfway up the stairs when it suddenly struck me—the blood was gone from the hall floor. I turned, looked back, crawled along the hall on my hands and knees, but of blood there was not a trace. Belinda always had a knack for employing good domestics; this maid was clearly worth her weight in gold.

It was hard to believe that this was the same house where a man had taken his life with a straight razor—where three men had fucked in the bathroom, where I'd fucked Morgan and sucked off PC Knight. Calm and decency had descended like a veil. The broken pane of glass, and the horror beyond, were covered up. The bloodstain in the hall was cleaned away. It was as if nothing had happened. Morgan and Belinda might simply have taken the children out for a walk. Fatigue hit me, and the reality of the case seemed to recede as a dream fades upon waking.

Food and coffee helped, and within an hour I was ready to start work. I smoked a cigarette in Morgan's den, and went over the facts.

Morgan and Frank Bartlett were lovers—they had been for 18 months, according to both Morgan himself and the evidence of Arthur Tippett, who witnessed their first encounters. The affair had continued, despite Morgan's occasional attempts to break it off—and Bartlett had bound him with gifts of money and property, possibly acquired through some shady dealing with his own business accounts. Finally, when Morgan had threatened a final separation, Bartlett staked his all on a final throw of the dice, naming Morgan as his heir in a new will that would make him a very rich young man upon his benefactor's death.

That, at least, was one interpretation of events. The other, less welcome, reading cast Morgan as an opportunistic gold digger who, realizing that Frank Bartlett was head over heels in love with him, proceeded to exploit the older man's infatuation by demanding ever more extravagant gifts, threatening to leave him, raising his price with every fresh round of negotiations, finally driving Bartlett to the desperate measure of disinheriting his own wife and then, despairing when Morgan threw it all back in his face, killing himself rather than facing the music. And that would leave Morgan sitting pretty. Sure, the will would be contested by Bartlett's widow—but it would surely be watertight. Bartlett and Ross, after all, were major City solicitors. Bartlett would hardly have gone to the trouble of making a will if it were not going to be done properly. It had been drawn up by his partner, Walter Ross—unwillingly, perhaps, and against advice, but this would not be the sort of impulsive will that the courts can blow apart. This would be a testament of stone.

Of course, I didn't know the terms of the will, whether Bartlett had made Morgan his sole heir or simply a beneficiary—but, if I allowed myself to imagine Morgan as this cocksucking Machiavelli, I thought it highly likely that his demands would have been absolute. All—or nothing. Vivien Bartlett would be thrown back on the mercy of her family while Morgan, acting surprised, moved his wife and children into the no-doubt-luxurious Teddington home and spent the rest of his life enjoying the fruits of the Bartlett estate. He would give up his job at the bank, travel around the world looking for more horny old men, selling his ass to the highest bidder…

No. It was not possible. Apart from anything else, Morgan wasn't clever enough to come up with a scheme like this. Setting aside my belief in his fundamental honesty—though that had taken one hell of a battering when I found out about the will—I just couldn't imagine Morgan having the application to work it all out. Maybe it just fell into his lap, and he was carried along on a tide of circumstance—that was much more like the Morgan I knew, powerless to resist temptation. But even so, there was a core of decency in the man that would never allow Bartlett to ruin himself and his wife in that way—wasn't there?

He's lied to you before, said that niggling voice of suspicion. He's lied to his wife.

But we all lie, all the time. That's the position the world forces us into. Just because there are certain areas of life in which a man is obliged to conceal and dissemble, that doesn't mean that the rot permeates every part of his soul.

We have to lie in order to survive—but we know the difference between right and wrong, between Good and Evil.

Don't we?

Even a quantity of cigarettes, which I usually regard as a universal panacea, were unable to quell these miserable doubts, and I was sinking into a slough of despond when the maid came up to the study with a fresh pot of coffee.

"Did you have a nice day off?" I asked, trying to sound casual.

"Oh yes, sir, thank you, sir. I went to the pictures, I did, with my sister and her young man."

"Fine, fine. What time did you get back here last night?"

"Not last night, sir. This morning. Mrs. Morgan's ever so generous. And what with her and the little ones staying away, and Mr. Morgan off on business—"

"Of course. Mr. Morgan spends a good deal of his time traveling, I suppose?"

"Yes, sir. Doing very well at the bank, he is." The maid sounded proud.

"Working for a big City law firm, I understand."

"Yes, sir. Mr. Bartlett visits a good deal."

"Did you see him over the weekend?"

"Yes, he arrived in time for lunch on Saturday."

"Did you—say, what's your name?"

"Ivy, sir."

"Ivy. Did you hear anything unusual on Saturday?"

"No, sir, I can't say I did."

I gave her two half crowns. "Thanks for looking after me, Ivy. If you remember anything—a conversation, for instance. An argument."

"Thank you, sir. But no. After cook had gone and I was finishing off I heard the gentlemen talking over something, but I couldn't say what."

"You're sure, Ivy? You're absolutely sure?"

"Yes, sir. Have I done something wrong?"

"Not at all. Just…just a bet I had with Mr. Morgan."

"Will that be all, sir?"

"Yes, thanks, Ivy."

And that cleared away another possibility—that the domestics had overheard Morgan and Bartlett in passionate discourse, and had—what? Blackmailed them? It was a desperate idea, of course, but I was sad to see it go. One last defense between Morgan and my horrible suspicions…

It was time to find out more about the dead man's home life, and then gauge the reaction of his widow to the news of her husband's demise. Perhaps she would reveal something about the relationship with Morgan that would—what? Consolidate the picture of guilt that was forming in my mind? Was that what I wanted?

I got Bartlett's address from the maid, and set forth.

The Bartlett residence, not far from Teddington station, was a substantial building that discreetly proclaimed the wealth of its occupants. And yet, this was a house of death and grief. You wouldn't know it from the gleaming brass door fittings, from the clipped box hedges around the parterres, from the high windows through which was visible the soft glow of expensive furniture—but behind this mask of peace and comfort there was the twisted face of horror and despair.

I rang, and was admitted. Almost immediately, Belinda Morgan ran into the hall and straight into my arms.

"Mitch. Oh, thank God it's you. I didn't know if you would come."

"Of course." I held her tight. "It's all right, Belinda. Everything's going to be all right," I lied. "How is…she?"

"It's awful," she whispered, as we walked arm in arm toward a high set of double doors. "Poor Vivie. She's absolutely destroyed. I don't know what to say or do. She's upstairs now. The doctor came and gave her something, and

I think she's sleeping. Her brother's here. He's been absolutely wonderful. Come and meet him."

She opened the doors to reveal a good-looking, well-built man of perhaps 40 sitting in an armchair by an open window, one of Belinda's children on each knee. He was teaching Margaret a trick with a matchstick; little Edward, my infant namesake, gurgled with delight, staring up with wide blue eyes, reaching out with his tiny hands to grab at a fine set of whiskers.

"No, no, little chap, don't pull my moustache!" He laughed, and gently batted away the grasping fingers. "Ah! This must be—hang on a moment." He carefully deposited the children on the floor; Edward immediately started wailing.

"Edward Mitchell," said Belinda. "Hugh Trent. Vivien's brother."

A large, square hand took mine and pumped it. He was a handsome man, for sure—authoritative, powerful, intelligent. Warm brown eyes met mine, dark brows contracted. "Terrible business, this," he said. "Good to know Morgan's got friends."

"Of course," I said. "How is your sister holding up?"

"She's not, poor girl. Doctor's put her to sleep for a bit. She's gone to pieces." Belinda was busy calming the baby, and Trent lowered his voice. "Can't say I blame her. Something damned fishy about the whole thing, if you ask me." Belinda stood up. "Thanks for everything, Mrs. Morgan," said Trent. "You've been an absolute brick to poor Vivie. Don't know what she'd have done without you. And of course, these two little rascals." He put out hands like claws and roared like a lion; Margaret screamed and giggled, while Edward wriggled and reached out to those irresistible whiskers again. The older Edward shared his desire to grab that moustache and sideboards, but for somewhat different reasons. My internal itch, described above, flared up again.

"I'll just get the children into their coats and shoes," said Belinda. "Everything else is ready. Don't forget, Mr. Trent, if there's anything else I can do... Anything at all."

"Thank you, dear lady. And likewise I."

Belinda left the room with tears in her eyes. It was characteristic of the woman to offer help to others even when she had terrible troubles of her own. Perhaps she didn't know how deep the trouble her husband was in; I'd have to break it to her gently on the way home.

"Glad to get you alone, Mitchell," said Trent, wiping his hands on a pristine linen handkerchief. "Messy things, children. They always seem to leave one sticky." He folded the handkerchief carefully and replaced it in his pocket. "You're a man of the world, according to Mrs. Morgan, there. Fine woman, by the way."

"The best."

"What's this husband of hers like?"

"Morgan? My best friend in the world."

One eyebrow lifted a little. "Indeed. Seems to have a gift for friendship, our Mr. Morgan."

"He was always popular, even at Cambridge," I said, not liking the tone of Trent's voice.

"I gather he's being questioned."

"Of course. He was the last person to see Frank Bartlett alive."

"Naturally, naturally. And they've kept him in."

"Well, I suppose there's a lot to be..."

"Discussed? Yes. There would be, in a case like this."

We held each other's gaze. Where was this leading?

"Mr. Mitchell, may I speak frankly?"

"Of course."

He stood in front of the window with his back to me, his large hands clasped behind him, like a teacher about to deliver a punishment. "My sister knew something of her husband's life," he said. "It was a marriage more of companionship than love, if you understand my meaning."

"I see."

"When she learned yesterday of this terrible thing, she was... How can I put this? She was not surprised."

"Ah."

"She has suspected for some time that things were not... as they should be."

"In what way?"

"Come on, Mitchell," he said, turning to face me, "you know the score." His eyes held the question that his lips could not frame: *Are you one of them as well?*

"Yes, I do."

"Thought so. Now listen to me, Mitchell. What a man does in his private life is nobody's business but his own. I don't judge."

Big of you, I thought.

"And I could see that Vivie and Frank were happy in their own way. Always thought it was a shame they never had children. Keep a marriage alive, children. I've got a son of my own—twelve years old now, and he's the apple of my eye."

Did all this family talk presage some kind of confession? I hoped so.

"But each to his own, or her own, and Vivie knew the score when she accepted Frank Bartlett as her husband. He provided well for her, as you can see."

"Absolutely."

"And there was never any breath of scandal. Bartlett was accepted in even the highest social circles, with Vivie at his side. But—well, she knew, and I knew, that he had other interests."

"Yes," I said. "So I understand."

"From Morgan?" The question snapped out of him. "What did he tell you?"

I saw the trap opening, and sidestepped it. "Not a thing. I spoke to Mr. Bartlett's colleague."

"That scoundrel, Tippett? Nasty little toady."

"On the contrary, Tippett seemed to be devoted to his boss."

"Devoted? Oh, yes, he gave that impression. I never liked the man, personally. I don't care for the type. No offense, I hope."

"None taken." Any hope I may have had of scratching that itch was fast fading.

"What did he say?"

"He mentioned that there may have been some financial pressures on Mr. Bartlett."

"Spit it out, man. Frank was being blackmailed."

"Who by?"

Don't say Morgan.

"Some dreadful person that he...knew."

"Do you have a name?"

"No, damn it, I don't, because if I did I would have the bounder drummed out of the guards and clapped in irons."

"The guards?" This had the ring of truth about it—guardsmen were a popular pastime for men of Bartlett's means, and were also notorious for biting the hand that fondled them. "You mean the blackmailer was a soldier?"

"A disgrace to the king's uniform."

"You don't happen to know his regiment?"

"Of course not. Frank didn't advertise the details of his indiscretions."

"Indiscretions hardly seems the right word, Mr. Trent. It seems to me that Mr. Bartlett was discretion itself. If, as you say, he was welcomed in the highest social circles in the land..."

Trent brushed away my remark. "Met him at the Parthenon, that's all I know. That bloody place should be shut down. It's a haven for immorality. Disgusting."

You mean they turned you down.

"Did Bartlett tell you this, Mr. Trent?"

"Yes. We had an awkward talk about it a couple of years ago. He came to me in desperate straits. Said this guardsman was dunning him for money. Didn't go into details—didn't need to, and he knew I wouldn't want to hear that kind of muck—I've got a wife and son of my own, I don't want to roll in the filth."

"Of course," I said, thinking of the dozens of husbands and fathers who had been happy, nay eager, to "roll in the filth" with me. There seemed little point in arguing with Trent, whose facial hair confirmed him as a man of set opinions—set in the last century. All I wanted from him now was information.

"Of course I offered to help, because I didn't want to see my sister dragged down, and with her the family name. I helped him out with a bit of financial jiggery pokery. Bartlett's a wealthy man—was a wealthy man, I should say. But it wasn't always easy for him to lay his hands on ready cash when he needed it. All his assets are tied up, salted away, sitting in the five percents paying for all this." He gestured around the room, and I could see the envy in his eyes.

"You lent him money?"

"God, no. I don't have much to spare, and what I do have I spend on my boy." That son of his again; how many times could Trent remind me that he was a family man? Was this a case of a "lady" protesting too much? I'd had to listen to these paternal litanies often enough before, sometimes just moments before the mouth was lowered onto my erect prick.

Not in this case, however.

"What, then?"

"I brokered a deal with a pal of mine in the city. Rustled up the necessary."

"A money lender?"

"That sort of thing, although he wouldn't thank you for calling him that. He prefers to be known as a venture capitalist."

"A rose by any other name," I said. "So Bartlett told you a little about his predicament, I suppose."

"I didn't ask, if that's what you're implying. There was no quid pro quo. I'd rather have had nothing to do with it. But as I say, I wouldn't see Vivie dragged down without a fight."

"And as far as you know, the blackmailer was paid off?"

"At first, yes. But now it seems that Frank found other ways to pay him."

"You mean—?"

"Think about it, man. He had his fingers in the till. Must have done. What possible reason could there be for him to do such a dreadful thing? He knew the game was up."

"But why would he do it at Morgan's house?"

"Last spark of decency in an otherwise corrupt soul," said Trent, with a note of appalling piety in his voice. "Didn't want to soil his own nest."

"So he soiled Morgan's instead."

"Birds of a feather," said Trent.

At that point, Belinda opened the door. The children were in their coats, all ready to go home. Just in time; I was ready to knock Trent's teeth out.

"Come on, Belinda," I said, "let's get you home and leave Mr. Trent"—I almost spat the name—"in peace."

We piled into a cab, much to the children's delight. There was much that I wanted to ask Belinda—what had been said, was there any mention of the will, did anyone suspect Morgan of wrongdoing? But, since the children demanded our attention, and I failed to think of ways of broaching the subject that did not implicate her husband in Bartlett's death, we reached Wimbledon without a single question being asked.

The children were taken upstairs by the maid. As soon as they were out of sight, Belinda's demeanor changed.

"Mitch, what's happening? Where is Boy?"

"He's at the police station. Helping with their inquiries."

"But…he's not—"

"No. Of course not." I was never sure just how much Belinda knew or suspected of her husband's true nature; perhaps, like many wives, she imagined that a certain amount of extramarital activity took place with male friends, she accepted it and found it to be no threat, and focused her mind on the good things about her marriage—of which there were many, this elegant house among them.

"I'm so worried, Mitch." Her eyes held mine, looking for answers or reassurance—neither of which I could give.

"Look, Billie," I said, "I can't do anything by hanging around here. You need to rest. You look exhausted."

"I didn't sleep. Poor Vivie was in a state."

"I'm going to find out what's going on. Stay here. If Morgan comes home, tell him Mitch is on the case."

"I will." She put her hands on my shoulders and squeezed. "Good old Mitch. You've been very good to us, you know. We both love you very much." She kissed me on the cheek and followed the children upstairs.

I took the train back to town, washed and changed in my hospital quarters, and wondered what the hell to do next.

# Chapter Eleven

IF I WERE A REAL DETECTIVE, AS OPPOSED TO A BUNGLING amateur with a supercharged libido, I would by now have formed some kind of overall picture of the case, and would be charging from one address to another asking seemingly irrelevant questions about minute details, much to everyone's bafflement. Then, suddenly, the pieces would cohere and I would finger the villain while leaning against a mantelpiece in an elegant drawing room, shaking my head in regret at the wickedness of humanity while all around offered me congratulations.

Unfortunately the "Mitch Mitchell Method," such as it is, involves blundering in a thick fog of confusion, from which cocks and asses occasionally emerge to demand my attention, until I trip over something so obvious that I should have noticed it right away.

I was pondering my general uselessness and lack of mental acuity, picturing that thick fog of confusion punctuated by male sexual parts—and this led me naturally to think about steamrooms, of which London is so gratifyingly full.

My first instinct was to visit one forthwith and see what was offered; my second thought was that Morgan had mentioned the steamrooms at the Parthenon Club as a regular haunt of the late Frank Bartlett—the place where their mutual attraction had first been revealed. Now, if anyone knew anything about the private pleasures of Frank Bartlett, it would be the patrons and staff of the Parthenon Club, one of those exclusive establishments where the pillars of the British Empire relax and unwind, without women, secure in the knowledge that what goes on behind that mock-Classical facade will never be spoken of beyond the Doric columns that guard the door.

Fortunately for me, my professor at the hospital is well connected in London social circles, and had equipped me with a letter of introduction to the Parthenon which would give me limited access as his guest; if he suspected what I would use it for, he did not let on, being the type of tight-lipped Scot to whom any mention of the physical, outside a strictly medical context, is unthinkable. Perhaps he, too, got his rocks off in the comforting obscurity of the steamrooms; if so, he would never tell, and I would never ask. But that letter stood me in good stead, and within minutes of presenting myself at the front desk I was being directed down a dark wooden staircase, flanked with portraits of prominent members, to the moist areas in the basement. It was barely noon, but already the place was busy; in the changing room, a Spartan arrangement of benches and coat hooks, there were perhaps 20 men, all of them over 50, dressing and undressing, or simply sitting wrapped in towels discussing the issues of the day. My arrival caused a discreet flurry of interest, and as I removed my clothes I was conscious of several pairs of eyes flickering in my direction. If I were a gigolo, I think I could turn a tidy profit in the lower regions of the Parthenon Club.

"Say, where can I get a massage around here?" I said to

a plump, rosy-faced gent who had been watching me more intently than most. It was a redundant question; I could see clearly into an adjoining room with four tables, only one of which was currently occupied by a man, facedown, who was being roughly handled by what looked like a Turkish wrestler. But I wanted to engage him in conversation; he looked like a regular, the type who would notice all the comings and goings, and would not be too discreet to pass on a bit of local news to a curious, attractive, and naked young stranger.

"I'm sure Tabib will be delighted to be of service, as soon as he's finished the Judge." The man nodded toward the tables.

"Is he good, this Tabib?"

A hand went up to his chest. "Oh! The best. Really, it's very lucky that you dropped in today. He's only here Mondays and Thursdays and he's much in demand. By about three o'clock they'll be queuing up to be manhandled by Tabib."

"This is my lucky day." I sat opposite the man on a slatted wooden bench, a white towel wrapped around my waist but otherwise naked, just as he was. This way, he could see just as much as I chose to show him. "Should I go next door and wait?"

"No! Stay right where you are." My plan, such as it was, was working. "Tabib! Customer for you! What's your name, sir?"

"Mitchell."

"Mr. Mitchell," he shouted again. "A visitor from the United States, I believe." I nodded, and he pursed his lips in satisfaction. "Tabib is a good friend of mine. He'll give you every satisfaction, I am sure."

"I sure look forward to that." I stretched my arms above my head, allowing him to see my hairy armpits. "I'm sore after a game of soccer. I need some steam, I guess."

"Let Tabib work his magic, and then relax through there." He pointed to a pair of double doors with glass portholes. "The Parthenon steamroom is the best in London."

"So I hear."

"Ah. You have...friends here?"

"Sure." There was no point in beating around the bush. "Do you know Frank Bartlett?"

"Oh." He rolled his eyes, narrowed them, pursed his lips again—a whole repertoire of facial tics to express knowingness. "Mr. Bartlett. Yes. We all know...him."

I thought for a moment he was going to say *her*. Perhaps, if we knew each other better, he would have.

"Great guy," I said, and then extended my hand. "Edward Mitchell, by the way. Pleased to make your acquaintance."

He took my hand. "Gerald Osborne, MBE, at your service." He tittered. "I'm sorry. I never can resist mentioning my order."

"I'm impressed."

This time he adjusted his features to express an unconvincing modesty. "Oh, really! No, don't be. Just for services to war veterans. One does what one can." I felt sure that Gerald Osborne, MBE, had done a great deal for war veterans in one way or another, though "another" was probably not what he'd gotten his medal for.

"So, you known Frank for long?"

"Oh yes. He's a regular. Always down here."

"Well, it's a swell place. Looks like a man can get just what he needs."

"Indeed."

"Massage. And steam."

"Absolutely." Osborne sucked his cheeks in, moved his lower jaw from side to side and did something complicated with his eyebrows. This telegraphed "understanding," possibly tempered with constipation.

"So, Frank..."

"Hmmm?"

"He enjoys the...facilities?"

"To the full."

"As it happens," I said, "another fellow was telling me recently what a great place this is. His name is—"—I made a pretense of searching my memory—"Oh God, what is it? I was talking to him only just the other day. How ridiculous."

"What does he look like? I know most of them."

"Tall, well-made guy," I improvised. "In the guards. Knows Frank, or knew him at any rate."

"Oh," said Osborne, with a look of disgust. "The person to whom you refer is no longer a member."

"You're kidding! He told me that—"

"Whatever that man has told you is not to be believed." Osborne crossed his arms over his ample chest. "I'm afraid that with the best will in the world, sometimes the Parthenon slips up and admits...a wrong'un."

"Gosh," I said, all hurt surprise, "and he seems like such a nice guy."

"So we all thought. At first."

"Oh well." I made a pretense of wanting to change the subject. "I wonder how much longer Tabib will be."

I knew that Osborne wanted to gossip, and would spill the beans much quicker if he thought I was slipping out of his grasp. "Actually," he said in a whisper, "he attempted to blackmail some of us."

"Who? Tabib?"

"No! McDermott."

"That's it!" I clicked my fingers. "McDermott. Of course. Met him in a pub on Shaftesbury Avenue."

"That sounds about his level."

"So, he's a blackmailer. Wow. I'd never have thought it. He seemed such a nice, genuine guy."

"Appearances can be very deceptive, Mr. Mitchell. Alas

for those of us who try to maintain some faith in human nature. All too often it's the most beautiful containers that conceal the most putrid rottenness."

This was getting a little too poetic for my liking, so I put one foot up on the bench, crooking my leg and revealing a bit of scrotum as I did so. "Well, he sure has one hell of a nice container, rotten or not," I said. "Good thing I didn't—you know."

"Come now," said Osborne. Was this a request, or simply a turn of phrase? "A young chap like you would never need to avail yourself of the services of a McDermott. If anything," he murmured, almost dreamily, "one would expect you to be on the other side of the coin. As it were."

His metaphors were muddled, but telling. McDermott, the blackmailing guardsman, was charging for what I give away for free. Judging by the glint in Osborne's eyes, he would drop a few pounds if I would drop the towel. The thought was not unpleasant; I often think that if I hadn't succeeded in my medical career, then prostitution would be the obvious path to follow. And though Osborne wasn't personally attractive to me, I found his keen interest arousing. My cock started to stir, and he watched it like an owl watching a vole.

"So, imagine that," I said.

"Mmmm?"

"McDermott a blackmailer. A disgrace to the king's uniform."

"Absolutely." Osborne was getting distracted.

"I don't recall which regiment he said he was in now."

"No…"

This wouldn't do; he was no longer paying attention, at least not to my words. I crossed one leg over the other, barring his view of the vole. He almost hooted in dismay.

"Oh well, I'd better go and talk to Tabib—"

"Scots Guards. Don't recall which battalion."

"Of course." I uncrossed my legs, and his eyes widened again. "McDermott. Scottish. How could I forget. And of course he's stationed at—" I made my cock jump a little under my towel.

"Wellington Barracks." The words tumbled from his lips.

"That's it. I've got a good mind to report him. Can't believe no one else did." I stood up, and my towel stood out, lifted by my now semierect cock.

"People are too scared," said Osborne with a sigh. "We've all got too much to lose."

"Not me," I said, and I was so grateful to the old boy that I readjusted my towel, opening it completely to give him a full flash, before fastening it around my waist again. "Well, looks like my massage awaits." Tabib was standing at the doorway, a big grin beneath his splendid black moustache. "Been nice talking."

"Yes." Osborne blinked and swallowed. "Perhaps I might—"

"Sure," I said, clapping him on the shoulder. "See you in the steamroom."

As I followed Tabib to the table, Osborne positively glowed, and nodded at various acquaintances to make sure that the whole world knew of our "date."

Tabib was huge: at least six feet tall, and at least 220 pounds, all of it solid, and most of it covered in dense black hair. He was wearing what looked like a long white cotton skirt, secured around his waist with a drawstring, and hanging to his shins; his upper half was bare, apart from his own natural pelt. His shoulders, arms, and hands were massive, his chest like a barrel, and his stomach a great convex mound, the muscles beneath shoving their way forward. I could only imagine what lay beneath his flimsy garment; if everything was built to scale, here was a man more than capable of scratching my inner itch, though getting my asshole fucked in the basement of the Parthenon Club would not help matters much. However, if Tabib gave satisfaction, I would make sure that we exchanged numbers, if nothing else.

I lay facedown on the table, as instructed in heavily accented English, and Tabib whipped the towel off me in one deft move.

"Arms by side," he said, grabbing my hands and pulling them down. "Head like so." He gently lifted my head and let it rest on its side. He was immensely strong, and very gentle.

The first touches, too, were gentle: small circles with his fingertips on the top of my back, fanning out over my shoulders and down my spine, until my whole body was awake and alive to every sensation. Needless to say, my cock, which had been half hard thanks to Osborne's ocular attentions, was soon fully erect; I'd taken the precaution of pointing it up against my belly when I lay down, otherwise things would have been very uncomfortable. As it was, I had to shift a few times as it grew to reposition it between the flesh of my body and the leather of the massage table.

Tabib was getting firmer now, using the heels of his palms to press against my rib cage, pushing the air out of my lungs and forcing me to breathe heavily. The rush of oxygen into my body was intoxicating—and of course my cock got harder. He knew exactly when to venture south, and soon his great hands were kneading my buttocks, working along the backs of my thighs, my calves, and down to my feet. When he pressed his thumbs into the softest part of my sole, I groaned aloud, and thought, for a second, that I was going to start coming. This caused a commotion in the changing room; I heard shuffling and scuffling, and then Tabib's angry voice, "Go on, get away, the lot of you!" and the clang of brass rings and the swoosh of fabric as he pulled the curtain across the doorway.

"Silly old men," he said. "Now we are private."

Tabib got back to work on my feet; I don't know exactly how he did it, but within a minute I was in a semitrance state, all thoughts of sex cleared from my mind (yes, I too found it hard to believe), surrendering instead to a great buoying wave of calm. I might have floated off on this into a happy slumber but for two things—first, the unmistakable prod of a very big, hard, cloth-covered penis against my leg, and second, a huge hand slapping my ass as a gruff voice commanded, "You turn over now."

I almost said, "Yes, sir!" but realized this would not be becoming for a guest at the Parthenon. Instead I raised myself on my forearms, twisted my body around, and settled back, my cock pulsing against my stomach. There was plenty of evidence of excitement, for those who knew where to look, other than the obvious indicator of my erection; the hair on my stomach was sticky with precum.

"Good," said Tabib, a man of few words. His hands went to my chest and started rubbing, the fingers occasionally catching a nipple and squeezing it; I wasn't sure if we'd crossed some kind of boundary between "giving a massage" and "having sex" yet, but we were certainly in some kind of disputed zone between the two.

Then he took hold of my cock, and settled the matter.

"You want relief?"

The answer, of course, was "yes," and despite the efforts of the previous night it wouldn't take him too long to bring me to a climax. But should I be saving myself? Would I need to perform again in the foreseeable future? There is an economy of spunk, and when a friend's life is at stake you have to ensure that every drop is spent wisely. So, if Tabib was going to get a load out of me, as his expert ministrations suggested he would, I must make sure that I get something in return, other than the best hand job of my life.

"Yes," I said. "But first, tell me something, Tabib."

"Sir?"

I sat up; he never let go of me. Now that I looked at him, I could see his prick straining against the thin fabric of his skirt; it, too, was colossal.

"What do you know about Frank Bartlett?"

"Mr. Bartlett very nice man."

"You do this for him?"

"Sometimes."

"Done it recently?"

"No, sir. He do it with Mr. Morgan."

Discretion was not one of Tabib's virtues, it seemed.

"And before Mr. Morgan?"

"Many men. Sometimes me."

"I see." Bartlett, it seemed, was quite active outside the legal profession. And, for that matter, outside the law. "And would you describe him as a generous man?"

Tabib looked puzzled and stopped. "Gener... What?"

"Does he give you money?"

"Ah!" He grinned again and resumed his stroking. "Yes. Mr. Bartlett very kind. Give me presents."

"And to other people?"

"I do'know. I don'ask. I think maybe. Sometimes."

"To Mr. McDermott?"

"Ach! He is bad man."

"So I gather. Did Bartlett give him presents?"

Tabib looked sulky. "I s'pose."

"Right." I lay back. "Go ahead, Tabib. I'll give you a nice present too." And you can give me one some time, I thought, with a glance at that great big cock.

He oiled up his hands and started running them up my shaft, one after the other, like a potter working a lump of clay on a wheel. My cock seemed to grow with each slippery pass, and I surrendered entirely to the feeling.

But part of my mind was still working. I had a sense of relief—not just the relief that Tabib was about to bring me—and I needed to analyze it. Something he said pleased me. What was it? Something about gifts. Ah, yes, of course: he had confirmed that Bartlett was given to spontaneous generosity, and if he was capable of showering gifts on a scoundrel like McDermott or a hairy giant like Tabib, then it made perfect sense that he would be even more liberal toward Morgan. Perhaps, after all, it was just as Morgan had said—the gifts of money and property, even the final grand gesture of the will itself, were unsolicited. Morgan had not asked or demanded; Bartlett had simply given, riding roughshod over any misgivings that his young protégé may have had. Yes, it seemed to me entirely possible, as Tabib worked his magic on my thick, oily prick, that Morgan was telling the truth.

And then I felt the tickle of coarse hairs on my supersensitive dickhead, and looked up to see Tabib's moustache making contact. His lips parted, and he sucked me in. This was my first experience of Turkish massage—but if this is what it's like, I'm booking my passage to Istanbul as soon as possible.

It didn't take long before I was squirting a load into the back of Tabib's throat; he precipitated matters by slipping one well-lubricated finger up my ass, and with the other hand making a ring of thumb and index finger around my balls, pulling them firmly down. When I started coming, I stuck my hands into his thick black hair and held him in place. Finally, he pulled away, just in time for a final glob of jism to land in his moustache. He licked it away and swallowed.

I gave him a pound, with which he seemed well pleased, and judged it money well spent. As I went back into the changing room to get the money from my wallet, Gerald Osborne made a great show of ignoring me, turning his back and engaging his neighbor in sudden animated conversation. Oh dear, I thought, I've let him down. Oh well; let him follow me into the steamroom if he relents. I'm sure I can do something to cheer him up.

I wasn't wrong; I hadn't been steaming for more than ten minutes before the door opened and a recognizably stout silhouette appeared in the doorway. It was hard to see too much in there, but I was pretty sure that Osborne was keeping our rendezvous. I was lying completely naked, only my towel between my ass and a marble ledge. Steam pipes hissed, and water dripped, but apart from that the room was silent.

"I hope Tabib gave satisfaction." Yes, it was Osborne all right; I didn't need to see his face to imagine the kind of dance his features would be executing.

"Mmmm…" I stretched out. "He sure did. I feel great."

"I'm sure you do."

"He ever do that for you, Osborne?"

"I don't know what you're—"

"Suck your cock?"

"Oh! Well. Really."

I expected to be told that we don't like that sort of talk in the Parthenon, but instead Osborne sat down—nearer to me than the otherwise empty steamroom necessitated.

"Swallowed it all, too. I like that."

"Yes." There was a long pause as he worked his way around to some kind of comment. "I could have done that for you, you know."

I feigned surprise. "You? An MBE?"

"Why not? And I wouldn't have charged you either. You could have saved your money."

"I'll bear that in mind for the future."

"I don't suppose…"

"Hey," I said, "you're welcome to try. But I'm afraid you won't get much out of me."

"Oh, I don't mind that," said Osborne, sounding much more cheerful. "I just like to…you know."

"Suck?"

"Mmm." He was down on his knees in an instant, and soon had me in his mouth. He certainly knew what he was doing, and after a great deal of effort he managed to get me up to a state of reasonable hardness. Further than this we were never going to go, and before long the sensation was too much, and I started to soften.

"Nothing personal, Osborne," I said. "In fact, you do that really well."

"Thank you," he said, reluctantly relinquishing me. "Would you mind if I just—"

"Make yourself comfortable?" I spread my legs. "Be my guest. All yours."

And so, nursing on my soft cock, burying his nose in my pubic hair, occasionally licking my balls, Osborne worked his hand between his legs and finally, with a long exhalation of breath through his nostrils, came over the marble floor beneath my feet.

I thought Osborne was the sort who would wipe up and run, but once his breathing had returned to normal he became quite companionable. I was getting far too hot, and longed for a cold shower and some fresh air, but Osborne was inclined to confidence.

"Your friend Bartlett needs to take care, you know," he said, making a little cushion of his towel and parking his rosy bottom on it. "We worry about him. Most of us are careful—too careful, I sometimes think, with all the opportunities that pass us by. But I'd rather end up alone if it means I don't have to face the horror of a scandal. Bartlett, on the other hand, believes in love."

Oh! The irony with which he laced that word.

"And you don't?"

"Love? For people like us? I don't think so. Fun and games, dear boy. Slap and tickle. A few quid here, a few quid there, something to keep you going, and all that. But no: not love."

I would have mentioned Vince, but somehow this didn't seem the time. "But Bartlett believed—believes in the possibility?"

"Yes. Always chasing rainbows, that one."

"And did he find his pot of gold?"

"He thinks so."

"And what do you think?" I lay back, my head in Osborne's lap. He stroked my hair.

"I don't know what to think. I know so little about the boy."

The Boy. Boy Morgan.

"You don't trust him?"

"One trusts nobody, does one?" His fingers ran over my face, feeling my eyelids, my lips, my chin. "The young gentleman in question seems respectable enough."

"Mmm…"

"And from what one gathers he has a good job at the London Imperial Bank."

"Oh yes."

"And so one can really only hope and pray that Frank won't be disappointed again. But lately…" His hand went down my neck, onto my chest. "Something's wrong. I know it is. I have a sixth sense for these things. I've seen Frank Bartlett in trouble before. I recognize the signs. There's a recklessness about him…"

"You think he's in trouble?"

"Yes. I'm absolutely certain of it." His fingers found my nipple. "I think he's being blackmailed again. I say, Mr. Mitchell," he said, noticing a stirring below my waist, "there really is no stopping you, is there? I don't suppose…"

I sat up. "Really, Mr. Osborne," I said, "I couldn't. Thanks all the same."

"Will I see you again?"

His voice was so soft, so sad, I couldn't bear to be unkind.

"Of course. I'll be back in a day or two, and you can suck me to your heart's content." I replaced my towel. "And it won't cost you a penny."

# Chapter Twelve

How to catch a guardsman? This is a challenge that has exercised minds since the first smartly fitted uniform was admired by a wealthy older man sometime in the remote historical past. Usually money changes hands, and, according to my sources, blows are frequently exchanged as the trade reasserts its masculinity after the act of congress. Guardsmen are popular game, but dangerous, rather like lions. You have to use a good deal of cunning in order not to get hurt—and Bartlett, it seemed, had not been quite cunning enough.

My visit to the bowels of the Parthenon Club was well worth while, quite apart from the expert oral and manual ministrations of Tabib and Osborne, two men who really knew their way around the male anatomy. I had uncovered what seemed to be the root cause of Frank Bartlett's problems—the blackmailer who had set him off on a disastrous chain of events that came to such a sticky end yesterday morning. I had a name—McDermott; a regiment—the Scots Guards; and a barracks—the Wellington, near Buckingham

Palace. If I couldn't get my man on the basis of that information, I might as well give up detective work forever and concentrate instead on being a decent doctor.

A doctor... Yes, that, perhaps, was the key. The medical profession is respected and obeyed at all levels of society, even the military, and if I could somehow use my qualifications to gain access to the barracks, then an unofficial interview with McDermott could easily be arranged. One only had to say a few carefully chosen words—tests, screening, contagion, results—and doors would be opened.

I hurried back to my room in the doctors' quarters, sweet-talked the nurse at the reception desk into giving me a couple of sheets of Middlesex Hospital letterhead, and jumped on a bus to Piccadilly. From there it was only a short walk through St. James's Park to the barracks, and on the way I scribbled a note to the commanding officer requesting an urgent interview with one McDermott in the light of recent medical tests, results, and so on, and requesting the use of a private office at his earliest convenience. My medical bag, containing a stethoscope and a few other props, seemed to convince the relevant parties that I was in earnest, and within half an hour of my request I was being shown into a small, windowless room—it looked like an interrogation room—by a deferential young guardsman who started asking me about the best cure for athlete's foot. Resisting the temptation to inspect him right there and then, I advised him to bathe the affected part in a weak solution of chloroxylenol, available from any pharmacist under the brand name Dettol. This seemed to satisfy him.

My friendly young companion stayed with me until the door was opened by a dazzlingly handsome creature in a pair of black uniform trousers, shiny black boots, and an open-necked white shirt. His hair was dark and neatly cut, his sideburns ended in a sharp line level with the lobe of his ear, and two regular black brows accentuated a pair of violet blue eyes. He may have been a guardsman, but nature had designed him to be a gigolo. In different circumstances—in a gentlemen's club, for instance, or a pub or nightclub—he would be absolutely irresistible, in his element, exuding the magnetic force that drew Bartlett and his kind like iron filings. But here, in a grim cube of a room in the barrack block, facing a doctor (I'd put the stethoscope around my neck to emphasize my status) and some mysterious medical problem, he looked far from comfortable. In fact, he looked worried. How much more worried will he look when the police catch up with him, I wondered. For I, unlike the Bartletts and Osbornes of this world, would have no hesitation in blowing the whistle on his nasty little racket. In my opinion, blackmailers are lower than shark shit, as we say back home in Boston, and I would take great pleasure in sending this specimen to meet his just deserts.

But first, I needed information, and in order to get that I had to play a part.

I consulted some papers—they were, in fact, random circulars about corn cure that I'd picked up at the Middlesex, but they were covered in long words and would do the trick.

"McDermott?"

"Yes, sir." He stood inside the closed door, "at ease," but ill at ease.

"First name?"

"Jack. John, sir."

"Very well, Jack McDermott. Have to make sure I've got the right McDermott. Bet there's a few of you in the regiment."

"No, sir. Just me."

"Ah." I indicated a chair. "Sit down, soldier."

"Sir." He pulled the chair up to the desk; he was close

enough for me to see tiny beads of perspiration on his upper lip, to smell the slightly smoky smell of masculinity at bay. There is nothing I enjoy more than seeing an arrogant cocksman like McDermott being taken down a peg or two. That is the only level on which I can get interested in sports, particularly those hypermasculine sports like boxing. I would far rather comfort the defeated boxer than congratulate the winner. McDermott did not yet reek of defeat—it was up to me to deliver the knockout blow—but he could sense a threat that his charm, his uniform, and his obvious physical strength could not overcome. He was afraid, and that's how I wanted him.

"You're probably wondering what this is about, McDermott."

"Yes, sir."

"When did you last have a medical checkup?" I had answers ready for any response that he gave.

"Just last month, sir. We all had to."

Good. Plan A. "Exactly. Now, a few anomalies have shown up during routine screening procedures on your endocrinological profile."

He was suitably blinded with science. "My—what?"

"In layman's terms, you're registering a chromosomal imbalance that may or may not be related to underlying renal and urological problems."

He stared at me, his mouth open. This was going well.

"Am I going too fast for you, McDermott?"

"Sorry, sir." He closed his mouth and tried to sit up straight and regain his composure. "It's just—" He flashed a smile: obviously this worked with most men, women, children, dogs, cats, and possibly plants, but not on Dr. Edward Mitchell. "I was never very bright at school. Never did science."

"Did you give a urine sample, McDermott?"

"A...what?"

"A urine sample. Did you make water?"

He was looking distinctly uncomfortable now. "I don't—"

"Did you piss in a bottle? I can't put it any more plainly than that."

"No."

"Just as I thought." I looked irritably through the papers in front of me. "The screening procedures in the military leave much to be desired. It's only by chance that these things are picked up."

"Am I—ill?"

"That remains to be seen, McDermott. First of all, we have to do a few simple tests." I had a glass flask in my bag, approximately half a pint in volume. I placed this on the desk in front of him. "Do you think you could fill that for me?"

"With…with what?"

"Well I'm not asking for a flower arrangement. With urine, of course."

"I…" He looked around him, hoping at least for a screen of some sort, but the room was bare, apart from our two chairs and the table between us.

"Don't be shy, McDermott. You're a soldier, aren't you? I imagine worse things happen in the field."

"Yes."

I handed him the flask. "Go ahead. I don't need a great deal."

"You mean I should just…get it out and…do it?"

I sighed. "McDermott, I am a doctor. I work at the Middlesex Hospital. I see dozens, if not hundreds, of patients in the course of a working week. If you think there is any reason to be bashful in my presence, forget it right now."

"Yes, sir." He unbuttoned the high waistband of his black trousers. "It's just rather unusual."

"I don't think you realize how important this is. Do you intend to have a family, McDermott? Are you the marrying kind?"

"One day, maybe. When I can afford to."

When you've squeezed enough money out of your victims, you mean.

"Then I suggest we get on with it. Because if we catch this problem now, a very quick course of treatment will mean that you can go on to father a whole race of little McDermotts. If we don't, you can forget any plans to be a father."

He started unbuttoning more quickly, pulling his shirttail out of his pants and working his way down his fly.

"Is this like...you know...VD, sir?"

"Good God, no. Nothing of that sort. I sincerely hope that you know how to protect yourself against that sort of thing."

"Yes, sir. We have lectures about hygiene."

"And do you follow the advice contained therein? Are you worried about VD?"

"I suppose all the lads are, sir."

"I see. Then I'll have to make sure there are no complications. If you've been taking risks..."

All that was left of his modesty now was the thin cotton of his army-issue drawers.

"I don't think so, sir."

"Are you sexually active, McDermott? Do you have a sweetheart?"

"No."

"Are you playing the field?"

"I suppose so."

I sighed, and scribbled on a piece of paper. "All right. I'll take a quick look around to make sure everything is in order. Meanwhile, if you wouldn't mind..." I gestured toward his open fly. "I don't have all day."

I bent over the desk, apparently uninterested, dismissive even, of my patient. He turned away from me and fumbled with the front of his pants; after a few seconds I heard the musical note of piss on glass. It sounded like a good steady stream.

"Try not to overflow, McDermott. I don't want to make a mess of the floor."

"Sorry, sir. I didn't think I needed to go so much."

The pitch of the note rose as he filled the flask from its broad bottom toward its tapering neck.

"Oh dear, I—"

"Steady, McDermott."

The stream stopped. "Just in time," he said with relief. I looked up.

"Let me see." He turned, with the full flask in one hand, his cock in the other. It was, of course, completely limp, and given the air of threat in the room I would have understood if it had shriveled to nothing, but even so there was enough there to keep a whole battalion satisfied.

"I'll take care of that," I said, taking hold of the flask; steam was rising from its mouth. McDermott started to tuck himself away, but I put a stop to that. "Now just drop your pants. I'll be examining you in just a moment."

"Drop them, sir?"

"Yes. No need to remove them completely. You may keep your boots on. That will give me access to everything I need."

"Yes, sir."

He pushed his pants down over his thighs, which were sturdy and covered in dark hair. His shins and calves were even shaggier. His cock rested on a pair of low-hanging balls. A single drop of piss hung at the tip, and I found myself involuntarily licking my lips, then it trickled off to lose itself among the hair on his scrotum.

"I won't keep you long. Sit, if you wish."

McDermott resumed his seat. His shirttail covered his genitals, and I had to content myself with those magnificent legs. But all would be mine soon enough.

I rummaged in my doctor's bag and produced a small envelope containing strips of litmus paper; this, I thought, was exactly the kind of hocus-pocus that would impress a soldier like McDermott. I stirred the bottle of piss with a glass rod, then wiped it carefully on my pocket handkerchief. Then, using a pair of tweezers, I took the little strip of litmus paper and dipped it into McDermott's still warm, delightfully fragrant urine. I held it up and scrutinized it as the color changed to the faintest of blues. McDermott leaned forward in his chair, entranced.

"Ah," I said, sounding grim, "just as I thought." Obviously he was as fit as a fiddle, but there was no need for him to know that.

"What, sir? What's the matter?"

"Blue," I said, investing the word with, I hoped, the ring of doom. "This confirms what the random endocrinology suggested. A hormonal, chromosomal imbalance, possibly related to an aberration in the pituitary gland."

"What does it mean, sir?" McDermott's knees were clamped together, his hands twisted over his groin, the very picture of anxiety. I think he might have run out of the room if it weren't for my authority as a doctor—and the fact that he was hobbled by his pants.

"To put it more simply, we sometimes find that certain men exhibit characteristics that are more usually found in women."

This was absolute bullshit, of course, the kind of thing you occasionally read in the more reactionary medical journals—but I saw no reason not to turn such crap into ammunition.

"Women? You mean there's something wrong with me?"

"Wrong? No, McDermott, I wouldn't necessarily say wrong. Not from a medical point of view, at least. But we have to be careful with this kind of profile. There are certain problems that can arise if we don't take precautions."

"Right. I see. So I'm not going to—die."

"Good God, no. What gave you that impression? This is

simply a matter of common sense. Now, McDermott, before I examine you more fully, I have to ask you a few questions. Please answer them honestly."

"Yes, sir."

"And remember, anything you tell me in this room is absolutely confidential. You understand?"

"Sir."

"It will not be put in your notes, and it won't be divulged to any of your colleagues or superior officers."

"Sir."

"McDermott, are you homosexual?"

He almost shrieked. "What?"

"Homosexual, McDermott. Do you know what that means?"

"I... I don't..."

"There are many other words for it, if you prefer them. 'Queer' being the most widely used."

"I'm not...queer. No, sir."

"Oh." I referred again to my "notes." "You're not? Well, that puts a very different slant on things. Usually, we find with this particular set of results that the subject is homosexual, queer, in which case a long and healthy life is perfectly possible. But in those case such as yours where the orientation is different... Well. Now." I cleared my throat, as if I were embarrassed by the bad news.

"What? What is it?"

"If, as you say, you are not queer, then these results may be indicative of something much more serious. Much, much more serious."

McDermott was as white as a sheet, and sweating. I was getting hard.

"Well, I mean, I might not be—"

"I'm going to have to examine you, McDermott." I cleared the papers off the desk and put my bag on the floor beside me. "Jump up here."

187

"Sir?"

"We can do this here, of I can ask your CO to send you to the hospital, where we can do it in a proper examination room with nurses and other doctors in attendance. It's up to you."

"Here, sir." He stood up. "How should I—?"

"Just sit on the edge here." I patted the table, and he obeyed, perching his firm, hairy, muscular buttocks where my hand had just been. "Now lie back. That's it." Soon he was stretched out before me—served up like a meal to a hungry diner. His knees bent over the edge of the table, and his legs dangled down, the heavy boots just brushing the floor. His torso was long, and the other edge of the table cut into his neck; he didn't know what to do with his head. He was obviously very uncomfortable, which suited me just fine. He cupped his hands behind his head and held his body tense.

"Now, then, McDermott, let's see what we've got here." I lifted back his shirttail in what I hoped was a convincingly scientific way, thinking all the while how rapidly I'd be debarred if this escapade ever came to the attention of the General Medical Council. His cock was lying to one side, his balls pushed up by his thighs, the whole ensemble topped off with a dense bush of soft, black hair, which thinned and tapered up toward his navel. As I lifted the shirt further, I had leisure to observe his abdomen, which was impressively defined; the uncomfortable position into which I'd put him obliged McDermott to tense his muscles, to great effect. Oh, what a successful whore he must be! How easily men would ruin themselves over this!

"Right. I see." I pressed my fingertips into his lower abdomen, delighting in the movement of the skin over the muscles. "Any pain, McDermott?"

"No, sir."

I moved to one side. "Here?"

"No, sir."

"Here?"

"No, sir."

"Good, good. That rules out any abnormal internal developments." God knows if he believed any of the nonsense I was spouting; all that mattered was that I had him at my mercy. "Now I'm going to take a look at your penis."

"Sir…"

"Normally, I would wear rubber surgical gloves for this kind of inspection, but since you've told me that you are free from infection…"

"Yes, sir. I take care of myself."

"You don't go with prostitutes, I take it?"

"No, sir."

"You sound very definite on that point, McDermott." And I know why, you being a prostitute yourself.

"I keep myself clean."

I picked his cock up by the tip of the foreskin, which stretched slightly as I lifted it, such was the weight depending from it. "Any discharge?"

"No."

"Normal function? Erection, ejaculation?"

"Er…"

"Or are there problems in that area?"

"No, sir!"

"You sound uncertain."

"No, honestly—"

"I see. Well, it looks all right. Now, let me have a look down here. Open your legs, please, McDermott."

He did as he was told, spreading his knees to the corners of the table.

"You have very large testicles, don't you?" I tried to make this sound like a bad thing.

"Do I?"

"Yes. Large, pendulous testicles. This can sometimes be

a sign of a much more complicated syndrome." I took his balls in my hand. "Are they sensitive?"

"Sir?"

"To the touch. If I do this—" I gently rolled his balls against each other in a way that many men enjoy, myself included.

"Yes."

"You feel something?"

"Yes, sir." Good—I kept rolling.

"Discomfort? Pain?"

"Not exactly, no."

"What, exactly, then? Hmmm? Go on." I could tell exactly what he was feeling, because his cock had stirred to life. It was not getting bigger yet; it had simply made that small movement that revealed to the practiced eye that the libido had engaged.

"It feels... Well, it feels quite...nice, sir."

"Nice?" I said, with a sneer. "Nice? What exactly do you mean?" I kept rolling.

"It feels good, sir. You know. Pleasurable."

"Ah! I see! Now we're getting somewhere."

"Is that a good sign?"

"Yes, it is."

"Thank God."

"Now, down here." I moved my index and middle fingers down below his balls, pushing against his perineum. "Good. Good. That feels very regular." His cock was definitely responding now, and had grown at least half an inch. "Any discomfort there? Or does that also feel 'nice.' "

"Yes, sir. That feels just fine."

"Right. I see. This is more serious than I thought. The fact that your penis is responding in this way worries me."

He looked stricken; I don't suppose anyone had ever complained when that handsome tool started to thicken and stiffen.

"Put your feet up on the table here."

"Like this, sir?" He was getting the hang of this nicely, but I didn't want him to feel any less uncomfortable.

"Yes, that's good. No. Wait a minute. I can't see a thing." His boots and pants were hindering my view of his hairy ass, which was my goal.

"Do you want me to take them off, sir?"

"There's no need for that." I cupped his heels in my hands, and lifted. "Just put your legs in the air. That's it. Now hold them back for me." He placed a strong hand on each hairy thigh, resting his knees back against his torso. His ass was completely exposed. I moved to the end of the table and bent down to inspect.

"Ah," I said, as if I had just made a great discovery. "Now we come to the root of the problem."

"What's the matter, sir?" came the voice from beyond the legs.

Nothing was the matter, of course; it was a beautiful ass, just how I like 'em, big and powerful, with enough hair to frame the exposed pink hole and remind me that this was a man, not a boy.

But I couldn't let McDermott know that, of course. We were approaching the psychological moment, so to speak, and now I had to put him even further at a disadvantage.

"Are you absolutely sure you're not homosexual, McDermott?"

"Why, sir? Is something wrong with me?"

"You have a convoluted sphincter."

"A...what?"

"It's a rare condition, but I'm almost certain that's what this is. That would explain the endocrinology and the urine sample. In a normal man, the anus is completely different. Yours exhibits all the characteristics of what we call the pathic or convoluted sphincter. I will have to examine you to be sure, of course."

"Is it dangerous?"

"Not in itself."

"Thank—"

"In men of that type. But if, as you say, you are not of that type, then we may have a serious problem."

"Are they really so different, sir?" Ah—a tremble in the voice. That was what I had been waiting for.

"Completely different, McDermott. Homosexuality is not, as some would have you believe, a mental or emotional deviation. It is purely physiological, of the body. Now, in a normal man, the anal sphincter goes this way." I ran a finger around his hole in a clockwise direction. "In a homosexual subject, it goes this way." My finger moved counterclockwise. "Yours most definitely goes this way." I kept moving my finger.

"What should I do?"

"All may be well. I'll examine further." I lubricated my finger with a little Vaseline—yes, I carry it in my doctor's bag, of course—and pressed against his hole. "If I knew that you were a healthy homosexual subject, that is to say, a man who enjoys having sex with other men, I would not be so worried." I penetrated him about an inch. "But if, as you maintain, you are interested in women, then we may have to…" I went further. "Oh, dear me. Oh. Oh dear."

"What?"

"It's as I feared. We will have to perform surgery."

His ring clamped around my finger. "Surgery?"

"Yes. As soon as possible. Today, even."

"No, please, I don't need—"

"But McDermott," I said, trying to sound warm and sympathetic, "if you want to live a happy married life and have children, it's absolutely essential. It's nothing to worry about. Just a couple of hours in surgery, and a week or so on the ward, then you'll be as right as rain in about six months."

"Six months?"

"Of course, you'll have to convalesce. We can arrange leave for you, that won't be a problem. You will have to abstain completely from all sexual activity in that time."

"What?"

"But what's six months' abstinence compared to a lifetime as a husband and father?"

My finger was still inside him. He was gripping his thighs so hard that the knuckles were white.

"I can't—"

"Yes, you can. Be brave, McDermott. It's actually a fascinating case, in its way. I would have staked my reputation on the fact that you were homosexual. You are almost a perfect specimen of the type. The way you're constructed..." I pushed my finger further in, until it made contact with his prostate, like a small potato covered in silk. "Yes! There we are! That's exactly what I expected to find. Fascinating, really fascinating. What a shame we'll have to operate. It may be more difficult than I thought."

"No, sir, really. You don't have to."

"Oh, really, McDermott. What's a scalpel and a pair of large metal tongs and a quick procedure with a saw compared to a fulfilled family life?"

"No—I was lying. I'm not like that. I'm what you said. You know. Homo-whatever-it-is."

"What?"

"Homosexual."

"I don't understand." I kept pushing against his prostate.

"Queer. I'm queer."

I clicked my tongue. "Oh dear, McDermott. I would have thought better of you. Telling lies just to avoid a simple, necessary surgical procedure. That's very silly. You're acting like a child."

"No, really, sir. I am queer. I go with men. I always have

done. I just didn't want to tell you before."

Now I pretended to be angry. "No, McDermott, this won't do. The medical profession is not something to be toyed with. I am a very busy man, and if I find you've been wasting my time I will be obliged to report it to your superiors."

"Honestly, sir, I'm sorry. Truly sorry. I couldn't tell you before. I didn't realize that it was important. But it's true. It really is. I am like that. I go with men. I don't tell 'em that I like it, but I do. I do like it."

"Hmmm." I scratched my chin with one hand, caressed his prostate with the other. "Why should I believe you? How do I know you're telling the truth this time?"

"You have to believe me, sir. I swear."

"I don't imagine your word is worth much, McDermott. You strike me as the sort of young fellow who is in the habit of saying one thing and meaning another. What about all these other men that you've lied to?"

"I did it because—I had to."

"We'll talk about that later. First of all, you need to prove to me that you really are queer."

"Sir?"

"Tell me what this feels like." I pressed harder on his prostate.

"Good, sir."

Another finger pushed against his ring, and joined the first inside him. He groaned and shifted a little. "And this?"

"Better, sir."

"You like the feeling of my fingers inside you?"

"Yes, sir."

"I don't believe you. I think you're lying to me, just to get out of having surgery."

"No, honestly sir. I like it. I do."

I started fucking him with those two fingers. "Do you?"

"If you don't believe me, sir—" He grabbed my free hand

and brought it to his groin. His cock was fully hard, and as hot as hell.

"Ah. That's a different matter."

"See? I told you so."

I withdrew my fingers from his ass. "Get up on all fours."

He was quick to obey.

"Take the shirt off."

He did so; his torso was magnificent, powerful, hairy.

"Now down."

"Sir." He rested his forehead on his forearm.

"For all I know, you're lying to me, McDermott. You're playacting. It's easy for a young man to produce an erection, isn't it? I have one myself, just from thinking about these things. See?"

It was my turn to grab his hand and bring it to my crotch. He squeezed what he found there.

"Yes, sir!"

"The only thing that will convince me that you are truly what you say you are is if you can ejaculate with something inside your ass."

"I can, sir. Honestly I can."

"My fingers?"

"Yes, sir."

"One? Or two?"

"Two, sir."

"That still won't persuade me. What about three?"

"Yes, sir. Or more."

"What about something really big? Like my penis?"

"Yes, sir. That would do it."

"You'd let me fuck you up the ass?"

"Yes, sir."

"You'd enjoy it?"

"Yes, sir. Very much."

"You'd come while I did it?"

"Yes, sir."

"You're lying."

"No, I'm not. Try it. Fuck me, sir. See how much I like it. I'll come for you. It won't take long."

"All right, McDermott," I said, unbuttoning and pulling out my painfully hard cock. "I hope for your sake you're telling the truth."

"I am, sir. Please." His hand was groping for my cock. I moved around to the front.

"You'd better suck it first. Get it wet."

He did as he was told, sucking vigorously while I held his head in place. Finally, when I was slick with his spit, I moved to the rear.

"This had better be convincing," I said, positioning my cock against the entrance to his "convoluted sphincter." I pushed, and I was in.

He sighed. "It will be."

"Are you enjoying that?"

"Yes, sir. Feel me." I did; he was as stiff as a pole.

I was up on tiptoe, and the position was uncomfortable, so I ordered him onto the floor and there, as he lay on his back and pushed his hard cock against my stomach to persuade me of how much he loved it, I fucked him with all the force I could muster. He came first, looking absolutely delighted with himself as the white spunk jetted all over the dark hair of his torso. Then, as his orgasm subsided, I hammered mine into him.

I lay on top of him for a while, both of us panting. Finally I withdrew.

"Well, McDermott, either you're telling the truth or that was the greatest performance since Gielgud's Hamlet. I'm inclined to give you the benefit of the doubt."

"Thank you, sir." He got up and started dressing; his pants had been roughly pulled over one boot and were in disrepair, torn up the side seam. That would take some explaining. "I really did enjoy it. I really am queer. Honestly I am."

"I believe you, McDermott." I put my cock away and tossed him his shirt.

"May I go now, doctor?"

"You may." I put things back in my bag. "Oh, before you go, McDermott, there was one last question I wanted to ask you."

He was his usual cocky, confident self now, and I found him almost painfully attractive. "Fire away."

"Did you know that Frank Bartlett's dead?"

"I..." Silence fell with an awful suddenness.

"Yes?"

"Frank...Bartlett."

"Dead. Yes."

The fear was back in his eyes, 20 times worse than before.

"I didn't do it."

"What an extraordinary thing to say, McDermott. Suggestive. You knew something about him, then?"

"I... No. I mean, yes. But I didn't—"

"I think, Jack, that you and I need to have a serious talk."

His hand groped for the doorknob.

"Otherwise I'm afraid the results of our little—test, shall we call it, may have to become public."

"You mean you—"

"Some people naturally tell the truth, McDermott. Others need a little persuasion. You fall well into the latter category."

"You mean you fucked me just to...to..."

"To compromise you. Yes. To force a confession out of you, just as you forced money out of Frank Bartlett and others. How many were there, McDermott? How many men have you driven to suicide?"

"That's not how it is."

"That's how it looks to me, Jacky boy. And that's how it's going to look to the police. Unless you can persuade me otherwise."

"You want to fuck me again?"

Yes.

"No. That will not be necessary. I simply want some answers."

"Very well." He stood up straight. "Not here. Somewhere else."

"Name the time and the place. And don't even think about not turning up."

"The Forces and Reserves Club. Four o'clock. I'll be there as near four as I can."

I knew the Forces and Reserves Club by reputation; this military lodging near Waterloo Station was regarded by some as an unofficial brothel.

"You'd better be, McDermott. Remember. I'm not fooling around."

"I know." He swallowed, stood to attention. "Sir."

This had worked out better than I expected. I couldn't resist a final embellishment. "One more thing before you go, McDermott."

"Yes, sir?"

I handed him the flask of piss, now cold and acrid.

"Get rid of this, would you?"

# Chapter Thirteen

A LETTER HAD BEEN SLIPPED UNDER THE DOOR OF MY ROOM at the hospital, my name neatly typed on the envelope, a sheet of weighty notepaper inside bearing the address of Bartlett and Ross, solicitors. Mr. Walter Ross requested my attention on an urgent matter at my earliest convenience. There was nothing else, no mention of Frank Bartlett—though it was clearly him, rather than my putative investments, that the note concerned.

Even more urgent than finding out more about the dead man, however, was the fate of the living. It was now well after lunchtime ("lunch," for me, had been a sandwich and a pint of milk, consumed on the hoof), and I still did not know whether Morgan had been released from Wimbledon Police Station.

I called Morgan's home from the phone booth in the hospital lobby, and got through to Belinda, who told me that Morgan was still "helping the police." She had no idea when he would be home. Morgan's solicitor had been to the station and was told that his client would be released as soon as the interview was concluded. Belinda's voice was calm—that was typical of her, coping in a crisis, keeping things on an even keel for the sake of the children—but I knew she must be feeling terrible, prey to all sorts of suspicions. I always imagined that she knew something of Morgan's "other" life—she would have to be blind to be entirely ignorant of the nature of our friendship—but, I suppose, like many a wife, she accepted her husband's extramural activities provided that they did not threaten her family.

I was a known quantity, a good and trusted friend who performed a valuable service for Harry Morgan. Belinda knew that I was never going to try to steal him away. But now, surely, she realized that there was something else—some unknown force at work. Did she suspect Frank Bartlett? Did she—as the police did, as I did—see something sinister in the fact that Bartlett died when he was alone with Morgan? Did she suspect that the friendship between the two men was somehow the cause of Bartlett's death? And, if so, did she take the next inevitable step of suspecting Morgan of wrongdoing? There was so much that we didn't know about Morgan—neither of us, it seemed, had the complete picture. There was a side of Morgan that, perhaps, only Frank Bartlett knew—and whatever it was, he could no longer tell.

If, at any time, I had hoped that this was all a horrible misunderstanding that would blow over once a few basic facts were established, that hope evaporated now. The police had held Morgan for nearly 24 hours. He had not, as far as I knew, been charged with anything, but neither had he been released. The police were biding their time. They believed they had their man; presumably they were now racing around town looking for enough evidence on which to bring a charge. Murder? Manslaughter? Something else? Whatever they were planning, it did not look good for Morgan. On one side, there was the might of the Metropolitan Police, eager for a quick conviction. On the other side there was—me. Mitch Mitchell, amateur detective, who had already half condemned his best friend in his own mind.

And what did I have? What information had I collected that might somehow help save Morgan? Little, or nothing. I examined my facts, and they slipped through my fingers like water. Someone was blackmailing Frank Bartlett—possibly it was still Jack McDermott, but after our recent interview it seemed unlikely that he had driven Bartlett to his death. Bartlett was known for his lack of discretion, so much so that he was the talk of the Parthenon steamroom—but again, it seemed unlikely that a man like that would take his own life. He might suffer an occasional fit of remorse, might even endeavor to clean up his act once in a while and be a good husband, but he would soon slip back into his old ways. I know the type. I'm probably one myself. And then there was his own brother-in-law's suggestion that Bartlett was stealing from his own company to pay off blackmailers—that this was not the first time it had happened. Tippett had hinted at the same thing. The web was so tangled, how could I—one man with an average intelligence and a low attention level—ever hope to extricate my friend from its deadly threads?

I had to stop groping in the dark. He who gropes in the dark tends to find things he wasn't looking for—and, looking back over the last 36 hours, I'd found more cocks, asses, and mouths than was altogether plausible. The one thing most likely to distract me from a case is, of course, sex—and sex seemed to rear its head at every corner. Was this a coincidence? It often seems to me, when I reflect on my experiences, that whenever I am in close proximity to crime, to murder, sexual opportunities arise with far greater frequency. Why is this? Is my libido suddenly exaggerated by the nearness of death? Is it, as the Freudians would have us believe, evidence of the close relationship between Eros and

Thanatos? Or is it simply that criminals know exactly how to keep me occupied by throwing sexually attractive men in my way whenever I get too close for comfort? Whatever the reason, my three encounters with suspicious death have coincided with peaks in sexual activity. I will leave further analysis to the experts.

I hurried over to the City. How very different it was today from the ghost town of Sunday! The streets were thronged with workers, every man wearing a hat, a collar, and a tie, the shoes polished, the trousers pressed. Everyone had a purpose—to get from A to B as quickly as possible. Woe betide the idler, the sightseer, who stumbled into the Square Mile on pleasure bent: he or she would be mowed down by the herds of workers. This was not a place for recreation; it was a place for doing business as swiftly and efficiently as possible. Fortunately, I knew where I was going, kept my head down, and let the crowd carry me to the front door of Bartlett and Ross.

Arthur Tippett's head was visible through the window, bent over a ledger, he hair neatly plastered down; what a different view I'd had of him yesterday. He looked up as I entered, and did not betray our recent intimacy by so much as a flicker of the eyelid.

"Good afternoon, sir," he said. "Mr. Ross is expecting you. One moment, please."

He squeezed between desk and filing cabinet to make his way to the back office; was it my imagination, or did his ass give a little wiggle as he went? Perhaps that part of his anatomy remembered me, even if the rest of him did not. It had every reason to.

Walter Ross was a big, avuncular man—broad from his neck to his knees, powerfully built and well padded, the sort who usually radiates welcome and good fellowship. He had sandy hair, possibly once carroty red, now faded with time and graying at the edges. He wore the uniform of the prosperous City solicitor—black suit, striped gray waistcoat, wing collar, bow tie, and a gold watch chain stretched across the ample dome of his stomach.

"Doctor Mitchell," he said, extending a hand. I said Ross was the type who usually radiates welcome—but on this occasion, he looked positively forbidding. I could not know exactly what Tippett had told him, but I assumed that he somehow associated me with the murky business surrounding his late partner. Whether or not Ross knew of Bartlett's lateness, I could not yet ascertain.

"Bad business, this," he said, indicating a chair. I sat; he remained standing.

"Sir?"

"Frank." He paced the room.

"Ah." I did not know whether to offer my commiserations, or to tut-tut over Bartlett's indiscretions. Ross was clearly building up to some statement; I would take my lead from him.

"The police were here this morning," he said.

He knows.

"I'm so sorry."

"Frank Bartlett was like a brother to me."

"Yes."

"But damn it all, Doctor Mitchell," he said, spinning around on the balls of his feet and banging his hands on the desktop, "why did he kill himself?"

"The police are sure it was suicide?"

"Of course." He frowned and searched my eyes with his. "What else could it be?"

I had no desire to promulgate any idea that this was murder, seeing as there was really only one possible suspect in the case. "I understand that they have to establish these things with a certain amount of evidence."

"Quite so. Well, it seems they have done so."

"Good." Good? What a ridiculous thing to say. But I was

baffled. If the police were satisfied that this was suicide, why was Morgan still being held? What of the mystery of the strychnine in the mouthwash?

"Between you and me, Mitchell, it might be better for all of us this way. Tippett, here, tells me that you are acquainted with Harry Morgan."

"Yes. Is that why you wanted to see me?"

"I want you to do me a favor, Doctor Mitchell. I know this is a lot to ask. You don't know me from Adam. Why should you help me? Truth is, we're in a damned awkward position, and I want as few people to suffer as possible."

"When you say 'we,' who do you mean?"

"The firm will close, of course. I was about to retire in any case. There's enough money in the bank, even after—well, enough to give Mrs. Ross and me a very comfortable few years. What's left of the business I will pass on to our Mr. Tippett. Ambitious man, Tippett, and very capable. If anyone can salvage something from this wreck, it's him. Good luck to him. But it's curtains for Bartlett and Ross. After all these years…" He sighed. "Well, so be it. Reputations come and go. It's no skin off my nose."

"Then—whose nose, exactly, do you wish me to protect?"

"Doctor Mitchell, let me ask you a direct question. I hope you do not object."

"Not in the slightest."

"Do you trust Harry Morgan?"

I hesitated just long enough to make my "yes" sound anything but convincing.

"The thing is, there have been a few irregularities in Frank's business dealings in the last couple of years. I'm not saying that Morgan is behind them, simply that they coincide with the period of their…acquaintance. A suspicious mind might think that Morgan was in some way…"

"Implicated?"

"Implicated. That's the word. You would make a good lawyer, Mitchell."

"I doubt that," I said, thinking of the job I'd done on the "ambitious" Mr. Tippett over a bottle of scotch in my room. "But thank you."

"The police came here looking for answers," said Ross. "They wanted to know if Bartlett had been stealing from the firm, not to put too fine a point on it."

"What did you tell them?"

"I said no, of course, but that didn't satisfy them. They asked me to look into it, and I had to comply. They have given us twenty-four hours in which to make a survey of Bartlett's financial dealings. Now, I know perfectly well that he had been borrowing from the firm in order to make…ex gratia payments to one or more individuals. Tippett tells me that these payments were sometimes made under duress. Do you follow me?"

"All too clearly."

"Some of the sums are large. Very large."

"Yes." The house.

"And then there is the matter of Frank Bartlett's will."

Here it was at last; the most damning fact of all, that change of will in Morgan's favor. "What of it?"

"Shortly before his death, Frank Bartlett revised his will to leave a very substantial part of his estate to Mr. Morgan."

"Oh. How much?"

"The lion's share, shall we say."

"And his wife?"

"She will be provided for."

"From the estate, or by…?"

"There is an annuity to be managed by the executors."

"You, I take it."

"Correct. This is damn unpleasant, Mitchell. Vivien Bartlett is a fine woman. I've always admired her. To be forced to hand her money in this way, as if I'm paying her wages, is humiliating for all concerned. She should have had everything."

"The house?"

"The house will probably have to be sold to pay the death duties. But what remains—and it's a considerable amount—will make Mr. Morgan very rich indeed."

"I see. And you are suggesting that Morgan somehow engineered this."

"It seems an irresistible conclusion."

"Is this what the police believe?"

"We did not discuss it plainly. But I imagine, yes, that is their theory."

"So they want you to give evidence that money was being signed over by Frank Bartlett to Morgan, and once they've established that, they'll have all the proof they need to charge him with extortion, blackmail—what else?"

"What else, indeed."

Driving Bartlett to kill himself.

Neither of us said it.

"I understood that the source of Bartlett's financial difficulties was elsewhere," I said, though I didn't believe it. Jack McDermott might be a blackmailing whore, I thought, but I did not think he was capable of such extremes.

"Where?" A light of hope shone in Ross's eyes.

"He had other...connections."

"I know that. He's always been one for the lads. We can speak openly, can't we, Mitchell? Bartlett never shared the details of his private life with me, but I've known him for many years, and one reaches an understanding. There are plenty of chaps like him in the City. Plenty in all walks of life—parliament, the church, the universities, even the armed forces. I don't judge and I don't condemn. Fine men, many of them, and Bartlett was one of the finest. A gentleman. Understood the importance of appearances. At least, he always did, until...recently."

"You think Morgan had undue influence on him?"

"I don't know what to think, Mitchell. You tell me. I understand you're Morgan's closest friend. He seemed like a nice enough chap to me—not the brightest of sparks, to be honest, but the sort of fellow you wouldn't mind marrying your daughter. Promising. Upright."

"He's all those things."

"And yet—it all comes down to appearances, does it not? Who would have believed it of Bartlett? A secret life. Secret passions. Borrowing from the company—sums of money that it would take him years to pay back. I call it borrowing, because I do not wish to call it theft."

"I cannot believe that Morgan is that kind of man."

Can I?

"I no longer know what to believe. What I am asking you, Mitchell, is to give me proof that Harry Morgan did not deliberately cause the death of Frank Bartlett. I know it won't bring him back. Poor Frank is dead whatever the outcome, and he must have been desperately unhappy and frightened at the end. It's an unbearable thought." He passed a hand over his brow, and suddenly I realized that it was only through a superb effort of will that Ross was keeping the agony of grief at bay. "I do not want any more damage to be done. I don't want Morgan and his family to suffer, and I don't want scandal to wreck the life of Vivien Bartlett. She's suffered enough already. I want to find out what happened, before the police jump to their conclusions. If Morgan is found guilty, the repercussions will not only destroy two families, but will quite possibly bring down the London Imperial Bank and set off a witch hunt, both in the City and in certain quarters of the West End, that could have cataclysmic results."

"I see."

"And on a personal level, Mitchell, I want to bloody well know what happened to my friend."

The poor man was reaching the end of his tether. I did not want to see him cry—I knew that would pain him more than it would pain me.

"I will do everything I can."

"Thank you, Mitchell." He pumped my hand. "I'm counting on you. I would help you, if I could, but—" His voice wobbled, but he passed it off as a frog in the throat. "If you require any resources, please speak to Tippett."

What was this—a private commission? Was I to be paid, like Hercule Poirot?

"Thank you, sir. I'm sure that won't be—"

"Anything you need!" He was shouting now, covering his misery in a blustering show of authority. I thought it would be best to leave.

Tippett was sitting at his desk as ever, scratching away.

"Ah. Doctor Mitchell." He handed me a thick envelope. "Mr. Ross asked me to give you this."

"I see." It felt like a substantial sum; I pocketed it.

"I hope you will be able to help."

"I hope so too, Tippett."

"There must have been someone else," he said. "Not Mr. Morgan. Don't you think?"

"I believe there was," I said, thinking of McDermott and the flimsy possibility that he was our culprit.

"That's a relief. Thank goodness. We're all counting on you, Mitch." He lowered his voice, and his eyes. "I know you won't let us down."

"I'll do everything I can."

"I knew it couldn't be Mr. Morgan," said Tippett. "It must be this other fellow. It must be."

God knows I wanted it to be, and I could have kissed Tippett right there and then for his faith in good and evil, right and wrong. Morgan was "one of us"—our class, our professional world, our little band of brother-loving-brothers—and he could not be guilty of such a crime as this.

It must be "this other fellow"—whoever he was, however scant the evidence. For a moment, I almost settled the question in my own mind; of course McDermott was to blame. Far too good-looking, far too easy with the answers and ready to please. Was he not the handsome, film-star type—and didn't that just fit nicely with Sean Durran's tale of a Douglas Fairbanks look-alike who had commissioned him to deliver that final, fatal package to Frank Bartlett? Whatever it contained—one last demand for money, one last threat of exposure—had driven Bartlett to suicide. Yes, that had to be it. It was not Morgan. Nothing to do with Morgan. He was just in the wrong place at the wrong time, caught up with a man with unsavory connections, a man whose chaotic, criminal ways had thrown the shadow of suspicion on all those who came into contact with him.

But just a couple of hours ago, I'd convinced myself that McDermott was thoroughly incapable of such a crime.

My head ached. I nodded a farewell to Tippett, who watched me leave with hungry eyes, and reentered the stream of humanity outside the office door. It was some time before my appointment with Jack McDermott—the interview that would establish whether or not we could pin Bartlett's death on him—and whatever I did with those precious minutes, I could not afford to wander, woolgathering, up and down the City streets. I must do something, talk to somebody, establish more facts. Facts—that's what I needed. I am a doctor, I said to myself, and I am making a diagnosis. Not the bogus bullshit with which I'd overpowered McDermott, but a real clinical diagnosis. I must first look at outward signs, then I must ask about symptoms, and finally, using my own knowledge, I must decide on a cause and a treatment.

Given that the principals were out of my reach, either temporarily (at the police station) or permanently (in the morgue), I would have to rely on secondary sources. It was around Morgan's character and integrity that this whole dismal business revolved, and it occurred to me that I knew little if anything of Morgan's professional standing, other than what he told me himself. (And even then, I was usually more intent on getting in his ass than hearing about his job at the bank.)

As it happened, my footsteps led me to a splendid edifice on the corner of Cornhill and Bishopsgate, an elaborate white stone building with green domes, crenellations, an antique frieze, and other signs of solidity and stability—the head office of the London Imperial Bank.

If I was going to find answers anywhere, it was here. But answers to what? How could I ask what I needed to ask without immediately raising suspicions? Presumably the police had got here before me as well—they would be investigating every aspect of Morgan's life, public and private, in order to find what they needed. God, even now they were probably back at his house in Wimbledon, subjecting poor Belinda to a none-too-delicate interrogation—perhaps even going so far as to suggest that she was in on it, that she had encouraged her husband to exploit Bartlett's interest in him, that she, a Lady Macbeth in petticoats, had pushed him further than he had ever intended to go, his weakness becoming her strength.

I felt angry and sick, and, bolstered up on that unpleasant wave, I marched into the London Imperial Bank looking like a very dissatisfied customer.

"I want to see the manager." The bank was full, and ears were straining—perhaps just idle curiosity, the delight we all take in another's discomfiture. Or perhaps more, if the police had already been here.

The clerk wasted no time and got me off the business floor as quickly as possible.

My unpleasant mood proved to be just what I needed. I'd started playing a part—I might as well see it through to the end.

"Are you the manager?" I barked at the first man over 40 that I saw.

"No, sir," he said, fawning a little, "but allow me to ask you what your business is and I will see if he can—"

"My business?" I sounded every bit the irate Bostonian brat. "I'll tell you what my business is. My business is going down the pan, thanks to your mismanagement. There's something wrong here," I said, gesturing up at the vaulted ceiling, the marble columns. "Someone's been playing fast and loose with my family's money, and I don't like it. No, sir. I don't like it one bit."

"Please, sir, do keep your voice—"

"I'll shout if I want to! Now please tell your boss that I demand some answers!"

The poor man backed away from me, moving his lips and making little sounds of concern, then disappeared behind a door.

What the hell was I doing? What did I hope to find? Why was I acting like a bull in a china shop, when surely a softer approach would have been appropriate?

A plan had started to form in my mind—vague, as yet, but I had nothing to go on but instinct, and I might as well follow it. Reasoning had led me only to the worst possible conclusions. It was time, now, for improvisation.

"If you'd like to come in, sir," said the nervous assistant, "Mr. Sturley will see you now."

"He the top man?"

"He is, sir."

"He'd better be."

If he wasn't, he was doing a good impression of it. Mr. Sturley sat behind a desk larger than the room in which I was currently staying, a masterpiece of the furniture maker's art, all adornment and elaboration. Behind him hung a large portrait of him in oil, a flattering version of the jowly, gray-haired reality. And above that, one cream-colored wall stretched up and up to an oval window and, above that, a ceiling surrounded by swags and garlands of plaster. I was way out of my depth, and my policy in these situations is to plunge ever deeper.

"So, you're responsible for this fiasco, are you?" I said, scowling.

"Would you take a seat, Mr.—?"

"Mitchell," I said. "Edward Mitchell. Of Boston." I sat.

"The Mitchell account, please, Mr. Moore," said Sturley, clicking his fingers at the poor, confused flunky. It would take him a long time to find it.

"What the hell is the meaning of this?" I produced a piece of paper from my jacket pocket—one of those useful circulars about corn cure that I'd already deployed for McDermott's benefit.

"May I?"

"No, you may not!" I replaced the letter in my pocket. "If you don't know what you've written to me, then you're an even worse fellow than I took you for. 'Funds lacking,' according to you, 'to meet your current monthly obligations.' I've never heard such nonsense in my life! Mitchell and Mitchell has never, I repeat never, failed to meet its financial obligations."

"I'm sure there's been some error, sir. As soon as Moore returns with the account file—"

"You know perfectly well that we recently deposited a huge amount from the sale of our London premises. And you have the nerve to suggest that this has somehow been lost?"

"Might I ask, sir, with whom you have been dealing?"

"You mean you don't know?"

"One handles many accounts, sir. One does not remember every detail." He was doing a good job of keeping a lid on it, I must say; if I ever do have money to spare, I might consider putting it in the care of the London Imperial Bank.

"Young fellow by the name of Morgan," I said, referring to that piece of paper again. "Yes. I remember now. Dark hair. Firm handshake."

"Ah. Mr. Morgan." Was that a frown I saw on Sturley's brow? Was I about to uncover a nest of vipers?

"Well?"

"If there has been an error, sir, I'm sure it is just that. An error."

"This Morgan—is he on the level?"

"Sir, the agents of the London Imperial Bank are absolutely—"

"Save your breath. I asked you a question. We're on the verge of pulling the account. Tell me straight: is Morgan on the level?"

"When Mr. Moore returns with the file..."

I stood up. "If I suspect for one moment that there has been some kind of wrongdoing here, I will have the law down on you. Mitchell and Mitchell is a respected name in Boston. You should know that. Your Mr. Morgan—he better not have done anything wrong."

"I'm sure there is a perfectly simple explanation, sir."

"Let me talk to him. I want answers."

"I'm afraid that will not be possible," said Sturley. "Mr. Morgan is no longer working for us."

That took the wind out of my sails. "What? As of when?"

"As of this morning. Pending...investigations."

To play my role to the full, I should have started yelling blue murder at this point, but I was so distressed to learn that Morgan had been fired that I could barely breathe. What had happened? Was the breath of scandal enough to lose a man his position? Or was there more? Had Mr. Sturley of the London Imperial Bank good reason to dismiss his employee?

The door opened, and Moore came in empty-handed.

"We don't seem to be able to lay our hands on a file for the Mitchell account just at present, sir. Would you be able to supply us with any details?"

Moore and Sturley exchanged a glance, and then both looked at me. I reached into my jacket pocket, then thought better of it.

"To hell with you!" I barged past Moore and out the door. "You'll be hearing more of this!" I yelled, and got out of the London Imperial Bank as quickly as I could.

The net was closing around Morgan. Tippett was right— if I could not prove that someone else had caused Bartlett's death, there was an overwhelming weight of suspicion that would send my best friend to his death, or at least to a life-time of imprisonment, and disgrace for his family.

Everything depended on one person: Jack McDermott. A gigolo.

It was nearly four o'clock.

I ran all the way from the City across Blackfriars Bridge and along the embankment to Waterloo, glad of the pounding of my heart, which sent blood racing around my body, clearing my mind. Anything was better than the horror of what was forming there.

McDermott was waiting for me on the street outside the Forces and Reserves Club.

"Come on up, sir," he said. "It's not busy. We can talk."

"I hope you've got good news for me, McDermott."

"I don't know about that," he said, leading the way up a narrow staircase. "But I'm going to tell you the truth."

# Chapter Fourteen

"AS YOU PROBABLY KNOW, WE DON'T MAKE A LOT OF MONEY in the guards."

"So I've been told. At least, that's the excuse most of you use for hustling, right?"

McDermott sighed. Away from the barracks, dressed in civilian clothes, he looked less obviously like trade. Less desirable, perhaps, but certainly more likable. We were seated in the corner of the Forces and Reserves bar, a shabby room that hadn't been decorated since the turn of the century, by the look of it. The fancy print wallpaper was faded and peeling, the green velvet upholstery had a tired, dusty look. At night, packed with servicemen, the air thick with smoke, illuminated by the yellow glare of electric bulbs, it would look inviting, exciting. Now, in the fading light of the afternoon, it simply looked depressing. But it was empty, apart from the obviously alcoholic old barman who was repeatedly wiping the same pint glass with the same dishcloth while staring into space. And McDermott clearly felt at home here, sufficiently relaxed to speak without the cringing fear of discovery that marked our earlier interview.

"I won't deny that I like it," he said. "What you did to me earlier. Being with another fellow. All that stuff. But you don't let on."

"Why not?"

"For one thing, I'd be drummed out of the army so fast my feet wouldn't touch the ground. Do you know what they do with queers? Military prison and a dishonorable discharge—and they're the lucky ones."

"So why not leave? You could make a good living on civvy street. You've got what it takes."

"I could never make as good a living as I do with a guard's uniform on my back. That's the other thing. The kind of gentlemen that I go with—they like you to be a real man. They like the uniform and all that goes with it. They don't want to think that you're like them; it's all part of the game. We pretend that we're just doing it for the money, that we're putting up with them for the few quid that we get at the end. Don't ask me why, but that's how they want it."

"So if you rolled over and told them that you liked a cock up your ass—"

"Shh!" Even here, with no one to hear us except one red-nosed old fart who was half asleep on his feet, McDermott was wary of plain speaking. "Look, what I might or might not like is neither here nor there. I'm trying to tell you how things really are."

"I understand. You play the man, and you make the money. The guards regiment looks after you pretty well, I guess. Barracks, companionship, three meals a day, clothes on your back, orders to follow. All the basic necessities of life. The bread and butter, so to speak. And for an enterprising young man with a handsome mug and a nice piece between his legs, the rest is gravy."

"Exactly."

"And don't tell me—you're saving up for the day when

216

you leave the army, so you'll have a nice little nest egg with which to start a new life."

"Yes. Why not?"

"Why not, indeed. I can see why gentlemen would be generous to you, Jack McDermott. You're very good. If you can give it as well as you can take it..."

"I can."

"I believe you."

"Want to find out?"

It was a generous offer, but I was exhausted enough to overlook it. "What I want to find out, McDermott, is why a good-looking, popular young man like you would turn to blackmail. Prostitution I can understand; you've got something to sell, and I'm sure you get a good price for it. Blackmail, however..."

The words hovered in the air for a while. I waited.

"You don't just wake up one morning, discover that your wallet is empty, and think, I know—I'll blackmail some old queer."

"What, then?"

"You don't know what they're like, some of them. They take you for granted. Especially the rich ones. They haven't got a clue what it's like to be poor."

I looked at McDermott's fine, clean shirt, his handsomely tailored blazer and sharply creased trousers, and wondered just how poor he thought he was.

"They think they can get away with murder, some of them."

Murder? Just a figure of speech, I suppose.

"Once they've had you a couple of times, they think they should get more for their money—or they think they qualify for a discount. I tell 'em all, it's the same rate for everyone. But they're clever, that sort. They 'forget' their wallets. They say they'll take you out for dinner instead of giving you hard cash—and then they can't find a date in their diary. They offer you presents instead of money—and while presents are all very well, they don't pay off your bookie."

"Ah. Gambling debts?"

"One or two. No more than any of the other chaps."

"You won't have much of a nest egg if you throw it all away on the horses."

"I know that. But sometimes I need a bit of cash in a hurry, and so... Well, I have to remind the gents that I'm doing them a favor."

"And how precisely do you remind them of that fact?"

"A word here and there."

"A threat, you mean."

"I wouldn't say that."

"But I would. Is that how you 'reminded' Frank Bartlett? Was he getting a bit stingy with his payments?"

"Mr. Bartlett was always very generous," said McDermott, "and what's more, he was one of the few that I really enjoyed going with. And he didn't seem to mind. I could be myself with him, more than the others. If I liked it, he liked it. I even let him do it to me. You don't usually."

"I'm sure. And you enjoyed it?"

"Yes. 'Course. Why not?"

"You don't have to explain to me, McDermott. I like a big hard cock inside me as much as you do. And, from what I've been told, Bartlett was very good at it."

"He was." McDermott's fingers plucked at the front of his fly; he was obviously getting hard.

"And now he's dead."

His fingers stopped plucking. "Yes."

"And I have to ask myself why."

He hung his head. Was this the moment I'd been waiting for—when McDermott would blurt it all out and let Morgan off the hook?

"I can't believe it," he said. "Dead. I just can't—" He looked up, and to my astonishment there were tears in his eyes. Morgan's reprieve receded a little.

"I think you'd better tell me everything, McDermott. And don't bother lying. I know you and your type better than you think."

"I won't lie, I promise." He rubbed his hands over his face, surreptitiously wiping away the tears; he didn't like being seen like that. "I met Frank Bartlett at the Parthenon Club. That's where I got a lot of them."

"Yes. You have quite a reputation down there."

"At first, he was just like all the others, except for the fact that he was younger and better looking than most of them. I couldn't understand at first why he would need to pay for it—but then, there's a lot I don't understand. You learn not to ask questions, and after a while you learn not to wonder much at all. Perhaps he was just one of them that likes the uniform. Married, wasn't he?"

"Yes."

"That's the usual explanation. They want what they're not getting at home."

"And that's what you gave him?"

"At first, yes. He sucked me off a couple of times down there, and when I asked for money he didn't put up a fight. Next time we met, he took me to a hotel in Euston."

The same place he'd taken Morgan. I disliked the fact.

"And what did you do that time?"

"Fucked him," murmured McDermott. "Good and hard. He liked that."

"And he was generous?"

"Like I say, flat rate for everyone. He paid up."

"And he came back for more?"

"He did."

"And then—the tables were turned?"

"One day, he started touching me back there. Saying what a nice bum I had. Trying to slip a finger inside me. I told him to get off, but he wouldn't take no for an answer."

"So you negotiated?"

"Yes. I named my price, and he agreed."

"Worth every penny."

"Didn't feel right, taking money from him after that."

"But you forced yourself, no doubt."

"Look, I—"

"It's okay, McDermott. I'm not judging you. Go on."

"Well, after that we saw a lot of each other. He was very generous. He took me out for dinner, to the theater, even took me on weekends out of town. He never forgot to pay me for services rendered, but there was an awful lot of extra gravy, as you would say. I thought for a while I was very nicely set up there. Thought we might have some sort of a future together."

"Did he speak to you about that?"

"Not in so many words. I suppose we both knew that the barriers between us were too great. Him a married man with an important job in the City, me a guardsman, stuck in the army. How could we ever have a life together?"

"You could have found a way."

"He could have bought me out, I suppose. That's what I used to dream about sometimes. He'd pay my way out of the regiment, and set me up in a nice house somewhere, and we'd be together as much as we could."

"A kept man."

"Maybe. But sometimes I thought... There might be... Well, not much point in dreaming about that now, is there? That came to an end a long time ago."

"What happened?"

"He changed. I don't know why. Nothing sudden. Just gradually he stopped wanting to see me all the time. There were no more weekends, then no more nights out, no more dinners, just occasional meetings in that bloody hotel room. And then that stopped as well."

"How long ago?"

"A year. Eighteen months. I don't know. Like I say, it was a gradual thing."

"So you started blackmailing him?"

"I didn't want to lose him."

"I don't suppose you did. The goose that laid the golden egg."

"That was part of it, I won't deny it. I'd got used to the money and the perks. It was nice. But there was more to it. I'd grown fond of him."

"You? A male whore?"

"Laugh at me if you want. I'd laugh at anyone else. But for a moment I thought this might be a chance for me. A different life—an opportunity I never thought I'd get. And when he took that away—when he didn't want me anymore—I was angry."

"So you got your own back?"

"I suppose so. I thought it was just a way of holding on to him at first. I told him that he had to see me at least once a week. When he said he couldn't promise that, I reminded him that I had letters from him."

"That's the oldest line in the book, McDermott."

"So? It worked, didn't it? He was nice again for a while."

"But then?"

"He stopped seeing me altogether. Said he had to leave town for a few weeks. Don't know whether that was true or not—but whatever he was doing, I never heard from him for ages. And then, every time I tried to find him, he gave me the brush-off."

"So you started blackmailing him?"

"What else could I do?"

That was such a bizarre question that I didn't bother answering.

"I admit that it was stupid and wrong. But I was desperate. I missed him, and I missed the money. I went back to seeing other gentlemen, and they just weren't the same. Older than him. Not as...nice. I didn't want to do it anymore. Not after him."

"How much did you get out of him?"

"I don't know."

"Come now, McDermott. Don't pretend that you've conveniently forgotten."

"All right. He paid me off in the end. There. Is that what you wanted? Five hundred pounds."

I whistled. "That's a lot of money."

"He could afford it."

Yes, I thought—with a bit of help from Bartlett and Ross. That would explain the financial trouble to which both Tippett and Trent had referred. Bartlett must have thought it was money well spent—the price of ditching one lover in favor of another. Because, by the time McDermott was cashiered, Frank Bartlett had taken up with his new lover—Boy Morgan.

Now it was with Morgan that he shared that hotel room in Euston.

It was Morgan whom he took to dinner, to the theater, on weekend trips.

It was Morgan—a respectable, presentable young professional with a wife and children—whom he welcomed into his home, introduced to his wife, brought into his business.

It was for Morgan that he bought a house.

It was in Morgan's favor that he changed his will.

What McDermott barely dared to dream of, Morgan had been given—or, at least, had taken.

But was it given freely? And at what point did Bartlett's desire to hold on to a lover become unbearable?

Did Morgan drive him to suicide?

McDermott was looking at me with such sad eyes that I had no choice but to believe that what he had told me was true. I left him as quickly as I could, with a hasty promise that I would see him again. Whether he wanted to tell me more—or whether he wanted to fuck—I do not know.

I left him sitting in that dismal barroom, and ran down the stairs to the street.

If only I could have run from the thoughts and suspicions that pursued me.

I returned to Wimbledon. What else could I do? That was where my duty lay—even if only to comfort Belinda. For all her strength, she must be feeling awful. Unless, by some unsuspected turn of fate, Morgan had been released and all was well.

I approached their front door with a sudden thrill of hope. While I was out in town, suspecting the worst, the truth had come to light, Morgan was home, and we would raise a glass together.

One look at Belinda's face told me all that I needed to know. She had been crying, and her cheeks were pale.

"Mitch." She didn't look particularly pleased to see me.

"Any news?" I stood on the porch, feeling like a door-to-door salesman.

"None." She sighed. "You'd better come in. We're in the drawing room."

We? Who was here?

"Ah, Mitchell." Hugh Trent, the dead man's brother-in-law, stood up to greet me. He did not look exactly thrilled to see me either.

"How is your sister?"

"Much the same," he said, stroking his moustache, "much the same. She keeps to her room."

"I'm sorry. I hope she will soon feel better."

"Better?" He glared at me. "No, I don't suppose she will feel better."

How different he was from the cordial, confidential character he had presented at our earlier meeting! Why the change? What had I done?

"Would you like a drink, Mitch? You look tired," Belinda said.

"I've been working," I said, though I didn't go into details. "I wouldn't say no to a whiskey."

"Of course." Belinda poured me a scotch—she knew exactly how I like it, with just a dash of water—while Trent continued to scowl. I was obviously *de trop*. Why was he here? What were his intentions toward Belinda and her family? What had he told her about Morgan and Bartlett?

"Cheers," I said, feeling anything but cheerful myself. Neither of them answered. I took a swig and was glad of the alcohol. "Any word from the police?"

"They've been here," said Trent, before Belinda could answer for herself.

"And Morgan?"

Trent cleared his throat, as if I had said something embarrassing. Belinda would not catch my eye. What had he been saying to her?

"Billie," I said—Trent raised an eyebrow at the familiarity—"things are going to be fine. We'll have him back soon enough."

"We?" said Trent, with an unmistakable sneer.

"Morgan and Mitch are very old friends," said Belinda, with a horrible note of apology in her voice.

"I see," said Trent.

Was he trying to turn Morgan's own wife against him? Was he so sure that Morgan had caused Bartlett's death? Had more evidence come to light? Why was nobody talking?

"Will you not have a drink, Trent?" I said.

"No, thank you."

"You will. I don't like to drink alone." I poured a large measure of Morgan's scotch into a glass, sloshed in some water, and handed it to him. "There. Good health." He could not decline without being rude, and I sensed that he was not yet ready for an open declaration of hostility. He

224

went to take a sip just as I reached out to clink glasses; in the confusion, I nudged his elbow, and he ended up with whiskey sloshing into his mouth, soaking his moustache, and dripping off the end of his chin. He flinched violently, turned away, and pulled a handkerchief from his pocket, holding it up to his wet face and hurrying out of the room.

"Oops," I said.

Belinda smiled for the first time. "Clumsy," she said.

"Yes. What a shame."

"Mr. Trent has been...very kind."

"Mr. Trent is a pompous ass," I said. "Why is he here?"

"He was kind enough to call," said Belinda, "to see if there was anything I needed."

"I see. And he was here when the police arrived?"

"Yes, as a matter of fact."

"What did they say?"

"Nothing much. They're keeping Harry in tonight."

"No charge?"

"Not yet."

"And Trent? Did he hear this?"

"Yes. He was most concerned."

"I can well imagine." Damn Trent for his curiosity. He was trying to protect his sister, no doubt—to get to the bottom of Bartlett's death, just as I was. I resented his presence.

"Look, Billie," I said, finishing my drink, "there's nothing I can do here. I'll be at the hospital if you need me. I'll call you first thing in the morning."

We kissed each other on the cheek.

"Just one thing before I go."

"Yes, Mitch?"

"Be careful with Trent. I don't know what he wants."

"You're so suspicious of everyone."

"Usually with good reason."

"I can take care of myself, thanks."

"I don't doubt it for a moment. Good night, Billie."

"Good night, Mitch."

I let myself out. As I walked down the half-dark street, a familiar silhouette approached.

"Mitch!"

"Stan!" My young blond cop was back in uniform. "How's your ass?"

Even in the twilight, I could see him blush. "Sore."

"Good. I look forward to making it worse."

"How's Mrs. Morgan?"

"Awful, thanks for asking. How's her husband?"

"Not too good."

"Shit." My guts churned, and I had a desperate longing to see Morgan. "Any news?"

"Not much."

God damn the Metropolitan Police—they were after a quick conviction, that was all, and the truth be damned. While I was out spending pints of semen in the name of investigation, they were simply cooking up charges that they would find a way to make stick. Morgan was done for.

"For Christ's sake, Stan, there must be something."

"Well, there was one thing that puzzled me."

"What?"

"The death certificate. It doesn't make sense."

"What do you mean?"

"The cause of death. They've put loss of blood as the primary."

"Well?"

"But then there's the secondary. Poison."

"So? They think he put strychnine in the mouthwash. In other words, either Morgan drove Bartlett to slash his wrists, or he poisoned him, or both. Either way, they'll charge him."

"But on the death certificate—"

"This isn't helping, Stan."

"When it says about the poison. It doesn't say strychnine."

"What?"

"It says mercury chloride."

"Mercury? But that's a completely different thing."

"I know."

"I mean, the symptoms are nothing like those associated with strychnine poisoning."

"Profuse sweating, skin discoloration, swelling and peeling of skin."

"Very good."

"I've been reading it up."

"You'll go far, Stan."

"I'd like to work at Scotland Yard."

"And strychnine?"

"Violent convulsions, asphyxiation, exhaustion. Victims frequently injure themselves during the fits."

"Good boy. So what happened here?"

"I don't know. Someone made a mistake."

"You don't make mistakes like that. Not in a suspected murder case."

"Or something's wrong."

"You bet your sweet ass something's wrong, Stan. And I'm going to find out what."

I was halfway down the street, but he ran after me.

"Mitch? When this is over—"

"Yes, Stan, I'll fuck you as hard as you could possibly want." I had some busy times ahead, it seemed.

The young copper went back to his post with a spring in his step; I ran up the road with a terrible pounding in my chest, as if I, too, had taken poison.

Something is wrong. Something is wrong. The words drummed in my head as the train pulled out of the station, heading back to town. Something is wrong. Something is wrong. I closed my eyes, watched strange blurred shapes drifting behind my eyelids, crossing, colliding, coming together, forming new shapes, new patterns, trying to show me something, trying—

The train stopped at Balham. I opened my eyes just as the sign on the platform appeared at the window. Balham. The Ring of Bells in Balham. Where Stan and I had found Bert, the giant with the proportional cock. Just last night.

I looked at my watch: eight o'clock.

And without thinking about it, I got off the train just before it pulled out, earning a dirty look from the guard in the process.

When Sherlock Holmes is faced with a seemingly insoluble problem, he retreats into an interior world, usually accompanying himself on the violin. When Hercule Poirot is approaching his conclusion, he gives up all attempts at investigation and treats himself to a good dinner, some fine wine, and a digestif. Like my fictional mentors, I felt that I had done enough running around in the last 36 hours—that nothing more could be gained from trundling up and down London's suburban railway lines, interviewing people, discovering contradictory facts, all of which somehow added to the horrible suspicion that Morgan was responsible for Frank Bartlett's death.

No—it was time to stop doing. Time to cast my mind adrift—to lose myself. And I could think of no better way of losing myself than by taking the biggest dick possible up my asshole. The moment I saw the word "Balham" on that station platform, that itch returned, and it needed scratching. It wasn't a complicated chain of reasoning: Balham—the Ring of Bells—Bert the laborer—the biggest cock I've seen in months—my hungry hole needs filling.

Holmes has his fiddle, Poirot his liqueurs—I have cock. We all have our methods.

I saw him as soon as I pushed open the pub door, sitting in the corner nursing a pint, the mug looking small in his vast hands. He looked up when I came in, as if he was expecting me. His face, none too clean after a day's labor, broke out in a smile. He stood and held his arms open.

"Mitch!"

"Bert."

"I knew you'd be back." When I was close enough to hear without him shouting, he said, "You want this, don't you?" and squeezed his groin. Ah, how simple the world suddenly seemed!

"Yes."

"You look done in. Bad day?"

"The worst."

"Your friend…"

"Still being held by the police."

Bert scowled and shook his head. "I'm sorry. I wish I could help."

"You can," I said. "You can take me to a room somewhere and spend the night fucking my brains out. That's what I need."

He knocked back his beer, smacked his lips, and thumped the glass down on the bar.

"Plenty of time for that," he said. "You need cheering up first. I want to fuck you, Mitch, but I don't want to fuck you while you've got a frown on your face. You need to relax and have a laugh."

What I needed was half a yard of hard penis in my guts, but I humored him. "What did you have in mind?"

"We're going to the music hall," he said. "We're going to watch a few turns, and we're going to eat pies and drink beer. And then, when I think you're ready, I'm going to take you back to my room and drive my cock so far up your ass you'll be tasting me."

"Thank you." This seemed an inadequate response, but I could think of nothing else.

"After what you did for me last night," said Bert, "it's

the least I can do. And look! I've already put a smile on your face."

A light rain was falling as we walked up the road, enough to wet the pavement. The facade of the Duchess Theatre was ablaze with lights, the yellows and reds reflecting on the pavement; it looked like the gateway to fairyland.

Bert hustled me through the door, handed over some coin, and pointed up a stairway. The place was elaborately decorated—vulgarly, some would say, with ridiculous torches projecting from the walls, their glass shades fashioned to resemble flame, the wallpaper a crazy mix of chinoiserie and regency stripe, the carpets thick and red but so worn down and covered in spilled beer and cigarette ash that they were starting to look like beaten earth. All around us, people were coming and going—workingmen like Bert and Sean, and women of the same class, their hair tied up in scarves, middle-class couples in suits and stylish coats, a few obvious "toffs" in evening dress, slumming it for an evening south of the river. Everyone was laughing and talking, their cheeks flushed, their eyes bright.

The stairs led up to the circle, which commanded an excellent view of the stage, where an old man in a dinner jacket with a red nose and long white hair was playing the "Barcarole" on a musical saw. The audience joined in with whistles, catcalls, and raspberries. The "artiste" did not seem to mind, nodding and smiling at the front rows of the Orchestra, so buoyed up with drink that he thought he was getting an ovation.

"Back here," said Bert, his hand on the small of my back, steering me to the rear of the circle. The view of the stage wasn't so great, but it didn't take long to figure out why he'd chosen these particular seats. All around us were couples whose attention was not entirely focused on the entertainment. Young couples kissed and cuddled; toward the very back, they did a great deal more. A few satisfied

230

customers snoozed with their legs over the seats in front of them. And I was surprised to see at least two pairs of men, their arms around each other's shoulders, their laps, in one case, covered by raincoats. I knew pretty well what that meant. Nobody but me was paying them the slightest attention. The Duchess was definitely my kind of theater.

We made ourselves comfortable, Bert's huge thighs pressing against mine, his heavy arm draped over my shoulder; he was a large, warm, and comforting presence. We watched and laughed at the exit of the old musician, who left the stage on a wave of fond, if ironic, applause, and settled back to watch a trio of acrobats introduced as The Three Adagios—a girl and two boys, one of whom, said Bert, had quite a reputation for his offstage acrobatics. They tossed the girl between them, they formed bizarre balancing shapes, they did a tricky bit of business involving a unicycle and a couple of flaming batons, at which point my attention wandered.

This was no reflection on the quality of their performance, but simply a response to the fact that Bert's hand had worked its way down my back and inside my pants, where one thick, blunt finger was probing between my buttocks. I shifted in my seat to give him better access; his finger found my hole and, after a bit of effort, penetrated me. The Three Adagios could have been levitating, and I wouldn't have noticed; my mind was clearing, my attention narrowing to that single point at which his flesh entered mine. He worked his finger further inside me; my dick was almost instantly hard, and I longed to get it out and relieve myself, but every time my hand strayed toward my groin Bert swatted it away.

"Save it for later," he said. "I'm in charge now."

This was exactly what I had been wanting to hear for the last two days—a chance to surrender myself, to relinquish control. I concentrated on the feeling of his finger—now fingers—moving gently inside me. His fingers were large—not as large as his cock, of course, but big enough to cause a certain amount of discomfort, and in order to transform that into pleasure I had to breathe deeply, relaxing my muscles, clearing my brain...

The world was narrowing down to two thick workman's fingers and one rather stretched rectum.

How long we stayed like this I do not really know; acts came and went from the stage, drums rolled, cymbals crashed, the audience laughed and cheered and sang along. People came in and out of the auditorium, sometimes in and out of our row, squeezing past us; at one point we even had to stand up to let a couple through, but Bert's fingers never left my ass.

Occasionally he leaned toward me and whispered some obscene endearment in my ear, or kissed me lightly on the neck, his stubble sending electric shivers up and down my body, nearly making me come. I was going into a trance...

What brought me around was the deafening volume of the audience singing along with the headlining act, a very clever male impersonator who came on as a perfect Mayfair dandy, in evening dress, top hat, and cane, sporting a fine set of whiskers, singing a jaunty, slightly saucy song about "strolling down the Mall, looking for a gal." "He" then did a quick change into a policeman's uniform, and gave us an equally popular number with the refrain "I've always got my truncheon in my hand," which became more suggestive with each verse. Bert was laughing so hard he was shaking, which added to the sensation inside me.

At the climax of the act, to the resounding cheers of the crowd, the policeman tossed his helmet into the wings, pulled out a couple of hairpins, allowing long locks to tumble around the face, and finally, as the *coup de théâtre*, whipped off the moustache, transforming a handsome young man into a very fine-looking young woman. The

illusion was shattered, and she skipped off the stage, blowing kisses and laughing as she went. Bouquets rained onto
the stage from men and women in the boxes; I imagine that
our little deceiver was madly admired by both sexes.

"Time to get you home," set Bert, wiping his fingers
on his trouser leg. My ass, empty and not happy about it,
agreed.

I followed him out of the Duchess Theatre like a devoted
dog.

# Chapter Fifteen

BERT LIVED IN A BOARDING HOUSE THAT BACKED ONTO THE railway tracks; from his room on the top floor you could see up and down the line that led from the center of town to the sleepiest southern suburbs. The whole house smelled of men—not unpleasantly so, but this was clearly an environment lacking the feminine touch.

The landlady, said Bert, was so fearsome she made her tenants look like kittens, and God help the lodger who was late with the rent, or who left the bath or the toilet in an unsuitable condition. She was, however, a heavy sleeper, and accepted with a degree of resignation the fact that men of Bert's class needed nocturnal company from time to time. She did not tolerate "living in sin"—but that was probably because she did not want two people getting a room for the price of one. Overnight guests did not concern her. She lived in the basement, said Bert, sleeping on a trundle bed in the kitchen so that she could rent every available room. Bert lived three stories up. We wouldn't trouble her, and she wouldn't trouble us. From what I gathered, most of his neighbors were either so drunk they wouldn't hear us, or so accustomed to the rumble and thump of the trains that a bit of extra noise wouldn't bother them. Or, like Bert, they were entertaining.

We wasted no time. As soon as the door of his room was shut and the key turned in the lock, his arms were around me, his mouth seeking mine. Bert was taller than me, and in order to kiss him I had to lean my head back. His face was rough, but his lips were soft and his tongue as hard and probing as his fingers had been. He grabbed my ass in his two huge hands and lifted me off the floor; God, he was strong. This was the strength of a man who spends his days digging up roads and carrying hods of bricks, and his nights fucking. It was the strength that I needed.

He lay me down on the bed—a single bed, of course; a double would have encouraged cohabitation, even though Bert could have filled it adequately on his own. He pulled off my shoes and socks, unbuckled my belt, unbuttoned my trousers, and soon had me naked from the waist down. I helped out by pulling my shirt over my head. My cock was as hard as it has ever been, lying up against my stomach, pulsing, the head already wet and sticky; all that warming up in the theater had caused precum to drizzle out of me like honey from a honeycomb.

Bert stood at the foot of the bed and looked down at me, his eyes half closed, one hand dangling in front of his crotch. Was that a sigh of regret? Was he wishing for a repeat of the fucking I'd given him last night? Was his ass, like mine, aching with emptiness? Possibly—but I'm a great believer in fair play, and, seeing as two men have the great advantage of being able to do exactly as they would like to be done, I had no hesitation in pulling my knees up to my chest, holding my buttocks apart, and saying "Fuck me, Bert. Fuck me now."

That was all the encouragement he needed, and in a flash

he was on his knees with his face between my cheeks and his tongue preparing the way that his cock was soon to follow. He worked saliva inside and around my ring, jabbing gently in a way that he knew would relax me and open me up, while his hands kneaded the muscles in my ass, causing the blood to rush down there, preparing me for maximum sensation. My dick stayed hard, but it was of less interest to me than usual; this was all about Bert's cock, and what it was going to do with me.

He tore his clothes off, dropping them on the floor, and soon he too was naked, his massive cock standing out at right angles from those powerful thighs. It looked big on him, even with all his bulk; on a smaller, slighter man, it might have looked freakish. It was certainly going to be one of the biggest things I had ever taken inside me—but if I was ever going to be ready for the challenge, I was ready now. Holmes's fiddle, Poirot's liqueurs—Bert's cock. He dipped two fingers in a jar of Vaseline, smeared it over his thick shaft and bulging head, and pressed against me. My ass lips opened, and he was in.

Any mental activity was instantly canceled by the sheer overwhelming sensation of that massive column of maleness working its way, inch by inch, into my hole. I knew well enough how to deal with this most difficult phase of the act of sodomy—and I knew that, once he was all the way inside me, and I was relaxed around him, this was going to be the fuck of a lifetime. I might not walk for 24 hours, but it would be worth it. However, for all my experience, my deep, controlled breathing, my efforts at muscle relaxation, it hurt like hell. I bit my lip; Bert stopped.

"Want me to pull out?"

"Never. Just give me a moment."

He caressed my chest, my face, my mouth. Finally, when the tide of pain receded, I opened my eyes and said, "Go ahead. I'm all yours."

And I was: completely, utterly his. When I felt his groin pressing against my butt, and I knew that I had taken all he could give me, I felt a sense of surrender and submission unlike anything I have ever felt before. I wondered if I had come; there was certainly something running from my belly down my side. Perhaps I had shot a load; perhaps it was just an extraordinarily large volume of precum produced by the immense pressure on my prostate gland. Either way, I wanted him to stay inside me, to start moving, to increase the tempo and the force until he was pounding me like a jackhammer.

Bert could read me like a book, and matched his actions to the demands of my ass. The fuck started small and slow—back a little, forward a little, the shaft of his cock moving within its sleeve of skin. And then a little more, so he was coming out of me a few inches, then pushing back in. When he judged me ready, he fucked me harder, pulling out further, reentering with greater force. Within five minutes, he was fucking me harder and deeper than I would ever have believed possible.

I would not say that I lost consciousness, exactly—I was fully aware at all times of where I was, who I was with, and what he was doing to me. But some part of my mind cut adrift of its customary moorings, freed perhaps by the intensity of the experience, unable to process rational thought, behaving more as the brain behaves during sleep and dreaming.

I started to experience sudden, vivid flashes—images that appeared to my inner eye, as it were, even as I watched Bert's heavy, handsome face a few inches above mine, his brow furrowed, breathing heavily though his mouth, sweat gathering on his upper lip.

Flash! The male impersonator at the music hall, handsome in her whiskers and uniform, the hair suddenly tumbling around her face, the moustache ripped away, dangling from her fingers like a little dead mouse…

Flash! The blood in Morgan's hallway, that haunting, horrifying smudge in the shape of a leaf, there one moment, gone the next...

Flash! Cigarette ash on the bathroom floor, a letter discarded or destroyed alongside the razor and the mouthwash...

Flash! Face after face after face, like images on a magic lantern—Sean Durran—Arthur Tippett—Hugh Trent—Jack McDermott—Stan Knight—Sergeant Godley and Inspector Weston—Walter Ross—Gerald Osborne, MBE—Tabib the Turk—Morgan's housemaid—Belinda—Morgan himself, ashen with fear...

Faster and faster they spun before my eyes, dancing and laughing and crying...

And somewhere behind this crazy parade were the two faces I had never seen—the face of the dead man, Frank Bartlett, and his wife, Vivien.

Something is wrong.

Something is wrong.

Something is wrong.

The blood.

The mouthwash.

The death certificate.

The will...

And this time, there was no doubt at all—I was coming. Bert too. He buried his face in my neck and fucked me with every ounce of that magnificent, hairy body, grunting and swearing as he emptied his balls into me—and I, carried on the wave of his pleasure, felt a boiling, burning eruption from the inside of my guts to my balls, through the length of my cock and out the end, the semen splattered and sprayed by our colliding stomachs.

He stopped finally, and we lay breathing heavily until he slipped out of me.

We did not speak.

I let him rest for a while—for an hour, maybe two, he slumbered beside me, as I lay wide awake, pressed against the wall by his huge, warm frame. And in that dark room, listening to the occasional rumble of the trains and the steady drone of Bert's snoring, my mind worked and worked without any conscious will on my part.

And when he awoke, at that darkest part of the night that precedes the first chilly gray light of dawn, his cock hard again, pressing into my thigh, a picture had formed in my mind. A picture so simple and strong that it had to be real and true.

I could not, yet, bear to analyze it—just as you dare not analyze a dream for fear that it will evaporate in the first conscious motion of the will.

So when Bert started moving his prick against me and murmured, in a voice thick with sleep, "You want it again?" I raised myself on all fours, pointed my sore ass in the air, and buried my face in the pillow. That was all the answer he needed.

I have been accused of an oversequential approach to narrative, a kind of plodding left-foot, right-foot way of recounting my adventures from crime to solution, from fuck to fuck. So the reader will excuse and, perhaps, applaud me if I skip forward some 16 hours from when Bert shot a third and final load into my ragged ass (this time with me straddling him as he lay on the floor) to eight o'clock that Tuesday evening.

We find ourselves in the drawing room of Mr. Henry Morgan's home in Wimbledon. A fire is burning in the grate, a tray of drinks has been prepared and left by Ivy the housemaid, and six men are sitting, with varying degrees of comfort, in a rough horseshoe of chairs that I have arranged around the room.

Belinda is doing the rounds of her guests, attending to

their needs, handing out drinks, distributing cushions, making small talk like the perfect hostess she is. She has a friendly word for all of them—for Sergeant Godley and Detective Sergeant Weston, who decline whiskey and sherry but are obliged to accept coffee from a beautiful Georgian silver coffee pot. For Walter Ross, the prosperous City solicitor, and Arthur Tippett, his meek, handsome young clerk, both dressed in their suits, both, apparently, grateful for a drink. For Hugh Trent, sitting with his feet a yard apart, a look of disgust and impatience on his face, his moustache bristling with indignation; he hadn't wanted to leave his sister's sickbed to be called out on "a wild goose chase in the middle of the night," he's already told us more than once. For Jack McDermott, beautifully at ease, his legs crossed, making small talk with the men, flashing that dazzling smile at his hostess.

There is a knock at the door, and all conversation suddenly ceases, all eyes turn—but it's only the maid, carrying little Margaret, smiling and blushing in her nightgown. "She wouldn't settle until she'd said good night to all the gentlemen," says the maid, curtsying. "I'm sorry, ma'am."

Belinda makes light of it, and ushers her small daughter around to the guests. "Say good night to Sergeant Weston... Say good night to Mr. Tippett..." and so on. As she stops at each chair, the little girl stands on tiptoe to deliver a goodnight kiss. When she comes to Hugh Trent, she gurgles with delight, remembering what great pals they were in a different house at another time. She might not know that it was just yesterday, or that the strange atmosphere in the house was one of death and suspicion—but she remembers the friendly, handsome man with the splendid whiskers, and as she reaches up to stroke his face he grasps her by the waist and lifts her effortlessly in the air with a "Wheee! Away we go, young lady!"

Little Margaret runs back to her mother, buries her face in her skirts, and giggles, delighted with the game. She would like to play all night—but we have other business to attend to.

"Thank you, Ivy," says Belinda. "I will put Margaret to bed. If you will excuse us, gentlemen." The men stand or half stand as Belinda leads Margaret out of the room. The maid follows, and closes the door behind them.

The men are alone.

I clear my throat. "Gentlemen," I say, and silence falls. I stand with my back to the door; they face me, six men in six chairs. There is a click and a rasping hiss as Trent lights a cigarette; he's been waiting for Belinda to leave the room before smoking.

"Thank you all for coming on such short notice."

"This had better be good, Mitchell," says Trent, exhaling a cloud, throwing the spent match into the fire. "My sister is very ill. I should be with her."

"I'm sure she'll be fine," I say, in a way he doesn't much like, judging by the expression on his face. "The doctor should be with her by now."

"Doctor? I didn't send for a doctor."

"Nevertheless, the fact remains. Does it not, Detective Sergeant Weston?"

The handsome plainclothes officer nods and sips his coffee. Sergeant Godley looks from Trent to Weston, from Weston to Trent, trying to fathom the sudden air of hostility between them.

"Now, if everyone has everything he needs, I'll begin."

"Fire away, Mitch," says McDermott, his hands behind his head, the muscles of his chest stretching the fabric of his shirt. Arthur Tippett steals a glance; now, there's a luxury that clerk's wages can hardly afford. And yet, Tippett looks greedy.

"Please do, Mr. Mitchell," says Walter Ross. "You have promised us the truth—or so your note said. I am sure I speak for us all when I say I am eager to hear it."

And so I began my exposition of the case as I saw it—a performance in the grand tradition, suitably located in a handsome drawing room.

There was much murmuring, which I silenced with an uplifted hand, like a conductor before an overture.

"Three of you knew Frank Bartlett very well. Mr. Ross—you knew him for many years."

"Twenty or more."

"And as partners in the firm?"

"Since 1919. After the War."

"And you would describe him, I suppose, as an honorable man?"

"Quite so. I admired him tremendously, until... Well... you know."

"Until his death? Or before then?"

"I have always known of Frank's...preferences. I do not judge a man by such things. He fought for his country with great distinction, he was a brilliant lawyer and a valued colleague. From what I knew of his home life, he was a good husband. Those things are far more important to me than what a man does behind closed doors."

"I wish more people thought like you, Mr. Ross. And yet, you were aware, I think, of certain irregularities in Bartlett's life?"

"Yes."

"Would you care to tell us what those were?"

"No. I do not speak ill of the dead."

"Then I will be obliged to. You knew that Bartlett was being blackmailed, that he was parting with large sums of money in order to pay off someone who threatened to make his private life public. Is that not so?"

"If you say so."

"I do. And you were aware, were you not, that Bartlett had called on company money when his own finances would not cover the sums in question."

Ross sighed. "So I gathered."

"And yet you did nothing to prevent this borrowing."

"I knew that Frank would pay it back. The idea of him stealing was unthinkable."

"And did he pay it back?"

"Yes."

Tippett shifted uncomfortably in his seat and coughed quietly. Ross glared at him. "Very well! If we must drag his memory through the gutter! There were some recent sums that, at the time of his death, were still outstanding. But I will not suffer any suggestion that Frank intended to rob me. From anyone," he added, looking pointedly toward Tippett, who blushed and stared at his feet.

"And then, Mr. Ross, there was the matter of the will."

Ross said nothing.

"The will, Mr. Ross, of which you are an executor."

"The will has not yet been read," said Ross. "Until it is, I can say nothing about its contents."

"All right. Once again you oblige me to speak. A few days before his death—a week or so—Frank Bartlett revised his will in order to leave a very substantial sum to Harry Morgan. Morgan, an employee of the London Imperial Bank, had been working on the Bartlett and Ross account for around eighteen months—almost exclusively for the last six months. During that time, Morgan and Bartlett had become close. Very close, in fact."

"That is none of your business."

I ignored Ross's interruption. "And, at the end, Bartlett felt so close to Morgan that, for whatever reason, he decided to leave him so much money that Morgan would be able to live comfortably without ever working again."

"And in doing so, he ruins my sister!" barked Trent. I was wondering how long he would be able to remain silent. "The swine!"

"Thank you, Mr. Trent, for pointing that out so forcibly. By leaving that money to Morgan, Bartlett effectively disinherited his own wife. Of course, under the circumstances this has become a more pressing matter than Bartlett could ever know: presumably, he was not aware that he was about to die. Would you say, Mr. Ross, that he was of sound mind when he made the will?"

"Certainly, although I advised strongly against it, as a friend and as his lawyer."

"But he was not insane, nor in despair, nor suicidal."

"Not at all. If anything, he was happier than I've known him for many years."

"Exactly. He changed his will in the full expectation of living another thirty, maybe forty years. Bartlett was a healthy man. He exercised regularly, he did not eat to excess, he drank and smoked in moderation. As a doctor, I would say that he had a good life expectancy. His wife, if she survived him, would have enough to live on for a few years. If she predeceased him, as she might well have—well, there were no children, no dependents, no heirs, were there? Bartlett's will was not designed to impoverish or disinherit anyone."

"Then why the bloody hell did he do it?" said Trent, throwing the end of his cigarette into the fire. "What witchcraft had Morgan practiced on him?"

"They were in love."

The words fell heavily into the room, thudding onto the carpet. Breaths were held. The fire crackled.

"Yes, gentlemen. We are not children. We know that Frank Bartlett was in love with Harry Morgan. And, perhaps, Morgan was in love with him."

"Absolute rot!" This was Trent again. "The suggestion is obscene."

I ignored this. "But Morgan was trying to end it between them. And every time he did so, Bartlett tried to bind him with another gift, another sum of money—the money that he'd been borrowing from the firm, Mr. Ross. Finally, when it seemed that no amount of money would keep Morgan from doing what he believed was right, Bartlett made this final, extreme gesture. He made Morgan his heir. To all intents and purposes, he adopted him as a son—but more than a son. He hoped that Morgan would feel the full force of that bond between them, and would stop struggling. It was a gesture—a crazy gesture, I suppose. But lovers are often crazy."

"Morgan forced his hand!"

"No, Trent. Morgan did nothing of the sort."

"Do you not think, Mitchell, that Morgan may have been partly responsible?" said Ross. "I saw the way he treated Bartlett. They thought we saw nothing—but it was hard to hide. Tippett and I—well, we watched it all, didn't we?"

"Yes, Mr. Ross."

"And we knew that things between them were not always happy."

"And those times tended to coincide with Mr. Bartlett's heaviest borrowing," said Tippett.

"Morgan was not blackmailing Bartlett. I'm sure of that now. I thought he was, but it doesn't make sense."

"Poppycock," said Trent. "It's the oldest trick in the book. Frank had been blackmailed before, and he'd paid up without a whimper. He was an easy mark."

"Doubtless," I said. "As you told me yourself, he'd been unfortunate enough to fall prey to an unscrupulous guardsman."

"Yes," blustered Trent, "and if I ever catch the bounder I'll horsewhip him."

"Feel free," said Jack McDermott, uncrossing his legs and half turning to face Hugh Trent. "You wouldn't be the first. Several gentlemen of your…class have paid good money to take a whip to my arse. The harder they do it, the more I charge."

"You!" Trent looked as if he was going to have a heart

attack. "Good God. In this room!"

"Yes, Trent, you have fallen among thieves. I'm sorry. I hope you will recover. This is Jack McDermott of the Scots Guards. A very popular visitor to the Parthenon Club, aren't you, Jack?"

"Before I answer that question," said McDermott, "do I have your assurance that this is all without prejudice?"

"Officers?"

Weston and Godley nodded their assent, looking at McDermott like something they had just found on the soles of their shoes.

"Right you are," said McDermott, stretching his legs in front of him; very shapely legs they were, too. "I don't deny it. I make a good living out of gentlemen like Mr. Bartlett. They like what I've got, and I don't mind giving it to them, if they're generous."

Tippett's lips were moving silently; I wondered if he was adding up his wages and savings to see if he could afford an hour of McDermott's company.

"But your friendship with Mr. Bartlett went beyond that, didn't it?"

"Yes. Frank and I—"

Trent spluttered with disgust.

"Frank," continued McDermott, emphasizing the familiarity, "was more than just a business arrangement. He led me to believe that we had a future."

"Preposterous!"

"Shut up, Trent. The less you speak, the quicker you will get back to your sister. Go on, Jack."

"But when he met Mr. Morgan, all that changed. I see it now. I always thought I had a rival, but like a fool I believed it was Frank's wife, trying to get him back. But, of course, it was another man. This time, he really fell in love; with me, it had only been about what we could do when we were in bed together."

246

The two cops were looking a little green around the gills; perhaps they wished, now, that they'd accepted something stronger than coffee.

"And so I tried to get him back by blackmailing him. That's not how I saw it at the time—not really. I thought I could persuade him by threats, and when that didn't work, I thought I'd get my fair share of what he was taking away from me."

"Loss of earnings?" I said.

"Yes," said McDermott. "But it was the loss of his friendship that hurt more. I know it was wrong. Eventually I saw that the game was up. He was generous enough."

"Because you forced him to be!" said Ross. "Do you have any idea how much this person extorted out of Frank?"

"Yes, I could make an educated guess. And I'm sure Tippett has it all down in black and white in the ledgers, don't you, Tippett?"

"Yes. Mr. Bartlett was most insistent."

"So, Jack—he paid you off, and that was the end of that."

"Yes. I found other gentlemen. Never the same as him."

"But the demands kept coming," said Ross. "More notes, more payments. If not you, then—who?"

"Morgan, of course."

"I don't think so, Trent."

"Then who?"

"Any suggestions, Tippett?"

"Me?" Tippett looked uncomfortable.

"Did you never recognize the people who delivered the notes to the office?"

"No. I told you. They came and went like a hundred other messenger boys."

"But surely, in a case like this, you would be watchful."

"I was not asked to be."

"And you never act outside the strict limits of what you're asked to do?"

"I am a clerk, sir. I am employed for my efficiency, not for my initiative." He looked to Ross for approval.

"Tippett is one in a million," said the employer. "He's been invaluable to the firm."

"So I hear. Nobody is accusing you of anything, Tippett. I merely ask if you have any idea where these continued demands for money were coming from."

"And I tell you—no. I don't."

"I see. That's a shame."

"Have you really dragged us all the way out here to hear this?" said Trent. "You have no more idea of what happened to Frank than I do. You're wasting our time." He got up.

"One moment, Mr. Trent. You're right, in a way. But I would like you to hear me out, all the same."

"Christ almighty—"

"Sit down, Mr. Trent," said Detective Sergeant Weston.

"I cannot tell you who delivered those notes—at least, not yet. But there was one delivery made to Frank Bartlett about which I do know. The letter that was delivered to him just before his death. Here, in this house, on Saturday night—or, rather, in the early hours of Sunday morning."

Six pairs of eyes were staring at me, expressing various degrees of disbelief. I opened the door and yelled, "Durran!"

Durran stepped into the room, holding his cap in his hands, shifting nervously from foot to foot, ill at ease in front of the police.

"It's okay, Sean," I said. "You just have to tell them what you told me."

"But, Mitch—"

"Who is this person?" said Walter Ross, who was almost as uncomfortable in the presence of the working class as Durran was in his.

"Sean Durran, laborer, of Clapham," I said.

"What is he doing here, Mitchell?" asked Trent.

"He's been here before, as a matter of fact. Haven't you, Sean?"

"Yes."

"Speak up."

"Yes. I have. I was here on Saturday night."

A murmur of astonishment.

"And what were you doing here?"

"I was invited here by Mr. Morgan—and Mr. Bartlett."

"You were—" began Trent, in his usual pompous tones— but then he suddenly stopped. "Ah," was all he said.

"Ah. Bartlett and Morgan met Sean Durran on Wimbledon Common, and then again in a pub called the White Bear. The White Bear is well known to the police, is it not, Sergeant Godley?"

"Yes," said Godley. "It's a queer pub."

"You know about these places," said Trent, "and yet you allow them to remain open? What the hell are we paying our taxes for, I'd like to know."

"We keep them under observation," said DS Weston, "and as long as there is no trouble, an occasional raid is sufficient to stop them from becoming a nuisance. If we closed them down, then the commons and parks of London would not be safe for decent folk to walk through."

"Thank you, detective sergeant. Now, Sean, perhaps you could tell us how exactly you got to know Mr. Bartlett and Mr. Morgan."

"I was told to meet them."

"You were told? By whom."

"A man," he said.

"Is that man here?"

Durran scanned the six faces—Trent, Ross, Tippett, McDermott, Godley, Weston. "No. I don't think so. Wait a minute." He looked back at McDermott, took a pace or two toward him. "Was it you?"

"Now, hang on," said McDermott, springing to his feet

and clenching his fists. "I've not come here to be framed for something that I had nothing to do with."

"No," said Durran. "It's not him. Looked a bit like. But no, this one was older. He's not here."

"So this mystery man instructed you to waylay Bartlett and Morgan?"

"It's like this," began Durran, returning to my side. "I was in the Ship one night—that's another pub of the same sort in Tooting. My regular, you might say."

"Good God," said Trent, "how widespread is this plague?"

Everyone ignored him.

"He asked me if I ever went down Wimbledon way. I says yes. He says, do I know the Common? I says yes. He says do I know the White Bear? I says yes."

"When was this, Sean?"

"Last Tuesday night."

"And what happened?"

"He gave me a letter to deliver to a certain party, and a message."

"What was the message?"

" 'Don't forget.' That's all."

"And did he tell you to do anything else?"

"Yes. He said I was to compo...compri... What was the word you said?"

"Compromise."

"Yes. I was to compromise the gentleman and his friend. In other words, I was to get off with them. Well, that wasn't so tough. They were good-looking, both of them. I didn't mind. And he gave me a tenner."

"Who did?"

"This bloke in the pub. And another fiver when I saw him again on Sunday night."

"And you're sure he isn't here?"

"No. I'm sure."

"So for fifteen pounds, you waited on Wimbledon Common, at a time and place you believed Bartlett would appear."

"Yes. This feller told me that he'd be staying at this house. Told me I was to keep my eyes in my head and follow him. If I could get him and his friend alone, I was to talk to them. So I waited around and I saw him arrive, and then after a while I saw him and the other gentleman coming out. I follows them over the Common, and I says good evening to them, with a smile and wink. Just to make sure they know my face. Then I keep an eye on them and they go into the Bear. So I think, right you are, my beauties, I'll have you in there."

"But they brought you home."

"Yes. Very nice too. Fun and games we had."

"I have no desire to hear the details," said Ross; Tippett looked disappointed.

"And afterward?"

"When the young gentleman is downstairs, the older gent, Mr. Bartlett, gives me a few quid. And I give him the letter, and I say, 'Don't forget.' He looks at me like he's seen a ghost, he does. Tries to say something, but the words won't come out. I feel bad and I leave him be. Other young gent sees me in the hall and we say good night and I go."

"And that's all?"

"That's all."

"Are you sure you're not forgetting something?"

"I don't think so." He was fidgeting, eager to leave—perhaps to get back to one of his regular haunts and put some extra bread on the Durran family table.

"Come now, Sean. What were you telling me earlier?"

"I don't know…"

"Yes, you do. And you promised you'd tell these gentlemen as well."

"I won't get into trouble?"

Durran had been eager to tell the truth when I tracked him down and interviewed him earlier this afternoon; now, however, confronted by a uniformed police officer and his plainclothes superior, he was losing his nerve.

"Detective Sergeant Weston?"

Weston nodded. "Go ahead, Mr. Durran. You can speak in confidence. Doctor Mitchell has already consulted me."

Weston had, indeed, given his word that Durran would be treated leniently if he cooperated—though he had been unable to promise a complete immunity from any prosecutions. I didn't think the time was right to mention this to Durran.

"All right, then," said Durran, staring gloomily at the floor. "There was something else that the bloke gave me. But I swear to God that I didn't know what it was. He told me it was like a love potion. Something to make things go with a swing."

"A love potion? Surely a young man like you doesn't need any extra lead in his pencil, Durran?"

"No, Mitch." Durran grinned nervously. "I don't. But it wasn't for me. It was for him."

"Who?"

"Bartlett. The gent told me to give it to him."

"And did he take it?"

"Well…not as such, no. I gave it to him without him noticing."

"You mean you slipped it in his drink?"

He took a deep breath. "No. It wasn't like that. It was in a little capsule—like something you might get from the doctor."

"And what did you do with it?"

"I did what I was told. I stuck it up his arse."

# Chapter Sixteen

THE REACTION WAS EXTREMELY GRATIFYING. HUGH TRENT turned a deep shade of red, and his eyes bulged out. Sergeant Godley, on the other hand, turned a rather unpleasant pale green, and looked as if he was about to faint. Walter Ross muttered and mumbled into his handkerchief, while Arthur Tippett was on the verge of tears. Only Jack McDermott and Detective Sergeant Weston remained calm—the former because he was basically unshockable, the latter because he knew what was coming.

"So, Sean," I said to my star witness, "you inserted this capsule, or suppository, or whatever it was, into Frank Bartlett's anus at some point during your…encounter."

"Yeah. I'd hid it in my sock, and then when my socks came off I held it in my hand until I had a chance to finger him. He liked that. He never knew I'd put something in him."

"And did it have an immediate effect?"

"I thought so," said Durran. "I mean, he was really randy. Especially for a bloke of his age. He was mad for it."

"So you thought that the love potion had done its work."

"Yeah. I suppose. I didn't think much about it."

"Did the man who gave you the letter and the capsule explain why he wanted Bartlett to be dosed in this way?"

"He said he wanted to make sure that Bartlett really let himself go. So that there was no chance that we wouldn't… you know. Go all the way. And then I was to tell him all about it."

"I see. He wanted evidence, in fact, that Bartlett was having sexual relations with other men."

"Suppose so."

"And the love potion was just to make sure that he got his evidence."

"Look, that's what he told me."

"You can sit down now," I said. That was more than I could do; after the pounding Bert had given me, I preferred to remain standing. Durran took his place in a chair next to Walter Ross; I saw the older man stiffen and edge away. His tolerance of his late partner's activities obviously had its limits.

"The contents of this capsule puzzled me," I said. "So I obtained a copy of the toxicology report from Frank Bartlett's post mortem. May I, detective sergeant?"

Weston nodded.

"The pathologist who examined Bartlett's body initially assumed that the cause of death was loss of blood from multiple wounds on the arms, inflicted by a razor that was taken by the police from the bathroom of this house. It seemed obvious, given the depth and severity of the cuts, and the amount of blood on the walls and floor of the bathroom. When Bartlett's body was removed from the house, there was still so much blood in those wounds that it spilled on the hall floor. Is that right, Sergeant Godley?"

"I don't remember. But yes, there was blood everywhere. It was a messy business."

"We'll return to that blood later," I continued. "But for now, I am interested in poison. Before the pathologist signed the death certificate, he noticed certain unusual things about the body. One: the face was bright pink, as were the fingers and toes. Two: there were scratch marks on the stomach, possibly the result of some vigorous sexual activity, but possibly also self-inflicted. Three: the ankles and neck were swollen. When he opened up the body, he discovered that the kidneys were damaged. All of these symptoms are consistent with mercury poisoning."

"Mercury? Good God," said Trent, "how horrible!"

"Very horrible. One of the nastiest ways to die, I believe. So, given the suspicious circumstances of Bartlett's death, the police removed more items from this house—specifically, the contents of Bartlett's overnight bag. They analyzed everything—his toothpaste, his mouthwash, his soap, his pillbox. And what did they find?"

"Mercury, I assume," said Ross. "But how did it get there?"

"No, Mr. Ross. They found strychnine. In his mouthwash."

"Strychnine? But you said—"

"Confusing, isn't it? Razor cuts, symptoms of mercury poisoning in the body, and strychnine in the mouthwash. Three possible causes of death for one corpse. Whoever killed Frank Bartlett wanted to make very sure that he died."

"Killed? Good God, Mitchell, you're not suggesting this was murder?" Ross looked horrified. "Frank committed suicide, surely. That seems clear. The trouble he was in... I mean, he did what he thought was right, didn't he?"

"That is what we were supposed to think."

"But for heaven's sake, man," said Trent, "he cut his wrists! You said yourself that there was blood everywhere."

"So he did, and so there was."

"I'm in the dark," said McDermott, with relish. I think

he regarded the whole affair as a sophisticated drawing room entertainment. "What happened?"

"I'm going to tell you," I said, feeling somewhat as if I were onstage myself. "But first, gentlemen, please recharge your glasses. Officers—you might allow yourself a drop of the hard stuff. This isn't a very pretty story. As a doctor, I recommend it."

The whiskey decanter was passed, and everyone helped themselves liberally. When everyone was ready, I began.

"Frank Bartlett and Harry Morgan were lovers. They had been for nearly eighteen months prior to Bartlett's death. There was a certain amount of overlap between Jack McDermott and Harry Morgan—but, as McDermott has told us, Bartlett made his choice, and paid the price for discarding his old lover in favor of the new."

McDermott looked pained, but nodded.

"At various points throughout their affair, Morgan tried to break with Bartlett—he felt he was in too deep, that he was endangering his marriage and family life, as well as compromising his professional relationship with the firm of Bartlett and Ross."

"He didn't try very hard, did he?" said Ross.

"Perhaps not. But we must remember at all times that, in his way, Morgan loved Bartlett just as much as Bartlett loved Morgan. I know Morgan pretty well—we were students together at Cambridge, and we've been in a lot of scrapes over the years—and I know that he's a passionate, impulsive fellow."

"He's a married man," said Trent. "He should have learned to control himself."

"Yes, he should," I said, "but he didn't. And how many of us do? Life is a constant temptation. Morgan was swept off his feet by Bartlett—but he still loved his wife and children, and had no desire to leave them. Bartlett made that easy for him—he didn't want to upset the apple cart any more than

Morgan did. He was a respectable City solicitor, with a reputation to maintain, and a very presentable wife at home."

"A wife who is now very ill from the shock," said Trent.

"Let us hope for a speedy recovery," I said. "As Bartlett bound Morgan tighter and tighter to himself, so Morgan realized that he was way out of his depth. When Bartlett came to this house for what he thought would be a romantic weekend, they argued. Morgan told him it was over. Bartlett was furious, crazy—he had only just changed his will, as an ultimate gift to Morgan, hoping that it would bind them forever. In a last-ditch effort to win Morgan back, he took him out and found another playmate—thinking, perhaps, that Morgan had tired of him, just as Bartlett had tired of Jack, here. But that wasn't the case. Morgan didn't want another man. The only man he wanted was Frank Bartlett."

"So why did they want me?" asked Durran. "Mr. Morgan seemed to enjoy himself."

"He did. Morgan's led by his dick. He's young and he doesn't always think before he acts." Neither do I, I thought, glancing rather ruefully at Arthur Tippett, whom I'd fucked in the name of the investigation and who, from the look in his eyes, was eager for seconds. "It wasn't the first time Bartlett had encouraged him to do something new, something dangerous, even. Bartlett had a great deal of influence over Morgan."

"That's absolute nonsense," said Trent. "If anything, it was the other way around. Who was giving Morgan money? Buying him a house? Making him his heir?"

"I'll come to that. But to return to the events of Saturday night and early Sunday morning. At some point, Sean Durran slipped a suppository containing mercury oxide into Bartlett's asshole. Subsequent investigations have found a concentration of the substance in the lining of his rectum. There is no doubt whatsoever that it was administered per ano."

"But the razor, for God's sake," said Ross. "Who cut him with the razor?"

I held up a hand. "When they had finished, Morgan left Bartlett and Durran together in the bathroom. Bartlett gave him some money, and then Durran handed over the letter and the message, and left. Frank Bartlett was alive and well when you last saw him, wasn't he, Sean?"

"Yes. I told you, he looked like he'd had a shock. But there was nothing wrong with him."

"When Morgan came back upstairs, he found Bartlett brushing his teeth at the bathroom sink, showing no sign that anything was wrong. They exchanged a few words, then Morgan saw Durran off the premises and prepared for bed. When he came back upstairs, Bartlett had locked the bathroom door. Morgan smelled smoke, and assumed that Bartlett was having a cigarette before coming to bed."

"We found ash in the bathroom," said DS Weston. "But it was not cigarette ash."

"No," I said. "In fact, Bartlett had burned the letter that Durran delivered to him, and tried to flush the remains down the toilet. A few pieces floated around the room and escaped his notice. He was not smoking a cigarette. He was trying to destroy a final note from his blackmailer."

"But I wasn't blackmailing him anymore!" cried McDermott, springing to his feet. "I told you. You must believe me!"

"I know. Please sit down, Jack. No—it was not you who was blackmailing him. Nor was it Morgan. It was someone else—someone who was threatening to expose Bartlett not only to his wife, but also to the newspapers and the police. To destroy his entire life. This final demand—whatever it was, we will never know for sure—must have been some kind of ultimatum. Perhaps Bartlett had refused to pay his blackmailer. Whatever the contents of that letter, it was enough to make Bartlett despair. Enough, in fact, to make him suicidal. He took the razor—which, only a few minutes previously, had been used to shave Sean Durran, and with which he had frequently shaved Morgan."

"And me," said McDermott. "He was keen on all that business."

"Thank you, Jack. Bartlett's shaving fetish was well known to all his lovers. He was not always discreet."

"So you're saying, in fact, that Frank cut his wrists after all?"

"Yes, Mr. Ross. There was no one else in the bathroom with him. The door was locked from the inside. Morgan could not get in, and Durran had left the house. There is no other means of access, apart from a window which was also closed on the inside. Frank Bartlett, stricken with horror at the contents of the letter, desperately sad after his argument with Morgan, perhaps remorseful after the orgy they had with Durran, decided to take his own life."

"Make your mind up, Mitchell. Murder, or suicide?"

"Both. Already the mercury oxide was absorbed into his bloodstream. He experienced a burning, itching pain over his torso—hence the scratch marks. His heart would have been beating fast, his mind disordered—he would have experienced a sort of panic. All these factors together drove him to cut himself with the razor. Whether it was the loss of blood that killed him, or the mercury poisoning, we don't know. The two causes would have been racing each other to take Frank Bartlett's life."

"Oh God," said Trent, "how horrible."

"But the strychnine in the mouthwash?" asked Sergeant Godley. "The lab found that right away."

"A red herring," I said, "or a precaution in case Durran failed to deliver, whichever way you look at it. Bartlett's interest in oral hygiene was even better known than his lust for shaving. Anyone close to him would know that he regularly rinsed his mouth out after sex."

"But if Durran had already poisoned him—"

"What puzzled me for a long time about this case was why, if the murderer had found such a clever way of killing Bartlett, he or she would go to such lengths to make it look like suicide. And then it struck me. Nobody would ever believe that Harry Morgan was a murderer—you only have to talk to him for five minutes to realize that. But it's possible, just possible, that he could be the sort who would drive a man to suicide. They were having a queer affair, weren't they?—and a man who is capable of that is capable of almost anything, certainly blackmail and extortion—in the eyes of the law. So the killer, who wanted Bartlett dead so badly, stumbled upon a brilliant way of deflecting suspicion, of disguising Bartlett's death as suicide, knowing that the police would look no further than the scandalous sexual relationship between the two men, and would instantly assume the worst.

The police would want a quick conviction—and when they found poison in the mouthwash, and Morgan with blood on his hands, they would put two and two together. Minor details like the toxicology report could be overlooked. Yes, it was a muddle—nobody would be sure if Morgan had simply driven Bartlett to suicide, or had a more active hand in his death by poisoning him or by wielding the razor himself. He had a cut on his finger, which he said was sustained while trying to shave Sean Durran—but who would believe that? And where was Durran, to corroborate all this? Gone. As far as the police were concerned, there was no such person as this mysterious Sean Durran. Morgan had just made him up as a desperate alibi. Perhaps he wouldn't even mention him—being a married man, a father of two small children. Perhaps he would lie all the way to the gallows. Whatever happened, the murderer was confident that Morgan would be found guilty."

"You keep talking about a murderer," said Ross, "but who is it?"

"You are about to find out."

"Bet it was the blackmailer," said McDermott, "whoever that was."

"You're right, and you're wrong, Jack. Bartlett certainly was being blackmailed, and he was paying out a large amount of money to his persecutor, as we can tell from the records he kept at the office. He told you to enter it all in a ledger, didn't he, Arthur?"

"Yes. He was very careful like that."

"Hoping, perhaps, that one day he might bring the blackmailer to justice. Well, justice worked a little too slowly for Frank Bartlett—but we will finish the job for him."

There was a gentle knock at the door.

"Come in!"

It was PC Stan Knight, my little blond cop, right on cue, looking very neat and fuckable in his blue uniform.

"Just to let you know, Doctor Mitchell, that I'm stationed outside the door as requested. And there are police officers at the front and back of the house, and at points along the road."

"Good man, Knight," said Weston. "Carry on."

Stan saluted, winked at me, and left the room.

"What the hell is the meaning of this?" said Ross. "You surely don't think that one of us—"

"Very useful, that ledger," I continued. "Proof that Bartlett was being blackmailed. All there in black and white. You're very efficient, Tippett. I know Frank Bartlett relied on you in all things."

"I did my best," said Tippett, with a slight break in his voice. His eyes were wet.

"I'm sure you did. But even you couldn't be expected to isolate and identify the person who was delivering these blackmail demands to the office. Perhaps they were posted and delivered by the postman. Perhaps they were brought by messenger. It's impossible to keep track of everything in a busy City law firm, isn't it?"

"If I had any idea who it was, I would have told you," said Tippett. "But I know no more about it than Mr. Bartlett knew. Or Mr. Ross."

"I assure you," said Ross, "I kept my nose out of Bartlett's private affairs."

"Like the good friend you were," I said. "But not everyone was so uninterested, or should I say disinterested, in Frank Bartlett's private affairs. Were they, Trent?"

"I should think not," said Trent, taking a swig of whiskey and smoothing down his moustache. "My poor sister had to put up with a great deal. She tried to turn a blind eye, but there came a point when there was so much money being paid that she couldn't help but notice. The staff's wages weren't being paid."

"Imagine that." I said. "And what did you advise?"

"Oh, I've never had any influence over Vivie," said Trent. "She's very much her own woman. I advised her against marrying Bartlett in the first place, and when we found out that the leopard hadn't changed his spots, as she rather hoped he might, then I advised her to leave him. But she didn't. She's a loyal old stick, my sister. I suppose, in her way, she loved him."

"She certainly enjoyed the material benefits of being married to him."

"That's a rotten thing to say."

"Maybe. But true nonetheless. There wasn't a great deal of money in your family, was there? I don't imagine your sister was too sorry to make such an advantageous match, whatever Bartlett's tastes."

"If you're implying that she married him for money, you're very wrong."

"All right. We'll call it a love match, if you prefer. Or a civilized arrangement between two mature adults. Perhaps it suited your sister to have a certain amount of freedom—"

"How dare you! Are you implying that Vivie was unfaithful?"

"Maybe. Or perhaps she was simply glad to be undisturbed at night."

"That's a disgraceful suggestion."

"They never had children, did they?"

"No. Thank God."

"No heirs at all, in fact."

"No." Trent looked a little nervous.

"So when Bartlett died, his entire estate passed to his wife, and when she dies... What do you know of your sister's will, Mr. Trent?"

"Nothing whatsoever."

"Well, then, I have the advantage. Mr. Ross has been kind enough to give us the details—"

"Under police duress," said Ross, flushing dark with anger. "This is all most abnormal."

"The whole case is abnormal, from beginning to end," I said, "but not in the way you may think."

"So—what did her will say?"

"Nothing, Mr. Trent. There is no will. Mrs. Bartlett has never got around to making one."

"Despite my constant suggestions that she should," said Ross. "It's ridiculous for a woman of her means to die without proper testamentary dispositions."

"Like most of us, I suppose, Mrs. Bartlett has no thought of death. The years go by, and these things slip and slide."

"So?" said Trent. "There's plenty of time to remedy that. She's a wealthy woman."

"Or will be," I said, "when Bartlett's last will is overturned and Morgan goes to prison. She will inherit everything. But she's also a very sick woman, as you keep telling us. I certainly hope the shock of her husband's death doesn't kill her. What would happen, Mr. Ross, if Mrs. Bartlett were to die intestate?"

"The estate would pass to her next of kin."

"Of course. And that would be...?"

"Her brother." He looked at Hugh Trent.

"This is ridiculous. Vivie's not going to die. She'll buck up in a few days. The shock has knocked her back, but she'll get over it. Bartlett's not such a great loss."

"And she has all that lovely money to console herself with."

This was too much for Trent, who stood up and made for the door. "I've had enough of this. The poor woman has just lost her husband under the most distressing circumstances, and you're suggesting—"

"Stop there, please, Mr. Trent," said Weston. "Let's calm down and sit down, shall we?"

This was not what I wanted him to do at all. It suited my purposes to wind Trent up to the highest pitch of anger, in order to justify my next move.

"Your sister is nothing more than a money-grubbing cheat," I said. "If the blackmailer didn't drive Bartlett to his death, his wife would have done it herself."

"How dare you!"

"In fact, I half suspect that she was the person behind the letters, the demands for money—"

"That is an outrageous suggestion."

"Outrageous? Or the most natural thing in the world? A woman disappointed, who sees money slipping out of her hands, and who discovers that she has been finally disinherited—in favor of a man? A queer? Like her husband?"

Trent lost his temper, pulled back his arm, and aimed for my jaw. I ducked just in time, but the blow struck me on the ear, and it hurt like hell. In pain and shock, I picked up my glass of whiskey—I'd filled it right up to the brim with neat scotch—and threw it directly in Trent's face.

"Now, Stan!" I yelled, and the door burst open.

Trent was spluttering, dripping with whiskey, wiping the stinging liquid from his eyes. But before he could move, Stan was behind him, grabbing his arms, securing them with handcuffs. Trent shouted and cursed, but he could do little more than struggle.

"Good God," said McDermott, who was the first to notice what was happening. "Look at the feller's moustache!"

All eyes focused on Trent's upper lip, where his splendid moustache, that feature that marked him so strongly as a man of property and propriety, was peeling away from his face.

Slowly, slowly, it came unstuck, finally hanging on by a corner, dangling down over his chin like a very large, bedraggled caterpillar. Trent watched it, cross-eyed. Finally, after clinging on for what seemed like an age, it fell to his lapel, and thence to the floor. Weston sprang forward, picked it up, and put it between the folds of a clean handkerchief.

"I'll take care of that for you," he said. "And the side-whiskers too, when they come off."

He was right: Trent's splendid sideburns were starting to curl up at the edges, as the whiskey dissolved the spirit gum that held them in place.

"Now," I said, stepping up to him and running my fingers through his hair, "we only have to do this"—I brushed the hair forward, changed the center parting to a side parting, arranged it roughly, and stepped back—"and I think we will all agree that Mr. Hugh Trent looks completely different."

"Jesus," said Sean Durran. "It's him."

"The resemblance to Douglas Fairbanks is striking, isn't it? Congratulations, Mr. Trent. You could have been a movie star. You could have made it in Hollywood. Instead you chose to be a murderer."

"You can't prove a thing," said Trent, looking guilty and ridiculous in equal parts.

"Oh, but I can. Durran here recognizes you, don't you Durran? Is this the man who gave you the letter and the capsule and the message for Bartlett? The man who told you where you could find him, and when? Who gave you fifteen pounds for your troubles—more than you could make from a dozen or more gentlemen?"

"It is. I swear to God it's him."

"You lying bastard—"

"Shut the fuck up, Trent," I said, fighting back an urge to punch him hard in the stomach and knee him in the groin. "You've said enough. Save it for the courtroom."

"So, you mean," said Ross, "that it was this man who drove his own brother-in-law to suicide? Who arranged for his death?"

"Yes. But he had an accomplice. Do you recognize anyone else in the room, Sean?"

"Yes, I do."

"Who?"

"Him." He pointed at Tippett. "The one at the Ship I told you about. Nervous type. One of my regulars. He was there the night that I met Mr. Trent."

Tippett was looking desperately around the room, like a trapped rat. "No! I never did a thing!"

"You told Trent about the original blackmail, didn't you, Arthur? You gave him the idea of carrying it on, and throwing the suspicion on Morgan. Yes, you know all about Morgan. You noticed the spark between them the very first time he walked into the office. You knew that Frank Bartlett was in love with Harry Morgan—and you realized that this was an opportunity. You knew that Trent was jealous of Bartlett's money, that he'd do anything he could to get his hands on it, so the two of you cooked up this plot to drive the man to his death and to send Morgan to the gallows."

This was the only hypothesis I'd been able to come up with, during the long dark night with Bert snoring beside me. It seemed ludicrous, nightmarish to me then—but, in the cold light of day I could think of nothing better, and when I outlined it to DS Weston at the police station, he didn't seem to think it was so ridiculous at all.

From the look on Arthur Tippett's face, Weston was right. I'd scored a bull's-eye.

"There's nowhere to run, Tippett," said Weston. "The house is surrounded."

"Do you have nothing to say for yourself, man?" said Ross. Tippett hung his head and kept quiet.

Trent, however, had other plans. Wriggling like an eel, he broke free from Stan's grasp, kicked open the living room door, and ran crazily across the hall. There was a shout, a crash, and a terrible thud, followed by the sound of wheezing and whimpering.

"It's all right, Mitch," came Bert's voice from the hall, where I'd stationed him in case we needed a bit of extra muscle. "I'm sitting on him."

Weston walked briskly into the hall.

"Hugh Trent, you are under arrest for the murder of Frank Bartlett. And for the attempted murder of your sister, Mrs. Vivien Bartlett."

Ross, McDermott, Godley, and Durran goggled in astonishment.

"Don't worry, Trent," I said. "The doctors are with her now. They think they found her in time. The mercury oxide you have been feeding her for the last forty-eight hours has not been enough to kill her. Not quite."

# Chapter Seventeen

It was time for me to leave London. I was not due back at work until Friday, but I could no longer stay in a town where painful associations seemed to lurk around every corner, waiting to jump out at me. The ghosts of happier times, perhaps. Or my own fears for the future.

Morgan came home that evening, after the police had taken Hugh Trent and Arthur Tippett into custody. I left with Jack McDermott and Sean Durran. Walter Ross declined the offer of company and took a cab by himself, looking very sick. I did not have a chance to talk to him. When Morgan returned, only Belinda was there to greet him. That was exactly as it should have been. I wanted nothing more than to take him in my arms, to kiss him, and to tell him that I had never stopped believing in his innocence—but that was not true. Only one person had done that—his wife. Only she had earned the right to welcome him home.

The case was closed, the villains apprehended, the innocent freed, and I was the hero of the hour. I did not feel heroic—if anything, I felt saddened by the whole ghastly affair. But there was some consolation: McDermott and Durran were both eager to celebrate, and to hear exactly how I had come to realize that Bartlett's death was a conspiracy between his employee Tippett and his brother-in-law, Trent. To that end, they had booked a large room at a hotel in Bayswater—the two whores, one high-class, the other rough trade, must have pooled a fair proportion of their immoral earnings to afford it, but they would not hear of compensation.

We waited with beers in the bar for the rest of the party to arrive, talking of this and that, the two of them bravely resisting the urge to ask questions until we were all here. By nine, the party was complete: Bert was here, and, when he finally got off duty, Stan Knight. And last of all, invited on a whim, Tabib and Osborne from the Parthenon.

We made a strange group, as the porter showed us up to our room, wheeling a trolley full of drinks ahead of him. His eyes were popping out of his head. Tabib, I noticed, was making a full inventory of the young man's assets; perhaps, when he came to refresh our supplies, he would be joining the party.

But before pleasure, there were questions to be asked and answers to be given.

"What I don't understand," said Durran, opening the proceedings, "is how Trent and Tippett knew that Bartlett would find me that night. That was taking a big gamble."

"Not really," I said. "Arthur Tippett was the perfect secretary. He knew everything about Bartlett's movements. He had made himself invaluable, and Bartlett had come to rely on him without thinking. It was inevitable that he would know that Bartlett was planning to spend the weekend with Morgan in Wimbledon, even if they pretended that business, rather than pleasure, was their aim."

"But Bartlett wanted to spend the weekend with Morgan," said Bert. "They were in love, weren't they? Why would he want to go out looking for trade?"

"Because he'd been told to. The blackmailer's final letter to him, delivered to the office on the Friday afternoon, just as the office was about to close, told him that his plans were known, and that if he wanted to keep his affairs secret, he was to go to the White Bear pub in Wimbledon, where he would be given further instructions. He was to do whatever the man he met told him to do. If he did not, then certain letters would be placed in the hands of the police and the newspapers."

"Letters between Bartlett and Morgan?" asked McDermott.

"Precisely."

McDermott frowned. "I've done the same thing myself. God, I regret it."

"Bartlett never knew who was blackmailing him," I continued. "Maybe, at first, he suspected it was you, Jack, but after a while he must have realized that he was up against a much more sophisticated criminal operation. The demands appeared in the office as if by magic. How? He would never have suspected Tippett—the good and faithful servant, the one who understood his need for discretion, who kept such careful note of all the money he'd spent, who had such sympathy for his master's predicament. And of course he would never in a million years have suspected Trent—his own brother-in-law, the person who had moved heaven and earth to extricate him from an earlier entanglement. Trent made a point of letting me know that he'd borrowed money on his own account to pay off Bartlett's original blackmailer—that's you, McDermott—so it was simply inconceivable that he would add to Bartlett's troubles by blackmailing him in his own right."

"The two people closest to him," said Stan Knight. "It's horrible."

"Yes, almost. There was Walter Ross, of course. At first

I thought it might be him. And there was Vivien Bartlett herself. The angry business partner and the wronged wife. I thought, perhaps, this was a conspiracy between the two of them. What could be more natural than for a woman in Mrs. Bartlett's position, starved of affection, to turn for comfort to her husband's business partner? An understanding would develop between the two of them, and out of that understanding, a plan. They would punish Bartlett for his infidelity, and then they would fleece him of his money, and to make sure of that, they would arrange for his death. The blame would be put on Morgan, the last will invalidated, the money would go where it always should have gone—to the widow—and Ross could wind up the company, put the blame on Bartlett, and look forward to a very prosperous retirement."

"My head is spinning," said Bert. "I wish we could stop talking, and start fucking."

"That's exactly what I thought last night, Bert, and it's thanks to you and your huge cock that I realized what had really happened. It came to me, I suppose, in the music hall, when you were fingering me."

"What?" they chorused.

"It was the false whiskers that finally made me realize. The girl on the stage of the Duchess Theatre, who appeared, at a distance, to have such a fine moustache and sideburns, and then suddenly, off they came and she was transformed. All along, I'd been looking for the man who gave Sean his instructions—and we couldn't find him anywhere. A handsome man, older than Jack, looked like Douglas Fairbanks. Clean-shaven. That didn't fit anyone involved in the case. But then, it suddenly occurred to me that false whiskers could be put on as a disguise—but real whiskers could also be shaved off. Nothing changes a man's appearance more. When Trent hatched the plan to use Sean as the final straw that would break Bartlett's back, he knew he had to adopt

271

a disguise. So he shaved off his characteristic whiskers, and appeared to Sean barefaced. And then, returning home, he put on a set of false whiskers which he had had specially made to conceal the change. In time, perhaps, the genuine article would grow back—or, when all this had blown over, he'd announce his decision to go clean-shaven. But for now, he disguised the original disguise—and he did it so well that even his own sister did not notice the deception."

"I suppose it was Frank himself who gave him the idea," said McDermott, gloomily. "Excessively fond of shaving, was Frank."

"Perhaps it was," I said, "or perhaps it was all just a horrible coincidence. It will all come out in the trial."

"They played me like a fiddle," said Sean. "I feel such a bloody fool."

"Nobody's blaming you, Sean."

"I must say," said Stan, "it was a bloody clever plot. I take my hat off to them. Had me fooled. I'm still not sure that I understand it. I felt certain that there was something wrong with Mr. Morgan."

"And that's exactly what you were meant to think. It was impossible to produce any single piece of evidence that would convict him—but the whole thing added up to one hell of a nasty stink, all of it coming from the general direction of Boy Morgan. And in a case like this, with so much at stake—a big City law firm, the reputation of a bank, and the scandal it would cause for Bartlett's family—it was better to pin it on Morgan and get the whole thing over and done with. That's what Trent and Tippett counted on, and they nearly got away with it."

"How did they ever dream it up in the first place?" asked McDermott.

"I don't know, for sure, whose idea it was originally. It could have been Trent, jealous of his brother-in-law's success, disgusted by his open infidelity, in need of money himself. Trent's broke; he's lost all his money, and his wife's, on one failed business scheme after another. They send their son to the most expensive private schools, desperately trying to keep up appearances, and they needed money—fast. I suppose Trent saw what Bartlett had, and he thought he was fair game, because he was queer."

"But his own brother-in-law," said Durran. "His wife's husband!"

"He was desperate, and all he saw was the money. But then again, it could have been Tippett's idea. Meek little Arthur Tippett, the perfect confidential clerk, lives with his dear old ma, wouldn't say boo to a goose. But Tippett had a secret life, didn't he, Sean?"

"He certainly did. He liked it rough."

"Tippett had been seeing Sean on a regular basis—and, I'm guessing, a number of other young men. That's an expensive hobby for a young man on a clerk's wages. He told me that he couldn't afford to have any fun—but the minute I got my cock up his ass, he was like a wildcat. This wasn't some tight little virgin I was fucking; this was someone with a taste for cock, who knew exactly what to do with it. I didn't figure it out at first; I just thought I was such a damn good fuck that I'd converted him on the spot, as it were. But no—Tippett was just as experienced as the rest of us."

"Good God," said Stan. "And to look at him…"

"Appearances can be deceptive. I mean, you'd never think that Bert, here, likes it up the ass as much as he does, would you? But take it from me—and Bert certainly did—he's a natural."

Bert cuffed me on the shoulder. "Go on," he said, but he didn't deny it. I'd already noticed him throwing lustful glances at Tabib. I hoped the ceiling below our room was well fortified.

"In any case," I said, "Tippett and Trent between them had ample motive for blackmailing Bartlett. His money represented a way out of all their problems. And they both knew that he was vulnerable. They exploited that knowledge, when they should have been the ones to protect him. So they started their little operation—Tippett would slip the blackmail letters in with the office mail, undetected, while Trent would arrange for the collection of the money. Bartlett suspected neither—but, sharing information from his home life and his work life, they had him covered. There was no escape. And they were doing very nicely out of him, until Morgan came along."

"And Bartlett fell in love," said Bert, a sentimental soul at heart.

"Exactly. And love made him brave—reckless, perhaps. He wanted to shake off these unknown parasites, to face the world—and if that meant divorcing his wife and starting again with Morgan, so be it. I think he was probably ready to do it, even though Morgan clearly wasn't. And I think Trent realized that, if Bartlett followed his heart, the game was up. And when Bartlett changed his will, leaving the bulk of his estate to Morgan, they made their final, deadly plan.

"Tippett would have found out about the will; Walter Ross was an executor, and Tippett only had to look through the files when he was alone in the office to find out what had been done. He told Trent, Trent was outraged—but then they realized that this gave them the perfect cover. They could get their hands on everything, all in one move, and they would never be suspected.

"Trent knew that his sister had not made a will, and that he, as her next of kin, would automatically inherit everything if she died intestate. So first, Bartlett had to die—and then, Vivien."

"My God," said McDermott. "That's vile."

"He was poisoning her with mercury oxide. Much smaller doses than the one administered per ano to her husband, but enough, over time, to kill her. But I'll come to that. Trent and Tippett worked out a way of killing Bartlett, making it look like suicide on the surface, but leaving enough clues around the place to arouse police suspicion. And if there was enough suspicion, they calculated that it would fall on the most obvious suspect—Morgan, Bartlett's lover, the beneficiary of this outrageous new will. Who else could possibly wish him to die? Certainly not Trent, his own brother-in-law. Certainly not Tippett, who stood to lose his job if the company went under. No, there was one obvious culprit—the man in whose house Bartlett died. The man whom the police arrested and questioned. Morgan."

"But how did they get him to cut his wrists? And why the business with all the different poisons?"

"I think I've worked it out, Stan. They knew that Bartlett was close to the edge, that they'd been threatening him so much he was in a tight spot. They guessed that his relationship with Morgan was at the breaking point, and that Bartlett was desperate to hold on to him. So they escalated their demands, asking for more and more money, making terrible threats—possibly threatening to hurt Vivien, or even Morgan himself, if Bartlett did not play ball. But they knew he wouldn't; they knew that Bartlett had the courage to stand up to them. He wouldn't cave in; they were counting on it. The one thing that gave him courage was the one thing they couldn't stand—his love for Morgan. Trent hated it because it threatened his standing with the family; Tippett hated it because it was something he knew, in his coward's heart, he could never have. He would pay to be treated roughly by men like Sean, but he would never have the courage to love another man. And that knowledge turned him bad.

"So they put into motion their final, most horrible plan. Tippett knew that Sean was reliable, so he told Trent to meet them in the Ship at a certain time. Some sign must have passed between them—and Trent went over to talk to Sean, giving the impression that he was cutting in on Tippett. He was the shy type, right?"

"Yes," said Sean. "Took him ages to work up to it."

"So Trent appears in his clean-shaven disguise, gives Sean the money, and tells him to pick up Frank Bartlett in the White Bear on Saturday night. Isn't that so?"

"Yes," said Sean. "I saw them on the Common first, and asked for a light; that was the arrangement, so that he'd know me later in the pub. We got talking in the toilet, and he asked me if I was the man he was meant to be meeting, and I said I was. He asked me what he was to do, and I said, You've to take me home and do whatever you want to do. He looked at me funny, but said he'd go along with it. So we go to Morgan's house, I stick the thing up his arse, give him the letter and the message. That's all."

" 'Don't forget,' wasn't it?"

"That's it. Don't forget. Don't forget what?"

"That if Bartlett refused to do as he was told, the consequences would be bad for him. So Sean played his part, not knowing that, one way or another, he was killing Frank Bartlett. The suppository was poisoned. And as the poison got to work, undermining Bartlett's reason, he read the letter. And what he read in that letter pushed him over the edge."

"What did it say?"

"I suppose," I said, "that it revealed the identity of his blackmailer. I can think of nothing else that, at that terrible moment, as the poison worked through Bartlett's system, sending him into a fever, would drive him to suicide."

"You mean," said Stan, "that Tippett and Trent showed their hand?"

"No," I said. "I think, even then, they lied. They used as a weapon against Bartlett the one thing that should have been his greatest defense. His love for Morgan."

"Oh my God," said Stan. "The letter told him that

Morgan was the one who was blackmailing him?"

"Exactly. What else could it possibly have been? What else would make Bartlett lock the bathroom door, shutting out the man he believed he loved, and take his own life in that terrible way? And, by doing so, he threw suspicion exactly where his killers wanted it. A queer affair—a suspicion of blackmail, or extortion—a suicide. It all falls so neatly into place."

"So why did they bother with the poison?" said Durran. "Why did I have to do that?"

"And the mouthwash?" said Stan. "It's madness."

"They thought it all through. That was their mistake. They left nothing to chance. The mercury oxide alone would have killed Bartlett. There's a good chance that the letter alone would have driven him to suicide. In combination, it was a sure thing. But then they laced the mouthwash as well—easy to do, given Bartlett's habits. If, for some reason, Sean failed to deliver the fatal suppository, and Bartlett was not driven to suicide, then without doubt his dental hygiene routine would do the job. Anyone who knew Bartlett well— and who knew him better than his own brother-in-law?— knew that the last thing he did at night was rinse his mouth out with Fresh-O."

"Yes," said McDermott. "Every time a coconut. I used to tease him about it. He always said that he wanted fresh breath for when he kissed me in the morning."

"So the killers had their perfect trap. If all else failed, the mouthwash would kill him. If the poisoned suppository and the razor did their job, then the strychnine would be another way of throwing suspicion on Morgan. The inconsistencies in the toxicology report would have been glossed over, I suspect. Judges don't look too much further than the ends of their noses in cases like this. Mercury oxide, strychnine—it's all poison to them, however different it looks in the pathology lab. Poison in the body, poison in the bottle, cuts on the wrists, and, as the finishing touch, Morgan's fingerprints all over the razor."

"It was a lucky day for Morgan when he met you, Mitch," said Bert. "You've saved his life."

"He's done the same for me."

"And how did you work it all out? Where did you even begin?"

"I said that, at first, I suspected Walter Ross. But then he begged me to clear Bartlett's name, to save Morgan—and, however hard I tried, I couldn't make that fit into a killer's plan. So I looked elsewhere. Who was left? A lot of people, it seemed, but there was one man I really didn't like, so I thought I'd try to pin it on him."

"Hugh Trent," said Bert. "Just because he wasn't interested in fucking you."

"Exactly. Everyone else... Well, let's just say he wasn't my favorite person. But I couldn't get anywhere with that, either. He seemed to be exactly what he appeared to be—a slightly pompous family man who doesn't like our type but wouldn't go so far as to kill us. But then there was that business in the music hall, and while Bert was fucking me, I started to remember the strangest things. Trent pulling away when little Margaret and Teddy tried to grab his whiskers. Trent running out of the room in confusion when I accidentally nudged his elbow and caused him to spill his drink over his face. He must have rushed off to the bathroom to fix his whiskers back in place—the whiskey in the glass would have dissolved the glue. Hence that little bit of business in Morgan's drawing room yesterday."

"A very effective *coup de théâtre*," said Osborne.

"And once I'd convinced myself that Trent was the blackmailer, I realized he must have an accomplice—and that would have to be someone on the inside. I'd long since dismissed you, Jack—you're a bad man, maybe, but not that bad."

"I'll turn over a new leaf."

"That's not all you'll turn over," said Bert, who was as eager as everyone else in the room to fuck the handsome guardsman.

"And the only person left was Arthur Tippett. Tippett, who, according to Morgan, had a mind like a steel trap. A very appropriate simile, as it turns out. So, between the two of them, they drove Bartlett to his death."

"And then set about murdering his widow," said Stan. "How did they think they'd get away with it?"

"Trent had put the mercury oxide into Vivien Bartlett's sedatives. She'd been taking them for some time, but when her husband died, she needed them more than ever. All he had to do was replace her sleeping pills, and it would be attributed to suicide, or an accident. And then he would inherit everything. He and Tippett would split the proceeds—"

"But how long before they turned on each other?" said McDermott. "I bet they would have done."

"They have already," said Stan. "Tippett says it was all Trent's idea. Trent says the same about Tippett. They're singing like canaries, hoping to save their necks."

"And will they?"

"I don't know," said Stan, "but I wouldn't put money on it."

A gloomy silence fell on the room, and we stared into our drinks. It was Gerald Osborne, MBE, who lightened the mood.

"Now see here, gentlemen. I was lured here on a promise of cock, and cock I will have. Much as I have enjoyed your meticulous reconstruction of the crime, Mr. Mitchell—and I have, I really have, it was as good as a play—I have not come all the way to Clapham to listen to sordid discussions of the motives of homicidal maniacs. I have come here to suck penises, something that I do very well, if I do say so myself. And so, before we all sink into the slough of despond, please allow me to give someone the benefit of a lifetime of unnatural vice. Come along, gentlemen. I am waiting."

There was a sudden mass fumbling for buttons—Osborne had spoken the magic words that broke the evil spell. I'm not sure which cock was the first out—I think it was a tie between Gigolo Jack and Constable Stan—but, in any case, the Member of the British Empire was very soon down on his knees, a cock in each hand, alternating his tongue and lips between them, and the rest of us were quick to follow.

In the hour that followed, we all came at least once.

PC Stan Knight came over his belly, jerking himself off while Tabib fucked him up the ass and McDermott dangled his huge balls in his mouth.

Sean Durran came inside me, fucking me from the rear—and it was true, he was just as good at giving as he was at taking.

Bert came once in Gerald Osborne's mouth—"I didn't mean to," he said, "but I couldn't help it"—and again while fucking Tabib, pulling out just in time to come all over the Turk's hairy belly.

Tabib came at the same time, his spunk mixing with Bert's. I had a feeling that this new friendship might last.

Jack McDermott came in Stan's mouth, while sucking my cock; Stan was learning fast, and even a hardened professional like McDermott was impressed.

Gerald Osborne, MBE, masturbated while rimming Sean Durran's tight pink hole, and produced a prodigious quantity of semen for a man of his years.

And I came, of course, shoving my aching cock hard up Stan's ass, fucking him so hard that, for a short while, all thought of Morgan and Bartlett was driven from my mind.

We lay quietly for a while, some of us dozing, some of us (Tabib, in particular) snoring. Then the porter arrived with fresh supplies of drink, which seemed to inspire the party to resume. Tabib stood with his back to the door, preventing the young man from leaving—which he clearly had no desire to do, as he was already on his knees, lapping at Jack McDermott's tasty cock, little knowing, perhaps, that in the normal course of events it would take him the best part of a month's wages to get anywhere near it.

# Chapter Eighteen

THE BOAT TRAIN FROM VICTORIA TO DOVER RATTLED SLOWLY through south London and into Kent. My heart was in my boots. Just three days ago, I'd traveled down to Wimbledon with my spirits high, my cock hard, thinking of nothing more than dragging Boy Morgan up to his bathroom and fucking his brains out before we'd even said hello.

But that was not how things turned out.

Morgan was home, safe, a free man, and grateful, as was his wife. They expressed their gratitude fully, properly, when I went to see them this morning. There was much warm shaking of hands, arms around shoulders, kissing (between me and Belinda, on the cheek, and between Morgan and Belinda, on the lips), many promises to see each other soon, to spend more time together, to visit Edinburgh, to take a holiday, perhaps on the Norfolk Broads, or in the Lake District, or even in France, perhaps Biarritz, perhaps the Riviera.

We laughed and smiled and hugged when I said goodbye, and waved to each other as the cab—paid for by Morgan, at his insistence—took me to Victoria. Waved and waved until I rounded the corner and could see them no more.

And I wondered if I would ever see them again.

Belinda had been at Morgan's side when I arrived, and she was at his side when I left. At first it seemed that I would have no chance for anything more than a formal expression of gladness and gratitude—that Morgan and I would not be left to talk alone. But, after Ivy served coffee and we'd made all the appropriate, sanitized observations about Arthur Tippett and Hugh Trent, after we'd expressed our hope that Vivien Bartlett—who was coming to stay—would make a full recovery from her recent bout of mercury poisoning, Belinda absented herself with her usual tact to take the children for an airing on the Common. Ivy cleared away the coffee things, and I was alone with Boy Morgan.

He stood at the drawing room window, looking out at the garden, waiting—or so it seemed—for the sound of the front door closing behind his wife and children. I kept quiet. It was up to Morgan to set the agenda for whatever was to follow.

He turned to face me and exhaled, as if he'd been holding his breath for some time.

"It's over, then."

"Yes, Morgan, it's over."

"Thank God."

"Thank Him if you like. Or thank Sean Durran. Or Jack McDermott. Without their evidence—"

Morgan passed a hand over his face, as if wiping away a cobweb. "Please, old chap," he said, "I can't bear to go over all that again."

"Without them, you might be facing trial for Frank Bartlett's murder."

For a moment, he looked angry. "I don't ever—" But he thought better of it, mastered himself, and continued in more even tones. "Frank Bartlett seems like part of a bad dream to me now. A nightmare from which I'm very glad to say I have awoken."

"I see."

"I think I went a little bit mad, Mitch."

"Do you?" Was this how we were now supposed to explain and dismiss his affair with Bartlett—a momentary madness?

"Frank was a very persuasive man."

"Ah." It was Frank's fault. And Frank wasn't around to set the record straight.

"I know I've been weak." He looked at me with pleading eyes, hoping, I suppose, that I would swallow this version of events. Perhaps this was how he'd explained himself to Belinda—or how she'd explained it to him. Weakness, madness, persuasion, a bad dream from which he had now awoken to be comforted by Belinda—just as she would comfort Margaret or Edward. The bogeyman is just a nightmare, darling. He's gone away now. Mummy's here. Everything's going to be all right.

"What will you do about the will?"

"We've discussed that," said Morgan, avoiding my eyes. "We think it would be best if we came to an arrangement with Vivien."

"I see."

"Obviously it's all watertight, and if that's what the old man wanted."

The old man. So that was how Bartlett was to be remembered.

"Well, I won't deny that some extra dibs would come in jolly handy. Just while I get myself back on my feet."

"Will London Imperial take you back?"

"I wouldn't go even if they did," said Morgan, straightening his back. "Belinda thinks I can do a lot better than that. And after the way they treated me…"

"Right. Well, I'm sure Belinda's right."

"I don't know what I'd do without her, Mitch."

And what about me? Without me your pretty neck would be in a noose.

"Will you stay here?"

"Probably not, old chap. With two children, it's already getting pretty crowded. And who knows? There might be more of us before long."

"Oh. Congratulations."

"Early days yet, old chap. But the timing's right. And then, we'll need a bigger place. Somewhere less…"

"What?" A house where your lover didn't slash his wrists, believing you to be his blackmailer? A house where every brick, every window, every tile on the hall floor, every drop of water in the bathroom doesn't remind you of Frank Bartlett, who paid for it all?

"Less cramped. Less suburban."

"Ah. You're going up in the world, I see." Just how much money would he "arrange" to take from the Bartlett estate?

"Yes," said Morgan, with no trace of self-consciousness—though he still would not look me in the eye. "We all have to think about the future, don't we?"

"I suppose so. But we mustn't forget the past."

"As for that…" He stood at the window, looking out on the garden, his back to me, silhouetted in the morning light. I knew that shape so well—the broad shoulders and narrow waist, the elegant neck, the well-proportioned head with its sheen of dark hair. And I felt then as if he was receding from me, moving into a future in which I had no part.

"I've made a lot of mistakes, Mitch."

"You mustn't say that."

"And it's time for me to set them right. I have responsibilities."

"You've had responsibilities for a long time, Morgan."

And they never stopped you from wanting a cock up your ass.

"And now I have to face up to them. I'm a married man. A father. You have to understand, Mitch."

I understood all too well. Whatever had been between us was over.

"Of course. I'm...pleased for you. And for Billie, of course."

"She's a wonderful girl, Mitch."

"I know it."

"Will we still be—" He turned, and finally looked at me. And there in his eyes was all the longing, all the lust, all the love of fun and adventure that I'd seen a thousand times.

"Friends, Boy? Of course. We'll always be friends."

The sparkle dimmed in his eyes. He blinked, cleared his throat. "Quite so. The best friend I've ever had."

And that's all? That's how I'm dismissed, after all we've meant to each other? Like Bartlett—the Old Man. Mitch—the Best Friend. The friend of my youth. I've moved on, I'm a husband and a father, but Mitch—well, perhaps Mitch is stuck. Perhaps his sort never really moves on. Never grows up.

I kept the bitterness out of my voice. "Thanks, Morgan." Damn it, that frog in my throat. I coughed. "Christ. I'm dry. Any chance of a drink?"

"Brandy?"

"Wouldn't say no." I could feel the symptoms of shock beginning to set in—a sensation of cold, though it was a warm day. Shivering. Just as Morgan had been when I found him, distraught and confused, on Sunday morning.

But who would comfort me? Who would hold me and kiss me and fuck me till I felt better?

He handed me a brandy, and took one himself.

"Here's to friendship," he said, and we raised our glasses. I could not think of a suitable reply.

At Dover I took the ferry to Calais, traveling light—I left

a suitcase with the porter at the Middlesex, and took only what I would need for a few days in Paris with Vince. I didn't pack many changes of clothes. I did not intend to wear many clothes. The ferry, of course, was swarming with interesting male passengers and crew whom, under normal circumstances, I would have been luring into an empty cabin for some tossing on the crossing, but, despite several expressions of interest, I ignored the insistent knock of opportunity and thought only of Vince.

That thought sustained me through the long, flat rail journey from Calais to Paris.

I had telegraphed ahead to warn Vince of my arrival; perhaps he had some little Parisian bed warmer to get rid of. Perhaps he had appointments, and would meet me back at his hotel.

What I did not expect—but should have, should have—was that he would be waiting on the platform at the Gare du Nord to meet me. That his expression would change from one of anxiety to one of sheer joy, like the sun coming out from behind a dark cloud, the moment we saw each other. That he would run to me, put his arms around me, kiss me, and say, "God, I'm so glad you're here."

"Me too."

"Couldn't keep away, eh? Missed me that much?"

"Damn right." My sore ass and weary cock told a different story—but if Morgan could put the past behind him, so could I. "I love you, Vince."

He took my case. "You came all the way from London to tell me that?"

"Yup."

"Gosh. The conference must have been even more boring than you expected."

"Ah," I said. "The conference."

"Was it ghastly?"

I was about to say, "Yes, absolutely," but at the last minute I changed my mind. "I have to tell you something," I said as we walked out of the station, into the bustle of taxis and newspaper vendors and beggars and pickpockets and tarts.

"Yes," said Vince, looking around for a free taxi, "I rather thought you might." He whistled, and a cab pulled up. "Could it possibly wait until we're in private?"

"Okay. When?"

He looked at his watch, made some calculations; I assumed he was going back to work. "Oh, about ten minutes, I should think, depending on *la circulation*. It's not far." He gave the driver an address, and we were off.

I am kneeling on a mattress in a small, elegant hotel room in Paris, just off the Rue de Rivoli, near Place des Vosges. In front of me, Vince is lying on his back, his legs pulled back, holding himself behind the knees. His ass—that hairy, muscular ass that I've fucked so many times—is open. I spit into my hand and rub it over my cock, getting it wet and slick. Vince's ass is already wet; I've spent the last ten minutes with my tongue up there.

His face is wet too, and so is mine, from tears and kisses. We have talked for—how long? An hour? Two hours? More?

I have told him everything—about Frank Bartlett, about Morgan, about the arrests and the subsequent celebrations. And more than that: I have told him that there never was a medical conference in London, that I had traveled there as I have gone before, solely to see Boy Morgan and to spend the weekend fucking him. I have told Vince that Morgan at first put me off, kept me at a distance, because he was busy getting it from someone else—that he only called me when that someone else lay cold and dead in a pool of his own blood.

I have told him about all that Morgan has meant to me, and all that was said at our last interview.

I have told him that Belinda has forgiven Morgan, and

taken him back—on condition, I assume, that he breaks utterly with "the past" and all that it means.

Principally me.

I have done all this with no expectations, no hopes other than the vaguest and craziest hope that Vince will find it in his heart to give me another chance.

Vince has cried, and I have tried to comfort him—I, the very person who has hurt him so badly.

And he has told me that he knew—has always known, ever since we first met at Drekeham Hall so many summers ago—that Morgan would always occupy the first place in my heart. That Vince, whatever else he gave to me or meant to me, would have to settle for second place. He struggled with it, and then accepted it, and tried to forget it—succeeded most of the time, and when the fact tripped him up in the middle of the night, he consoled himself by counting his blessings, being grateful for all that we had in our lives together—for the part of me that he did have, even if he knew that he would never have all of me.

Now it is my turn to cry.

And so we go, crying and explaining, explaining and crying, until there are no more confessions to be made, no more tears to be shed, all that is left is the future, whatever it holds for us.

We have made no decision. It is too hard.

And finally, when words run out, we start to make love. I would like to say that we express in the act of love what words cannot express, but I think it would be truer to say that we both seek oblivion in physical pleasure, that we are exhausted by talking, exhausted by each other, and want only to stop.

So here I am, holding on to my hard cock, about to stick it into Vince's tight, wet ass, hoping that if I can give him the greatest fuck of his life, he might look more favorably on the idea of our future. That he might think, taking everything on balance, that I am worth holding on to, even if he can never trust me again.

His eyes are closed, his brow furrowed, his lips pressed together, as if anticipating pain. And then, as he feels the first touch of my hot, hard cock against his hole, he opens his eyes and looks straight into mine.

"I love you, Mitch," he says.

"I..."

"It's all right." He smiles. "You don't have to say anything. Just fuck me."

And there, dear reader, you must leave us, on the brink of an uncertain future, on the brink of what I hope will be the greatest fuck of my fucking career. If my cock can express all that my words have failed to do—my love for Vince, my remorse for the past, my faint but desperate hope for a future that I know I don't deserve—then, perhaps, all the practice that I've had will be worth it.

Because right now, all I want in the world is lying before me on a mattress in a small hotel off the Rue de Rivoli, looking up at me with kind, unwavering eyes, his lips parted, and then, as I press gently into him, whispering the only word I want to hear.

"Yes..."

THE END

# About the Author

The winner of the 2008 Erotic Award for "Writer of the Year," James Lear is an internationally bestselling author whose titles regularly appear at the top of Amazon rankings. His novels are "elegantly orgasmic," rip-roaring good reads that receive accolades from *Time Out London, XX Magazine,* and *BOYZ. A Sticky End* is his sixth novel; other titles include *The Back Passage, Hot Valley, The Low Road, The Palace of Varieties* and *The Secret Tunnel.* James Lear lives in London. Find out more at www. myspace.com/ jameslearfiction.